# Praise for Dan Walsh's Other Suspense Novels

**When Night Comes (Jack Turner Series - Book 1)**
"Though Walsh steps into a different genre, fans will not be disappointed. He continues to infuse historical facts into his books, bringing history to life in this character-driven tale. The pace quickens as events unfold, making it challenging for the reader to predict the twists and turns." – *RT Book Reviews, 4.5 Stars*

"Dan Walsh surprises with his new novel, *When Night Comes*. This engrossing mystery/thriller is a break from his normal superb Christian fiction and proves Walsh is more than one-dimensional." – *New York Journal of Books*

**The Discovery**
"Dan Walsh's novel is rich with intrigue, history and romance…The Discovery is a sublime delight that shouldn't be missed." – *USA Today*

"Yet again, Walsh has crafted a novel so engaging that you will lose all sense of time as he draws you in and makes the reader a part of the story." – *RT Book Reviews Magazine, 4.5 Stars/Top Pick!*

# Remembering Dresden

A Jack Turner Suspense Novel
Book 2

Dan Walsh

# 1

**The Present**

How was it that just being in a certain place could give you the creeps? Jack Turner never understood it.

He wasn't superstitious. He was a rational, level-headed guy with a fairly disciplined mind. Nevertheless, he was on his way to check out a lakeside cabin after selling another perfectly good cabin on the same lake less than three miles away.

Just one reason.

The other cabin gave him the creeps.

They'd start the moment Jack would drive onto the property and intensify by degrees the closer he got to the front door. Once inside, the tension would become almost unbearable. Jack hadn't even been there when the murder was committed. The first time he had actually been inside the cabin, everything had been cleaned up. But he had seen the crime scene photos and video. And Sergeant Joe Boyd, the officer in charge of the case, had explained what happened. In detail.

Jack could see it all in his mind; imagine the entire scenario as it unfolded that crazy day and night almost one year ago. He could see where the body lay, a single gunshot wound to the chest. The dead stare in the eyes. He could feel the fear the victim must have felt in the moments before the fatal shot. He'd known the same fear when the same killer had come after him.

As bad as it was, some good had come out of the tragedy. Jack had inherited the dead man's condominium and his cabin on Lake Sampson.

The cabin that gave him the creeps.

After a few months, Jack had been able to sell it to a trio of fishermen who couldn't care less about its history. He decided to use the money to buy another one. There were hundreds of them in the hills and lakes around Culpepper.

"Turn right in one-quarter mile. Your destination is on the right." The GPS lady's voice interrupted Jack's thoughts.

He looked at the screen then at the row of trees on his right, expecting an opening to appear. It did. A moment later, she stated the obvious, and he turned right. She failed to mention it was a dirt road. Jack hated dirt roads. He wasn't driving a pickup but a BMW sedan. The car vibrated through the first fifty yards until the road began to smooth out. It stayed smooth until he passed a dirt road on the left. He kept driving till he reached a clearing. The cabin was on the right, a beautiful unobstructed view of the lake on the left.

As he did, his phone rang. It was Rachel. "Hey, Rach. What a nice surprise."

"Well, I had a few minutes before my next class. Thought I'd take a chance and see if I could reach you." Rachel Cook was attending Culpepper University. Once again as a student. She'd worked there a few years after getting her bachelor's as a professor's assistant but was now studying for her master's.

"I'm glad you did," Jack said. "I actually just pulled up at the cabin a few seconds ago."

"How is it?"

"Haven't gone in yet, but the outside's nice. Definitely bigger than the other one. Doesn't look like anyone has lived here in a while." He stepped onto a porch that wrapped around the front and side. "No evidence of a woman's touch."

"Why do you say that?"

"No wind chimes or little gnomes. No potted plants or flowers." Something caught his eye about twenty yards away. He stepped off the porch. "Wow, I like this."

"What? What is it?"

"I'm seeing you and me about two months from now when the evenings cool down, sitting here on these two adirondack chairs facing the water. A fire pit right in front of us. Two cups of hot chocolate."

"I like the sound of that, but will you still be out there two months from now? I thought you were only leasing the cabin for a month."

"You're right. I am. But if this little getaway goes smoothly, and if the cabin looks this nice on the inside, I might just buy it. The owner really wants to sell, but he was open to the idea of leasing it to me for a month, to see if I like it."

"It's going to be hard not seeing you for a month," she said.

"Who said anything about not seeing each other?"

"I thought you were on this retreat with strict orders to get your doctoral dissertation hammered out."

"Not the whole thing, just the main outline. Maybe the first few chapters. I'll need some peace and quiet for that. But that's why I came out here. To get away from all the hassles at the school, not you."

"I'm glad. So when should I come out?"

"How about tonight? Give me a couple hours to get set up."

"No, not tonight. That's too soon. That'll get you started off on the wrong foot. You really need to get this dissertation going. Last week, you went on and on about how much pressure the school's putting on you to get it started. Your publisher, too."

When the school had offered Jack his old Professor's slot, it was with the understanding that Jack would finish his doctorate. He'd completed half the course work two years ago before coming to Culpepper, then completed the second year of classes this past year...while teaching three of Thornton's classes. But he hadn't any time to work on his doctoral dissertation. "You're right. Okay, I'll behave. But seriously, I didn't set up this retreat to take a break from you. You are not a distraction. Well, maybe you are. But a good one."

"So, have you figured out what the dissertation is going to be about?"

"I've narrowed it down to three things. My goal in the first few days is to get it down to one."

"Well let's make that our goal then. I'll come out when you finalize your topic. What three things are you wrestling with?"

"They're all World War II related." Jack's first two published books were about World War II. That's what his publisher wanted for his next book, too. "One idea contrasts the success we had rebuilding Japan and Germany after the war compared to the total failure of trying to rebuild Iraq. Another explores why German technology was so much more advanced than ours, and why none of it helped them win the war."

"Those sound promising. What's the third one?"

"It's a little different and, oddly enough, the one I'm leaning toward. It's about Dresden."

"Dresden? Okay...why? The other two make some sense to me. What could you say in a dissertation about Dresden?"

"See? Your reaction proves it. It's a fairly obscure topic. That could be a plus. A way to help it stand out in a crowd. You probably haven't heard hardly anything about Dresden, have you?"

"Maybe a little. I think we bombed it or something during the war, right?"

"We more than bombed it. We literally burned it to the ground, killed tens of thousands of civilians in the process. Ever heard of Kurt Vonnegut?"

"The author?"

"Yes."

"I think we read one of his books in a class."

"Probably *Slaughterhouse Five*?" Jack said.

"That's it."

"Well, he wrote that partly about Dresden. He was there during the fire-bombing as a POW, witnessed all the horrors that occurred after. But hardly anyone's ever heard anything about it. It's almost a forgotten chapter of the war's history. To me, it's one of the most intriguing and tragic stories to ever come out of World War II."

"Well, I'm sure you'll make the whole thing come alive. Anyway, I better get going. Call me again, soon."

# 2

Dresden, Germany
February 13<sup>th</sup>, 1945

Some say life is not measured by the multitude of our days, but by the most significant moments in our experience. Whether good or bad. For Luther Hausen, there was only ever one moment that mattered. One day by which all other days were measured. And it wasn't a good day. It was beyond bad. The very definition of horror.

The day began late in the afternoon as Luther walked with his big brother Ernst along the Augustus-Brucke, a wide bridge that crossed the river Elbe. Luther was eight years old, Ernst twelve. They were on their way to the beautiful Altmarkt to meet their sister, Eva, who worked in a bakery there. Eva was twenty-eight. Luther thought she was very pretty. Having Eva was like having two mothers. She always treated him well. Ernst was just alright as big brothers go. At the moment, he was pulling too hard on Luther's arm.

"We don't have time to stop and watch the boats." Ernst didn't look back as he spoke.

"I wasn't looking at the boats. I just wanted to rest a minute. I'm running out of breath."

"We can't rest either, Luther, or we'll be late. Mother said we must be on time to meet Eva. She doesn't know we're coming, remember? If she leaves before we get there we'll never find her in this crowd."

"Would you let go? You're hurting my arm."

"I'm sorry," Ernst said. "But you see these crowds. Do you know what would happen if we got separated? I'd never find you. One of these strangers would walk off with you and then—"

"Why would they do that?" Luther said.

"Never mind. Just keep up." Ernst looked back, gave him a quick smile. They were almost completely across the bridge now.

Luther looked ahead toward the Altmarkt, the beautiful big buildings on either side of Schlossstrasse. Just to the right was the big Catholic cathedral, the Hofkirche. Luther had never seen the inside. Mother said Protestants weren't allowed. Beyond that was Hausmannsturm, the Palace Tower.

Eva was so lucky to work in the town center. It was such an exciting place. The Altmarkt was often crowded, but today there seemed to be more people than ever. And they all looked so poor. "Who are all these people, Ernst? Where have they come from?"

"They are called refugees. I don't know where they're from. From all over, I suppose."

"Why are they here?"

"Because they have nowhere else to go. Their towns have been destroyed by bombs or else taken over by the Russians. They come here because Dresden is the only safe place to go. They know the bombers never come here."

"Will they live here forever now…in the streets?"

"No. Someday our mighty Luftwaffe will rid the skies of all these

7

Allied planes. And the Wehrmacht will drive the Russians back to wherever they came from. Then all these people can return to their homes."

"Stupid boy!" A harsh voice came from out of nowhere.

Luther and Ernst turned to face an older boy leaning against a brick building. His face and clothes were dirty, his coat sleeve torn. Trash gathered at his feet. "What did you say?" Ernst said.

Luther suddenly felt afraid. The boy stood straight. He was bigger than Ernst.

"I said you are a stupid boy. The mighty Luftwaffe, did you say? The Luftwaffe is gone. The Brits and American bombers do as they please now with no one to stop them. The war is lost."

"You're wrong!" Ernst shouted. "What kind of German talks this way?"

"I'm not wrong. I've seen it with my own eyes. The Allies bombed my city and not a single Luftwaffe plane rose to meet them. Then the Red Army came and chased us away. Soon we'll all be speaking Russian. That is, if they don't kill us first. You wait and see."

"You are a traitor to The Reich," Ernst yelled.

Luther was angry, too. This boy shouldn't say such things about The Fatherland.

"What do you know?" The older boy stepped closer to Ernst. "I see the way you look at me, like I'm some kind of street rat. Back home, before the bombers and Russians came, we had a large house—with lots of servants. People like your mother probably did our laundry."

That was it. Luther didn't even think, he just walked up and kicked the boy in the shin.

"Ow! You little—" The boy grabbed Luther's shirt.

Ernst didn't hesitate. He punched the boy hard in the stomach.

The boy doubled over. Ernst grabbed Luther's arm. "Run Luther—now." They took off. Luther heard a loud thump. Ernst groaned but kept running.

"Come back here, cowards," the boy yelled. "Go ahead then, run away. But remember what I said…you'll be on the streets next."

After running a full block, they slowed down. "What was that thumping sound, Ernst?" They started walking normally.

"He punched me in the back."

"Are you all right?"

"I'll be fine."

"Thanks for saving me."

"He had it coming. You just got to him first." Ernst rubbed his head and smiled. "We showed him, didn't we?"

"We sure did," Luther said. "He shouldn't have said those things about Mother. Or The Fatherland."

"There's Eva's store up ahead," Ernst said. "Don't tell her about this, she'll just get upset and tell Mother."

They walked a few moments in silence, weaving through the crowd. Ernst gripped Luther's arm again. "Ernst, do you think what that boy said is true? Could the bombers come here next?"

"No, he doesn't know what he's talking about. He's just bitter from living on the street too long. Has our town ever been bombed, in all the years since the war started?"

Luther shook his head no. They'd often heard air raid sirens go off, but nothing ever happened.

"And it never will," Ernst said. "I heard an old man say we have some kind of deal with the British. They have a historic town in England, called Oxford. It has all kinds of architectural landmarks like us. The deal is, our planes don't bomb Oxford, and their planes won't bomb Dresden."

"What did that boy mean about the Russians coming soon? The

Russians are bad, aren't they?"

"Very bad. But they can't come here, either. The Wermacht will make sure of that. Herr Goebels said so on the radio. We have nothing to worry about."

Luther felt much better. "Ernst, how much longer before we win the war? Father has been gone so long." If it wasn't for the picture over the fireplace, Luther wasn't sure he'd remember what their father looked like.

"It can't be that much longer," Ernst said. He didn't look at Luther as he said this.

He never looked at Luther when he spoke of their father.

# 3

Later that night, Luther sat calmly clutching his third-grade reader, warming himself by the fireplace. The world at the moment consisted of two children named Heinrich and Hilda doing various things that didn't take more than four letters and one syllable to accomplish. He loved to read. For now, he'd have to do all his reading and other schoolwork at home. When they'd showed up that morning, he and Ernst were told all the school buildings were needed as temporary housing for the refugees.

A few hours ago, just after dinner, Ernst had left for a special meeting with the Hitler Youth. He said it also had something to do with the refugees but wouldn't say more. Ernst never told Luther much about what went on at his meetings, always pretending he was guarding great military secrets. Lately, whenever Ernst left for his meetings, Mother and Eva would say things about the Hitler Youth Luther knew would anger Ernst. They were doing it now at the dining room table. He glanced down at the pages of his book as he listened.

"You know what all these refugees really mean," Eva said. "The war is coming closer to Dresden."

"Don't be so dramatic, Eva. It's not as bad as that. Besides, show

11

a little charity. They've been thrown out of their homes. They have nothing left but what they can carry."

"It's not a question of charity, Mother. It's a question of money. Mr. Von Esch said, between what these people steal and what he's been forced to give away he's hardly making any money anymore. If he's not getting paid, then he can't pay me. We haven't seen one of Father's checks from the military for over three months. How will we live?"

Mentioning father seemed to pull Mother out of the conversation. She didn't answer Eva right away. She just sighed and looked away. "I hope he is well."

Neither said anything for a few moments. Eva sipped her tea. "Things are not going well with the war, Mother. The things the refugees are saying—and not just a few of them, totally contradict what Herr Goebbels is saying on the radio. All the land we gained at the beginning of the war, the Allies have taken it all back. Now their bombers are bombing every major city in Germany, one by one. The Luftwaffe is nowhere in sight."

"Keep your voice down, Eva," Mother scolded.

Luther could feel their eyes looking in his direction. He put his finger on the left page, pretending to follow along with the words as he read.

"With your eyes, Luther," Mother said. "Read with your eyes, not your hands."

"Yes, Mother." They continued to talk, but he could still hear their loud whispers.

"The Americans and British," Eva continued, "have reached the Rhine, and the Russians have already crossed into Germany. Everyone is saying it is just a matter of time before the war is completely lost."

"It's already lost if you ask me," Mother said. "The Fuhrer is a madman. He has brought all this destruction on Germany himself with his ambition and greed. I've seen this coming for years. I tried to tell your father." She held her head in her hands. "If he does not return to me…" her voice trailed off.

"Don't say that, Mother. Father will return. One of these days he'll come right through that door. Remember that accident at the cigarette factory before the war? Twelve men around him were hurt; only father escaped unharmed. He has luck on his side."

"God was watching over him," Mother said. "But I think God has abandoned Germany now." A look of dread came over her face. "We have done too many terrible things. Especially to the Jews. I never thought it was right. Never. Calling them Christ-haters. The Bible says they are God's chosen people. Christ was a Jew. The apostles were Jews. He taught we should love our enemies. But what have we done?"

"Our family has done nothing against the Jews. We were always kind to them when they were still here."

"Yes, when they were here. But where are they now? We stood by and said nothing when they were all taken away."

Eva sighed. "What could we have done? Nothing. How can God blame us for that?"

A strong smell of baking bread wafted into the living room. Luther thought about how nice it would be to have some butter to put on that bread when it was done. Maybe after the war they would have butter again.

There was silence for a moment. Luther looked over at his mother and Eva. Eva got up from her chair and walked to the window. She stood holding the edge of the drapes aside with one hand, just staring outside.

"What is it, Eva?"

Eva was still looking out the window. "It's nothing."

"What? Tell me."

"It's just…I've been looking around the city lately, and I've noticed…" She halted again.

"Noticed what?" Mother said.

"I notice there are no young men left my age. Even among the refugees. They are all boys like Ernst, or else old men."

"But that is because the young men are at war."

"Is it?" Eva said with some anger.

"But what else could it be?"

"What if this war has taken away any chance for me, and I am to become an old maid?"

Poor Eva, Luther thought. Two of the young men Eva courted before the war had been killed. One on the Russian front, the other in Belgium.

"They cannot all be dead," Mother said.

"Haven't you heard? They've come for Gerhard Hammel? They've put him into the war, straight from the Hitler Youth. He is only two years older than Ernst—a boy. What else can that mean, except that they have gone through all the young men?" Eva began to cry.

Luther looked up again. Mother had her arm around her shoulder.

"I wish I had left years ago…with Arthur."

"That boy from America?" Mother asked. "You hardly knew him."

"But we were in love, Mother. I know that now. It could have worked. Then maybe I could have sent for you all before America got into the war."

"Eva, do you think your father would ever have consented to such an idea? To leave Germany for America? Our family has always lived in Dresden…for more generations than I can count."

Eva sighed. "I know. It all just seems so hopeless now. You and father were married at nineteen. I am twenty-eight. There will be nothing for me but old men and cripples when this war is over."

"Oh Eva, don't say that." She looked over at Luther, noticed him paying attention. "Luther, it's getting late. You need to start getting ready for bed." She motioned for him to get up and pointed toward the hall.

Luther obeyed.

"Where is your brother?" Mother said.

"Remember?" Eva said, "Ernst's group went to that circus in town after their meeting. He told you about it at dinner."

Luther remembered. When they had picked up Eva at the bakery, Eva's boss, Mr. Kleindeist, asked Ernst if he was going. He had taken his family the night before. Ernst told him he didn't have the money. Mr. Kleindeist had offered to pay Ernst's way if he would stop by after the circus ended to help him move some boxes into his storage room.

"That circus should be over now, shouldn't it?" Mother said.

"It probably is," Eva said. "I guess he's still at the bakery."

His mother sighed. She entered the hallway. "I just wish there was some way to get Ernst out of the Hitler Youth altogether. You know they'll come after him next."

A loud, frightening noise pierced the air outside.

"Luther?" Mother called. "Into the cellar. Now! Eva? You too."

It was the air-raid sirens.

Luther followed Mother and Eva through a narrow doorway in the dining area that led down to the cellar. "But the bombers never come here," Luther protested.

# 4

Fifteen minutes had passed. Luther, Eva and their mother continued to sit in the cold, damp cellar, without making a sound. Finally, Luther spoke up. "Mother, can we get out of here now? It's just like all the other times. No bombers are coming. Ernst told me this afternoon they're never coming here."

His mother said nothing. It looked like she was thinking. Eva joined in. "I think Luther's right. There's no reason to stay down here."

Alright," his mother said. "I suppose there's no harm."

Luther got up and opened the cellar door. A few moments later, he was in the kitchen. He heard Eva's footsteps right behind him, then his mother's.

"It's still time for bed, young man," she said.

"Can't I just go outside a moment? To get some fresh air? The cellar stinks."

"For a moment," she said. "Then you get right back in here and get ready for bed."

"I will."

"I think I'll join him," Eva said. "He's right about the smell down there."

"It's not that bad. But go ahead. Make sure he comes in soon."

Eva joined Luther who was standing out on the sidewalk looking south toward the *Altstadt*, the Old Town area. The air was crisp and cool, the night sky a pleasant dark blue. Although most of the city lights had been dimmed because of the air raid, you could still see specks of light here and there downtown.

"Smells much better out here," Eva said.

Luther nodded.

"But you should be wearing a jacket."

"We're only out here a minute."

Suddenly, Luther heard something, a deep droning sound up in the sky. At first, he didn't know what it was.

Eva said it before he could. "Those sound like planes."

"You think they are bombers?"

"I don't know," Eva said. "It doesn't sound like there are too many of them."

Then Luther saw something strange. "What is that?" He pointed to the sky above the downtown area, in the direction of the stadium. "What are those?"

"I'm not sure," she said. "But it doesn't look good."

"They look like flying green Christmas trees, all lit up," he said. "See? They're falling from the sky. Some of the neighbors had come out from their houses and were also pointing to the green lights in the sky. The sound of planes faded. But he noticed something else. "They're coming down on little parachutes. See?" Luther also noticed, green light appeared to be dripping and falling to the ground in big drops.

"Those aren't Christmas trees," Eva said. "I think they're flares. I've heard about them. Those planes we heard must have dropped them. They're here to light up the city."

"Light up the city…why?"

"We need to get back in the cellar, right away." She turned back toward the house.

"Eva, what's the matter? Light up the city for what?"

Moments later, Luther had his answer. A new sound. Eva heard it, too. She stopped just before the front door and turned around, her head shot upward. It sounded like swarms of monster bees coming.

"What is that, Eva? Are those…bombers? Are they coming here?"

She reached out her hand. "C'mon. We have to get to the cellar. Now."

Every one who'd been outside began running back into their homes. Others ran down the street in the opposite direction.

"But what about Ernst?" Luther said. "He's right down where those green lights are falling." Eva sighed. She looked up at the lights, the first few were close to reaching the ground. She looked toward the Altmarkt area, then back at Luther. He didn't understand the expression on her face. The sound was getting louder.

They didn't sound like bees anymore.

Luther knew exactly what they were.

"I don't know what to do about Ernst, Luther. I'm sure whoever's in charge of their group will take them to a shelter. That's what we have to do—now! Come on."

Mother appeared in the doorway. "That sounds like planes." A frantic look on her face.

"They are, Mother. And they're coming here. We have to get back down to the cellar."

Luther came up behind her. "But what about Ernst? He's still downtown."

Eva pulled Luther through the front door. "Don't worry about Ernst. He'll take shelter. Just follow Mother, quickly."

18

"Oh, Ernst," Luther heard his mother say. "God, please take care of him."

"Ernst, what are those? Come here and see."

Ernst looked over at Albert. Albert was Mr. Kleindeist's oldest son. A little younger than Luther, and the reason Mr. Kleindeist had offered to pay Ernst to come and move all these boxes into the storage room. Albert was frail. There was no way he could have lifted even a single box on his own. "What are you talking about?"

"Come see. There are strange green lights coming down, all over the sky."

Ernst walked out of the storage room. About twenty minutes ago they had heard the air raid sirens go off, but since nothing had ever come of them, Mr. Kleindeist said they could keep working. Ernst looked up into the sky. He'd never seen anything like this before. "I don't know."

People were coming out of buildings up and down the street, all of them looking up and pointing. The sky was becoming so bright.

"What is happening?" Albert asked.

Ernst had an idea, but he wasn't sure. Before he could answer, he heard a sound he did recognize. Bombers off in the distance. Sounded like hundreds of them. Occasionally, they had flown near Dresden but always on their way someplace else. It almost sounded like they were getting closer. Between them and these strange green lights he became convinced—as hard as it was to believe—they *were* coming here!

The back door of the bakery swung open. Mr. Kleindeist appeared. "Bombers," he screamed. "They're coming." He ran out and grabbed hold of Albert's hand. "We have to go. Quickly. I can't leave my family alone at the house."

Ernst knew Mr. Kleindeist's house was several blocks away. "What should I do?"

"You can come with us or take shelter in the bakery cellar. I don't think you have time to make it home. The planes are getting louder. The bombs will start falling any moment."

Ernst didn't know which way to go. "I think I'll stay here. It's closer to my house. What should I do about the rest of the boxes?"

"Leave them," Mr. Kleindeist said, as he turned toward the direction of his house. "Get in the cellar. If I can, I'll come back after to check on you." He ran down the street, dragging Albert behind him. Albert looked back just once, his face full of terror.

By now, everyone had begun to leave the street. Some ran back into the buildings they had come out of, others fled in different directions. No one ran toward bomb shelters. There were none in Dresden. No one imagined they'd ever need one. Ernst headed into the bakery and closed the door behind him. He wasn't even sure where the cellar door was but quickly found it. After locating a small chain dangling from a lightbulb on the wall, he pulled it. It provided enough light to see the bottom of the stairs, but not much else. He had barely made it halfway down before he heard the first explosions. The whole building shook. He almost tripped.

Then more explosions, one right after the other. The ground rumbled beneath him. He couldn't see much beyond the stairs, but he made it to the nearest wall and slid down.

The explosions were getting closer.

One went off right outside. He crunched into a ball, as dirt and dust fell from the floorboards above. The light went out.

It was pitch black.

# 5

For the last twenty minutes, Ernst sat curled up in the basement of the Kleindeist Bakery in that same position, eyes closed. Until moments ago, the ground had been shaking violently, nonstop like an earthquake. The explosions seemed to come from every direction. The noise was deafening. At any moment, he was certain the building above him would crumble and crush him to death.

Now it sounded like the planes had gone. He became aware of a new sensation. The chilly cellar walls began to feel hot. The air, too. Like breathing in front of a large fireplace. He had to get out of there.

He wondered what had become of Mr. Kleindeist. It sounded like a lot of bombs fell in his direction. What about his own house? Were Mother, Eva and Luther all right? Surely the bombs didn't reach out that far from the town center. It had suddenly become even harder to breathe. He forced himself to stand.

Feeling his way up the wall, he climbed the cellar steps. The wall was much hotter than it had been just moments ago. Smoke began to seep through the crack of the cellar door. Was the bakery on fire? He began to cough. When he reached the top, he put both hands on the door. It didn't feel too hot. He tapped the brass doorknob. It was warm, but it didn't hurt to touch it.

As he opened the door, the intense heat in the hall almost forced him back a few steps. But he couldn't stay in the cellar. He'd die there if he did. He remembered a pile of towels in a laundry basket by the bottom of the stairs. Hurrying down, he grabbed one. Right outside the cellar door was a bucket filled with dirty mop water. That's what Mr. Kleindeist had been doing just before he left. Ernst dipped the towel in the bucket and wrapped it around his head and shoulders then took a few steps toward the front of the store.

Everything was all wrong.

He realized why. The ceiling had caved in, crushing all the displays. The Kleindeist Bakery had occupied the ground floor of a four-story building. He looked through a huge hole and could see at least three floors up. Suddenly, a flaming black object came hurtling down through the whole. Ernst backed out of the way, barely in time, as it thumped to the ground.

He backed out further toward the rear doorway, in horror at the sight. It was the body of a woman, charred and smoldering. Out through the back door, he was soon standing on the sidewalk near the street. He almost stumbled over a heap of bricks and stones now piled up in front of the bakery. Half the buildings across the street were gone. He could actually see into the next block. Those buildings were on fire. In fact, most of the buildings were on fire. Everywhere he looked.

He ran toward the end of the street and gazed out toward the Old Town area. The panorama before him shocked his senses. It was like a scene from Dante's inferno, an image of hell itself. Flames leapt high into the sky from every direction, as if every building in the downtown area had been hit and was on fire. The air felt hotter than the cellar and seemed to grow even hotter by the second. Hundreds of sparks, like devilish snowflakes, swirled through the air all around him.

Where had this sudden wind come from?

He had to get home. Running toward the bridge, he stayed as close to the center of the street as possible. Still, he constantly dodged flaming debris falling from buildings. Everywhere he looked people were screaming and running in every direction.

He turned at the last corner before the bridge and came to a three-story building totally engulfed in flames. The central beams of the structure burned through. The remnants of the roof fell onto the floor below; their combined weight crashed down upon the remaining two floors. An eruption of sparks and flames shot out through the openings that had once been windows. Horrific screams came from beneath the blazing mass. Ernst realized, people had taken refuge in the cellar below. There was no way to help them.

Seconds later, the screams died out.

Ernst turned and continued running toward the bridge. The wind grew more intense. Now he could tell it was coming from across the river moving directly toward the center of town. He became aware of a dull roaring sound behind him. It was getting louder. He was about to turn and look when suddenly, out of the corner of his right eye, he saw a ball of flame come out the front door of a bombed-out building. As he stepped out of the way, he could make out three figures holding hands, fully engulfed in flames. Was it a mother and two children? He gasped as the realization took hold. After a few more steps, the mother collapsed in the street, face first. The two flaming children fell on top of her.

Ernst took the towel off and ran to them. Another man with a blanket helped him try to put out the flames. The three blackened figures didn't move or make a sound. Ernst and the man, both coughing, stopped and looked at each other. "They're dead," the man said. "They are better off than we are." He ran off.

Ernst decided against putting the towel back on his head. Besides being filthy, it was completely dry. He continued his trek toward the bridge. The heated wind had picked up speed. He had to lean forward as he ran to push against it. When he arrived at the bridge, it was mobbed. Hundreds were trying to cross it.

He fell in line behind a thin bald man, his head blackened and sooty. The man turned when Ernst bumped him. Ernst gasped. It wasn't an old man, not even a man. It was a young woman. Her hair had burned off. Ernst apologized quickly; the woman turned around without reply. Ernst wasn't sure even she understood.

They had barely made a few yards' progress when Ernst saw a small group of men pushing through, going the opposite way, toward the fire. As they got closer, Ernst realized many of them were boys his age, some from another chapter of Hitler Youth. He wished he still had that towel around his head, so he could hide.

An older man in the back of the group recognized him. "Ernst, is that you? It is you. Where are you going?"

"I'm heading home to look in on my family."

"If they're behind us, they're probably fine. Most of the bombs didn't reach across the river. Come with us. You can look in on them later."

Ernst nodded. The man made room for Ernst to get in line. He turned around and began to go with them.

The wind was now at his back. Hot and howling. He couldn't believe he was heading back into this horrible nightmare.

# 6

It was hard to stay close to Eva, especially moving against the crowd and especially since Eva didn't know Luther was following her. The bombing had stopped ten minutes ago. Thankfully, their neighborhood was untouched, but it was the scariest experience of Luther's life. Eva had left the house against their mother's wishes, insisting she had to find Ernst and make sure he was all right. She'd thought by now he would have certainly left the circus for the bakery.

That's where she was headed now.

When his mother wasn't watching, Luther had snuck out. He and Eva were making their way across the bridge, toward the fires. Almost everyone else was going the other way, fleeing the center of town. When they had made it across, it became a little easier to move, and to keep his eye on Eva. But he was so distracted by the terrible sight before him. It looked like the whole town was on fire. It was hard to even recognize any of the buildings. And the heat was so much worse this side of the bridge. He found it hard to breathe. The hot wind he'd begun to feel as they neared the river was much more intense.

Eva stopped for a moment, so he stopped too, trying to keep the same distance between them. She was looking at a collection of boys, teenagers, and old men carrying shovels and pick axes. They stood together staring at the blaze. She waved and called out Ernst's name. Luther looked more closely at the group. There was Ernst! He turned and saw Eva.

She waved at him again and started walking closer.

"Stay there," Ernst yelled. "I'll come to you."

When he reached her, they embraced, which wasn't normal, but Luther wasn't surprised.

"I thought for sure you were dead," she said.

"For a while, I almost was. Eva, you can't believe it. It was so horrible. The bakery is destroyed and so were most of the homes and buildings around it. You can't believe the things I've seen just getting from there to here." He started to cry.

She hugged him again. "Is Mr. Kleindeist okay?"

"I don't know. He and Albert ran off as soon as the bombers came. He wanted to be with his family. I don't know if they're okay, though. It sounded like so many bombs landed in that direction."

She kept her arm around his shoulder. "Come, Ernst. Let's go home."

He pulled back, looked up at her. "I can't, Eva. I have a duty."

"No, Ernst. There's no putting out fires like these. Surely you can see that. There are far too many."

"But Eva—"

"Ernst!" She grabbed both shoulders. "Look at me. These fires are completely out of control. And you are just a boy. There's nothing you can do."

"I'm not a boy."

"I'm sorry. I shouldn't have said that. You were very brave to come out here like this. But please, Ernst. Now is not the time to listen to the Hitler Youth voices in your head."

An older man dressed in fireman's gear walked up. "Ernst," he called. "Let's go."

"Shut up, old man," Eva shouted, over the sound of the wind. His face registered shock.

Luther was surprised by it, too. He had never heard her talk disrespectfully to her elders.

"We have to help," he said. "It's our duty."

"If it's your duty," Eva shouted back, "you go help. Ernst's duty is to look after his family. He's the man in our house now."

It seemed to work. The old man looked back at the fires. They had spread to even more buildings in the few minutes they had stopped. And the wind continued to grow more intense. Where was it coming from? Luther wondered. There were no storms in the sky. Only smoke.

"She's right, Ernst," the man finally said. "Go take care of your family. We'll be—"

"No," Ernst said. "It *is* my duty. Our neighborhood was spared. You go home, Eva. I will come soon."

"Ernst, please." She stared at him for several moments. His eyes never flinched.

Luther knew he wasn't coming.

"Be careful," she finally said. "Don't stay a moment more than you have to." They hugged once more and she turned to go.

Luther quickly hid behind an older couple until she passed. He watched until she disappeared into the crowd flowing across the bridge toward their home.

Who should he follow now, Eva or Ernst?


They were almost home now. For obvious reasons, Luther chose to follow Eva. It was just too hot on that side of the river. And way too scary. Eva was just about to turn down the street that led to their house. It was time to catch up. Things would go much better with their mother if he came home with her. "Eva, wait up." She didn't seem to hear, so he yelled louder.

She stopped and turned. "What are you doing here?" She was angry.

"I followed you. I wanted to make sure Ernst was okay."

"You shouldn't have. It was too dangerous. You could have been hurt by falling debris or lost in that crowd, and we would never have found you."

"I'm sorry."

"Okay." She hugged him tight. "Let me do the talking with Mother."

They walked together the rest of the way home. Every so often Luther looked back. The entire Old Town area was on fire, from one end to the other, the sky glowed orange-red.

When they got home, they didn't see Mother outside. It was quite late, almost eleven. But Luther couldn't imagine how she could be sleeping.

She wasn't. Eva opened the front door, she was standing by the sofa. "Oh thank God, you got him."

"What?" Eva said. "No mother, I didn't." She stepped aside revealing who stood behind her. "I found Ernst, and he's fine. But some of the firemen are working with the Hitler Youth and Ernst insisted he be allowed to stay and work with them."

"What?" Mother saw Luther step out of the shadows. "What are you doing here? I thought you were in bed."

"I couldn't sleep. I was too worried about Ernst, so I followed Eva."

"I didn't know he did this," Eva said. "I never saw him until we were almost home."

"Come here," his mother commanded.

Luther braced for a spanking. Instead, she almost smothered him with hugs. After, she scolded him and repeated the same things Eva had said outside. She led him to the sofa and sat, pulling him down beside her. "Sit," she said to Eva, "and tell me…are you sure Ernst will be all right?"

"I hope so." Eva sat in the upholstered chair.

"I hope so? You don't know for sure?"

"How can I be? He wouldn't come home with me." Eva sighed and buried her head in her hands. "It was so awful, Mother. The whole downtown area, all of Dresden's beautiful buildings…they're all gone. Either blown up or burned up in the fires. And the fires are still raging. You can't even imagine the sight. It was so hot across the river, I could barely breathe. It's pointless, what Ernst and his group are trying to do. There's no way to stop fires like these." She looked up. "I only hope those in charge will realize this and let him come home."

"What do you think will happen if they don't?" Mother asked.

Eva looked at her but didn't answer.

The look on her face was answer enough.

# 7

A few hours had passed since Eva and Luther had returned home. After being given some cookies and milk, Luther was sent to bed. But he couldn't sleep. How could he after the things he'd seen? Even more so, with Ernst not lying in his bed? They had shared the same room every night. With his father gone so long, Ernst was the one Luther turned to whenever he had a bad dream.

He sat up and looked at the far wall. Another reason he couldn't sleep. It was glowing a bright orange. Every other night the wall was either dark or reflected the soft white light of the moon. He quietly stood and walked to the window. The buildings across the street were right where they belonged. It was the sky that was all wrong. That's where the orange glow came from. Luther knew why. Everything on the other side of the river was still burning.

Where Ernst was.

But surely they couldn't be working all night. Ernst was just a boy, only two years older than him. He needed to sleep. In his bed. Next to Luther.

Luther decided to sneak out once more, to go find Ernst and bring him back home. That was the only way he would ever get any sleep on a night like this. He quickly dressed and opened his bedroom door a crack. The rest of the house was dark. He listened a few moments. Not a sound. His mother and Eva must've gone to bed. But sometimes his mother waited up in the living room, in the dark, if Eva had ever come home late on a date. That hadn't happened in a long time. But Luther couldn't take a chance that she might be waiting up for Ernst.

He decided to sneak out the back door and went the opposite direction down the hallway.

Outside, a wave of fear stopped him. Could he really do this? He'd walked this same path to the river then over the bridge, even around the Old Town area many times. But never at night, and always with Ernst. He knew the way. And with these fires, it really wasn't all that dark out. And there was no way he could ever get to sleep without Ernst.

He started walking. Quickly, before he talked himself out of it.

It had taken an extra ten minutes to get here, but Luther was now on the last street before reaching the bridge. The darkness hadn't slowed him down; it was the bomb damage. Apparently, some bombs had fallen on this side of the bridge, knocking a few buildings down right in the middle of the street. This had forced him to find another route. But at least he'd never felt lost. The ever-present glow of the night sky had kept him on track.

He turned the corner. The once-familiar Augustus-Brucke was across the street. Nothing else looked even remotely familiar. From left to right, everything was still on fire. One massive wall of flame. And the intense heat he'd felt on the other side of the river hours ago had reached this side. The hot wind he'd felt before was also much stronger now. It was actually pushing him forward, toward the bridge.

Small groups of people huddled together along the riverbank on either side of the bridge. As he got closer, he saw all of them had blankets or towels wrapped around their heads. The bridge was still crowded with people, though not as many as before. Most of them coming this way.

He walked up to a few of these groups near the riverbank, hoping to find Ernst among them. He didn't. Then he realized, if Ernst wasn't with the Hitler Youth anymore he wouldn't stay down here; he'd go home. Luther certainly hadn't seen him on his way here. Ernst had to still be on the other side.

Luther decided to try and make it across the bridge. Since so many people had left the Old Town area, maybe it wouldn't be so hard to find Ernst's group. He could just ask people if they had seen any Hitler Youth fighting the fires. How many of them could there be?

He squinted his eyes against the heated wind and began walking toward the bridge. At the base, he bumped into a woman with her arms around two children.

"Where are you going, little boy?" she said. "You can't go back there. The fires are too hot, and they're coming this way."

"I've got to find my brother. He's over there with the Hitler Youth trying to put them out."

"No one is trying to put out fires anymore. It's no use. We were told to get over the bridge right away. There's nothing to stop the fires from burning all the way to the river now. But I did see some young boys a little older than you working with some old men. They were carrying the wounded on stretchers toward the riverbank. Maybe he's with them."

"Okay, thank you." That had to be Ernst's group. He started pushing his way through the crowd. When he had almost reached the far side of the bridge, everyone suddenly stopped walking. An eerie silence swept through the crowd. The only noise he heard came from the wind and the roar of the flames.

Every eye instantly looked up.

"Listen," someone yelled. "Hear it?"

Luther did now. So did everyone else. The low droning sound of bombers coming from the west. Just like before. Another wave was coming. Pandemonium broke out. People started screaming and shoving. Two people instantly went over the stone rail and plunged into the river. The mob around him instantly turned and headed back in the other direction, the same direction Luther had been going. No one wanted to be stuck on the bridge. The sound grew louder. The planes weren't just getting closer, there were more of them. Many more.

Luther noticed a man carrying a child in his arms with a woman right beside him. She held another child by the hand. He followed them. The man got off the bridge and turned left, then down the riverbank. Luther was right behind him. The man ran away from the bridge.

"We've got to get to that open area," the man said. "See it? They didn't bomb the open areas or by the river last time. Maybe we'll be safe there."

Luther tried to keep up, but he tripped. When he got up, the family was too far ahead. But he could still see them, so he started running again.

The plane noise was so loud now. All along the riverbank people were looking up and pointing. Luther stopped a moment to look. The first few squadrons of bombers were just reaching the city. You could see them perfectly outlined by the reflection of the fire on the wings and fuselage.

Then the bombs started falling again. He could actually see them falling from the bottom of the planes.

Everyone started screaming.

# 8

The first explosions were the loudest sounds Luther had ever heard. The ground beneath him rumbled and shook with each one. He began to scream but couldn't hear a thing coming out of his mouth. He glanced back toward the Old Town area as three huge explosions went off, one after the other. Three fiery mushroom clouds followed, rising high in the sky. Luther buried his face again into the riverbank.

More explosions came, this time on his right and much closer. He lifted his head. It was the railway station, already on fire from the first raid.

Soon explosions came from every direction. He curled into a ball and clamped his palms around both ears, but it made no difference. Images of his mother and Eva flashed into his mind. Why had he come out here? He could be safe at home with them. And what about Ernst? If he was anywhere else but right here near the riverbank, how could he survive?

How could anyone?

Luther was certain any moment a bomb would fall right on top of them. What did it feel like to die that way? Did it hurt? Anything would be better than burning to death.

Luther continued to lay there on the riverbank for the next twenty or thirty minutes, along with a mass of strangers. The bombs continued to fall, almost nonstop. Only a few came close. Luther became more aware of two other things besides the terrifying explosions. The wind and the heat. Both had gotten much worse since the second round of bombs began. In the last few minutes, the wind had gotten so strong, Luther had to dig his heels and claw his fingers into the mud to keep from being pulled away.

But it did seem like the explosions were finally starting to cease. The hot wind made the greatest noise now, followed by the roaring sound of flames. The heat was so bad, Luther found it hard to breathe. Suddenly, a towel had blown from somewhere right into his face. He clung to it, then crawled carefully toward the edge of the river. Dipping the towel into the water, he wrapped it around his head. It offered only a tiny bit of relief.

When the explosions finally did stop, some of the people around him stood. Luther saw the father and mother with two small children coming this way. Everyone standing had to lean forward into the wind.

"We have to get out of here," the father yelled, not just to his family but to anyone who would listen. "Get back across the bridge to the other side. The fires will be here soon and this wind—the fire is causing it. Can't you see? It's sucking the air all around it into itself. If we stay here, we'll be sucked into the flames."

What a horrible thought. Luther got up. He had to crouch to fight against the wind. He glanced over his shoulder at the wall of flame, now only a few hundred yards away. The father was right. Closer to the edge of the flames, Luther saw all kinds of objects being lifted off the ground and sucked into the fire. They had to get away.

The father started leaving, heading toward the foot of the bridge. Luther followed but noticed over half the people stayed put, unwilling or unable to move. Those who did leave walked quickly but each step filled Luther with fear. To get to the foot of the bridge they had to backtrack a bit and actually move toward the flames. The wind was so strong, Luther was afraid it would suck him right in. He moved to the middle of the small crowd to shield himself.

Finally, they made it to the bridge and began to cross. The wind picked up speed with each step. A third of the way there, Luther heard screaming over the stone rail. He looked and saw a large number of people fleeing from the buildings closest to the river. Some were already on fire. When they tried to cross the road that ran along the river, something terrible happened.

It took a few moments for Luther to realize what he was seeing. The people only got so far across the street, screaming in agony the whole while. One by one they stopped, as if their feet could not take another step. Luther realized why. The asphalt on the street had melted from the heat. Their shoes were becoming stuck in the liquid tar. Seconds later, they'd fall right into it and their bodies would catch fire.

He couldn't watch any longer.

The wind had become even worse halfway across the river. Luther had to hold tight to the railing with each step. Their group was met by another group going the other way, toward the flames. For a brief moment, Luther got excited, because it looked like another combination of firemen and Hitler Youth. But Ernst was not among them.

The father who led their group yelled to their leader, a middle-aged man. "You have to stop, or you'll all die. The fires are almost to the riverbank, and this wind. It's because of the fire. It's sucking all the oxygen into itself."

"We have our orders," the older man said. "There are people over there who need our help. Step aside."

"Please," the father pleaded. "Turn back. It's too late to help."

The fireman ignored him and continued leading his group toward the fire. As they crossed paths, Luther looked at the faces of some of the youth. Their eyes looked straight ahead, terrified by the sight. It made him shudder to think Ernst would have been led by someone just as foolish. And that Ernst might already be....

Luther couldn't finish the thought. He kept walking, one foot after the other, against the hot, violent wind. Soon it became too hard. His legs started feeling weak. An extra strong gust knocked him on his behind. He started to roll down the bridge, the wrong way. He couldn't stop or get up. "Ernst!" he screamed, not knowing why.

The wind dragged him a few feet more then someone grabbed his wrist. "Give me your other hand." Luther looked up. It was the father. Luther did, and the man pulled him to his feet. He helped Luther back to the group he'd been leading. He took the child he had been holding back from its mother and they all continued their trek. The father held Luther's hand. Luther was more than happy to let him.

Right when they reached the far side, they heard shouts and screams coming from the other end of the bridge. Luther let go of the father's hand and braced himself behind a stone piling, then turned to see. The line of firemen and Hitler Youth had reached the street but so had the sucking wind.

Luther was horrified by what happened next.

The older man who'd been leading the group was flying through the air, reaching back with his hands toward the others, screaming for help. They couldn't help. They linked arm in arm, trying to stay together. Suddenly, the next man in line lifted off the ground. For a few moments, he still clung to the third man's hand. But he couldn't hold on, the sucking force was too great. He started flying away.

The first man continued to fly up and back toward the wall of flame. Before reaching it, his clothes caught on fire. In a few moments, so did the second man. The rest of the group broke rank and fled across the bridge toward Luther.

He slid down to the ground, his back against the stone piling and covered his face with his hands. It was like the fire had come to life, like some huge monster, swallowing up everything and anything in its path. All he could think of was to flee. He had to get away from this sucking wind before it reached him. He knew the way home from here.

He got up and ran as hard as he could. But as soon as he reached the first street, he knew it wouldn't be that simple. The street was gone. So were all the buildings on either side. Now just a mountain of smoking bricks and rubble.

The bombs from the second raid had reached this side of the bridge. Oh no, he thought.

*Mother and Eva.*

# 9

The sucking wind had become less intense the further Luther got from the river. But the heat still made it hard to breathe. All around, new buildings were on fire. Ones left untouched after the first raid.

The biggest problem was how to get home. He had no trouble seeing; the fires continued to light up the ground and sky all around him. But the roads he'd used to get here were now blocked by the rubble. He started walking in the general direction of his house, hoping something would begin to look familiar before long.

He tried to keep his eyes focused in front of him. It was all so frightening. Luther had only seen one other building on fire before tonight, and it was just part of a top floor. Happened about a year ago. He, Ernst and some friends had stood on the far sidewalk and watched the firemen put it out with their hoses. The whole thing took less than an hour. The boys had talked about it for days.

This was too much to take in. There were almost as many buildings on fire as not. And some were just...gone. Completely gone.

He hadn't seen any firemen trying to put the fires out, at least not yet. When he'd made it beyond the first few blocks, he finally saw a few working on one building. He stopped to watch. It didn't seem like what they did made any difference. He wondered why they even bothered until he heard the faint cry of people screaming from the cellar. The stairwell was blocked by chunks of debris.

Just then a boy about his age tapped him on the shoulder. Luther turned and was startled by the boy's face. It was completely black. Only his eyes and teeth were white.

"Do you know where my house is? I know where it used to be but everything's changed. It's not where it's supposed to be."

Luther shook his head no. "I'm trying to get back to my own house. Do you know where your mother is?"

The boy didn't answer. He repeated the same thing, almost word for word, then walked away. Luther realized he should keep moving. He really did have to get home, see if mother and Eva were okay. What if they weren't? What if the bombs had reached his neighborhood? If they were gone, he'd be totally alone. He hadn't found Ernst yet. Would he ever?

Luther looked toward the Old Town area for a moment. His view was partially obstructed by a collapsed building. He stepped to the side to see better. Another row of bombed and burning buildings blocked his view of the river, but above them the tops of the flames spread out from one side of the sky to the other.

That's where Ernst was. Somewhere back there.

Tears began to roll down his face. As he turned and began to run toward his house, it felt like he was saying goodbye to his brother. But he didn't have any choice. He had to make sure Eva and his mother were okay.

How could he make it without them?

A walk that used to take fifteen minutes took three times that, but Luther finally made it to his neighborhood. As he neared his street, he took some courage that far less homes had been bombed here compared to the area by the river. He turned the final corner. His eyes shot halfway down on the left. A great sigh of relief. Their home was intact. Two homes at the far end of the street, however, were gone.

He somehow found the strength to run. There was plenty of heat and smoke here, but it was less intense. He came in through the side door, which led to the kitchen. The house was dark. Someone was crying in the living room. "Hello? It's me, Luther. I'm here?"

"Luther! Oh thank you, God."

His mother's voice. "Is Eva with you?"

"Eva? No, why would she be?"

She ran up and hugged him. "She left about twenty minutes ago, looking for you."

"I didn't see her."

Still holding his shoulders, she pulled back a little and bent down. "Where were you? Where did you go?"

"I couldn't sleep without Ernst. I went out to look for him. I made it to the river, then more planes came."

"You could've been killed." She hugged him some more. "Did you see Ernst?"

"No. I couldn't find him anywhere," he said, still leaning against her. "Mother, it was terrible. The fires are everywhere. The whole Old Town area is gone. It's one big fire from one end to the other. And it was so hot, I could hardly breathe."

She walked him back to the couch where they sat, side by side. She started crying again.

It made him cry. "I don't know if Ernst is safe, Mother. I don't know how he can be. The whole area his crew was working on is on fire. And it's not just fire. There's this terrible wind that is sucking everything into it. I was standing on the bridge when it started sucking me in. I fell down and it started dragging me into the fire—"

"Oh, my gosh!"

"Then this man grabbed my arms. He pulled me back—" Luther was seeing everything all over again in his mind…the people running toward the river, their feet getting stuck in the street, them falling and catching on fire. The men being dragged into the air, right off the bridge, catching on fire. The wind sucking them into the wall of flames. He buried his face into his mother's sweater and sobbed.

He heard her pray, "Please God, bring Eva home safe. Speak to her. Let her know she should come home. And if Ernst is still okay, please keep him safe. Bring my children back to me."

She had barely said the words when a loud bang came from the same door Luther had just walked through.

"I can't find him anywhere. I've walked all around the neighborhood and all the way down to the river. If he's on the other side—" It was Eva.

"He's in here," Mother said. "He's alright."

She stood, so Luther stood.

When Eva saw him, she ran to him and gave him a hug, crying the whole while. "I thought we lost you, too."

What did she mean by that? Did she know something about Ernst? It sounded like she believed he was gone for good. They all sat in the living room. "I had to try to find Ernst," Luther said. "He never came home, and I couldn't sleep. So I went down by the river to the last place I saw him, but it wasn't like before. The whole place was on fire. Then more planes came."

Eva wiped her eyes with a handkerchief. "Mother, you can't believe what's happened, what the bombs have done. The whole downtown area, not just the Old Town, is completely destroyed. It was so hot and so windy I didn't dare go near the bridge."

"That's where I was," Luther said. "Except across the bridge. But it got too hot, then the fire started coming toward us. Then the wind grabbed me—" He started feeling all the same feelings and seeing everything all over again in his head. He burst into tears.

Eva put her arms around him and let him cry into her lap. "We were sound asleep until the planes came again. We kept calling your name as we ran down the cellar, but you didn't answer. I ran into your room. I couldn't believe my eyes. Neither one of you were there." She started to cry. "Don't ever do that again!"

They all sat for a while. When Luther was done crying, he lifted his head. Eva looked like she had stopped too. "What are we going to do? What if more planes come back again? Where can we go?"

For a moment, no one answered. "What else can we do?" Mother said. "Just go back in the cellar. And pray. There is nothing else."

"I'm so tired," Luther said. "Can we at least sleep out here? I don't want to go back in my bedroom alone."

"You can sleep in my bed," Mother said.

"That's okay," Eva said. "I'll stay out here with him. I don't know how much sleep I'll get, but we'll try to make it work here on the couch. You go on back to bed."

Mother got up, leaned over and gave both of them a kiss on the forehead. "You come wake me if Ernst—*when* Ernst—comes home."

"I will."

# 10

Luther awoke totally disoriented. It was definitely daytime. Light came in through the windows. But where was he? He couldn't be in his bedroom. The wrong walls were staring down at him. He smelled smoke. Why smoke? Where was it coming from?

Then he remembered.

The planes. The bombings. The explosions. The fire. It all came rushing back.

He was in the living room, on the sofa. He sat up. He had been leaning against his sister Eva, who was still asleep. Rubbing his eyes, he looked around. Except for the lingering smoke which hung in the air like fog, everything looked the way it should. He stood, then remembered something else.

*Ernst.*

He ran into the bedroom they shared, desperate to find him there. But his bed was empty. Still made from the day before.

He fell across the bed and burst into tears, his fists grabbing Ernst's bedspread in bunches. He could think of only one reason Ernst had not returned. He would have come home if he could. He was gone, perished last night in the fire and the flames.

Lying there, he tried to imagine Ernst's face. Instead, horrible images replayed in his mind. The people running in the street toward the river, all of them getting stuck in the melting tar. That man on the bridge with the crew of workers, the look on his face as the sucking wind pulled him up and away. His screams and others as he flew through the air and disappeared into the inferno.

Luther lifted his head off the bed and opened his eyes, trying to dispel the scenes. Eva came into the room and hurried to his side. They hugged, tightly.

"It's okay, Luther. It's going to be okay."

But he could hear her crying. She knew what the empty bed meant.

"He's gone, Eva. Gone."

"Maybe not, Luther. He could still be down there working." She lifted his face to look into hers. "There was so much work to do. Maybe his crew worked through the night. Don't give up hope yet."

"You think it's possible?"

She nodded. But her eyes didn't seem very sure.

Just then, their mother stood at the doorway. She looked down at Ernst's empty bed. Tears filled her eyes.

"Not you too, Mother. I'll tell you the same thing. Ernst might just still be working with the Hitler Youth. So much of the city was destroyed last night. There's so much work to be done. I'm sure that's why he didn't come home. Why don't we all get some breakfast, then we'll head down there and look for him together?"

Luther liked that idea. That's what they would do.

It was nearly noon.

No one said a word as they walked from their house down to the river. Luther knew they hadn't seen the worst of it yet. But in the light of day it was already beyond anything they could have imagined. The sky was gray and dingy. Nothing looked the same. Not a single road was clear and passable, not a single block of buildings was intact. Smoldering rubble lie everywhere. Smoke and fire also, increasing in intensity the closer they got to the river.

Although his mother and Eva constantly shifted their gaze from side to side, trying to absorb what their eyes almost refused to see, Luther kept his focus straight ahead. So many people had died last night in these buildings, and he didn't want to see any more of it. When they reached the river, ignoring it became impossible.

Death was all around, everywhere he looked.

Work crews were dragging charred bodies out from the cellars of nearby buildings and stacking them into a pile in the street. What they carried didn't even look like people, more like burnt pieces of shriveled wood. But Luther knew what they were. He wished he didn't. It was almost hard to look away. The three of them had to stop walking a moment as a man dragged three blackened bodies by, their limbs intertwined.

Eva gently turned his head. "You don't need to be seeing that."

They kept walking until they reached the row of bombed buildings that faced the river. All of them gasped when they stepped into an opening, as the full panorama of destruction lay before them.

"My city, my beautiful city," his mother said. "Everything is gone."

Eva just stared, her head moved slowly from one side to the other then back again.

Luther looked at their faces then at the scene itself. He had already seen more than his young mind could absorb. Nothing in his world made sense anymore. He might just as well have been walking on the moon. Nothing felt real. His mother was right. The city was gone.

But they had come down here for a reason, to find Ernst. If he could be found. Luther's eyes immediately focused on the bridge, which was still intact. People were still walking across, though in lesser numbers than last night. The Old Town area was still on fire. Thick billows of smoke still rose high into the air, but it wasn't nearly as bad as before. And the sucking wind was gone. Just a regular wind now, carrying with it the thick smell of smoke and other smells that Luther didn't like or recognize.

"I don't know if I can do this," his mother said. "There are too many horrible things to see, everywhere I look. I feel like I'm going to be sick. And the smoke, I can hardly breathe."

"We have to do this, Mother," Luther said. "We have to find Ernst. You said we would do this together. We have to try and find him. If he's alive, he's somewhere over there, across the bridge."

Eva pointed to an area across the river, near a block of burned-out buildings. They were still smoldering, but it appeared the fire there had burned itself out. "We could start looking near those buildings. See the groups of people walking around it? Maybe Ernst is with them. And see over there?" She pointed in a different direction. "Someone brought a wagon full of food. See all those people standing around eating. We could check there, too. C'mon, Mother." She gently tugged on their mother's arms. "We'll just take it slow."

Luther knew Eva was trying to snap their mother out of the gloom she had fallen into. They needed to get her moving, get her mind off the destruction. He took her other arm and nudged her forward. Soon she was walking in step with them.

"Try not to look at anything too long," Luther said. "That's what I do."

They made their way across the bridge, which was usually wide enough to allow two full lanes of traffic plus ample sidewalks on either side. It was so cluttered with junk and debris left by people fleeing the firestorm that they had to step carefully. As they neared the other side, the stench of the smoke grew more thick and foul. So did the visual horrors. The streets were littered with hundreds of charred bodies, limbs sticking out in strange angles. Workers had already created a pile that was over Luther's head. Every minute or so, more bodies were added.

He tried to focus on the faces of those doing the work, hoping to recognize his brother. No one even came close. He looked back at his mother. Her eyes were clearly irritated by the smoke, and she had covered her nose and mouth with her shawl.

"Why don't we walk toward the cathedral?" Eva said. "I see a lot more people over there. Maybe Ernst is working with them."

So they did.

Once they got there, Luther saw just more of the same, lots of people dragging dead bodies from the rubble. But none of the workers looked young enough to be Hitler Youth. His mother and Eva walked back and forth hoping to find some sign of Ernst. Luther was beginning to feel this was a hopeless task but then he saw a group of young men walking in single file down by the river, carrying pick axes and shovels.

He watched them a few moments. They were too far away to see their faces, but some seemed the right size and height. He turned to tell Eva and saw they had continued walking closer to the bombed out church. "Eva, Mother," he yelled. "See that group walking down by the river?" He pointed. "I'll be right back. Ernst might be with them." He started to run.

"Wait, Luther," Eva called out. "We need to stay together."

"I won't be long," he yelled. "You stay there. I'll be right back."

He ran as fast as he could. When he had cleared half the distance, he began to hear the most dreadful sound. At first, he wasn't sure. Then, there could be no doubt. He stopped in his tracks. Everyone stopped whatever they were doing and looked up toward the west, toward the sound.

Bombers. Hundreds of them. Coming this way.

Again.

# 11

"How could they do this? How could they come here again?" A woman next to Luther yelled. "Haven't we suffered enough?"

People began to scream and run in different directions, but mostly toward the riverbank. It appeared to be the only area that wasn't bombed the first two times. The sound of the planes grew louder.

Luther tried to locate his mother and Eva, but there were too many people running between them. He headed back in the direction where he'd last seen them, looking up at the sky as he ran, trying to spot the planes. He collided with a man carrying a small boy and was knocked flat on his back. His head banged hard against the sidewalk.

"I'm sorry," the man yelled. But he didn't stop.

Luther sat up rubbing the back of his head. Another crowd of people were running this way, straight for him. He needed to get back to Eva and his mom, but he couldn't get through all the people. Seeing an abandoned wagon off to his left, he made a dash for it, hoping to hide there until this surge of people passed. The sound of planes filled the sky now. Luther remembered from last night…when they got this loud, bombs started to fall.

"Look," a man shouted right in front of him. "There they are." Luther's eyes followed where he pointed. "Good God, they are Americans. Those are B-17s. Now the Americans are bombing us, too?"

Luther remembered something Ernst had told him, once when they'd talked about the war. He'd said the British commanders were all devils, bombing German cities and towns without mercy, even going after civilians on purpose. The Americans, Ernst said, only bombed military targets, not civilians. At least not on purpose.

Luther stood and looked up. Through the patches of smoke and haze he could clearly see row after row of bombers, stacked high in the sky. Brilliant white vapor trails streamed off their wingtips. But then he saw something else. He could actually see little black dots falling from the planes. That had to be the bombs coming. Others had seen the same thing. Now they were starting to scream even louder.

Coming out from around the wagon, he scanned the area in front of the cathedral, desperate to find Eva and his mom. Enough people had cleared the space between them. He saw them standing a few hundred yards away. They were looking in this general direction, scanning the crowd from one side to the other. But they didn't see him. He waved his arms frantically and jumped up and down.

He wanted to run to them, but he knew they'd be safer if they came this way. Then they could all take shelter by the river. Suddenly, the first bombs began to explode. They seemed quite a distance away, but the ground began to shake and rumble with each one.

Now the bombs were falling all around.

Luther hit the deck then crawled underneath the wagon. He saw his mom and Eva still in the same place, though now crouching to their knees. They had to get out of there. Why weren't they running this way? Everyone else was running away from the buildings toward the river. Then he realized…they were staying put *because of him.* They were afraid if they moved away and he came back, he wouldn't be able to find them.

He crawled out from under the wagon, fixed his gaze on them and had just started running when a huge explosion hit right where they were standing. A brilliant flash of fire and smoke. A second later, a massive shockwave knocked him to the ground.

Again, his head hit the pavement.

This time, it knocked him out cold.


When Luther awoke, he was still lying flat on his back. He didn't know where he was. The sky above was gray and cloudy, the smell of smoke still hung heavy in the air. He wasn't on the pavement; he felt the earth beneath him, even some grass under his hands. His head hurt. When he sat up, he was aware something was wrapped around it. It felt like bandages.

He was near the riverbank but far from the river, on the other side of the bridge. The side where he lived. How did he get here? Who had brought him? All around him in neat rows, other people were laying down also. Many looked badly burned. Some were unconscious. Or were they dead?

A man and woman were tending them. The man wore a soiled white coat. Was he a doctor? Luther tried to stand. He could but felt wobbly, like he might pass out if he wasn't careful. His head started to pound. Slowly, he turned to take in his surroundings.

Everything looked the same. The city, totally destroyed. Not a single building intact. Fire and smoke still rose into the sky in several places. Other buildings smoldered. On the fringes of the burned-out areas, several crews of workers dragged debris and bodies from the buildings, just as before.

Where were Eva and his—

He remembered.

The explosion, the flash. The invisible force smacking into him, knocking him to the ground. The moment just before that surfaced and froze in his mind, like a photograph only in color. His mother and Eva were standing near the rubble of the cathedral, searching the crowd for him. He had started to run toward them.

Then they just…disappeared in the explosion.

"Momma," he cried. "Eva." He fell to his knees, then curled up in a ball on the grass and cried some more. They were gone. And so was Ernst. Luther was all alone now. What would he do? Who would take care of him?

He lay there a few minutes, sobbing. Then felt a firm but gentle hand on his shoulder.

"Little boy, you okay?"

A man's voice. Luther looked up into the face of a soldier. Or was it an older man dressed as a soldier? He shook his head no. He was not okay. "I lost my mother and my sister. And my brother, too."

"Don't worry. We'll find them. When did you last see them?"

"I'm not lost. They're not lost. They're dead. I saw it happen. The bombs." He started crying again and buried his hands into his face.

The man patted his shoulder again. "That's okay. You just cry then. You have every right."

Luther must have cried himself to sleep. When he opened his eyes, he could tell some time had passed. He saw the old man dressed like a soldier about thirty yards away. He and a younger man were carrying an unconscious woman this way. He guessed this must be some kind of temporary hospital.

The other man in the white coat, whom Luther guessed was a doctor, walked toward the woman and pointed to a place in the grass. The men laid her there, and the doctor began to examine her. Luther didn't know why, but he decided to walk toward this older man. When the man saw him, he nodded and came toward Luther.

"How are you?" the man said. "Are you doing any better? No, don't answer that. Of course you're not. How could you be?"

Luther did what he said and offered no reply.

"Which of the bombings killed your family?"

"The one today," Luther said. "Except for my brother. I think we lost him last night during the second one. He started to come home with my sister and me until some men took him to help the people from the first bombing."

"Oh," the man said. "But how could anyone have known the Brits would come back to attack us again? Twice in the same night."

"My brother said we would never be bombed. He said we had some kind of deal with the British. They have a city like Dresden. If we didn't bomb it, they wouldn't bomb us."

"I've heard that before. Oxford, I think. Well, obviously it wasn't true. Last night may have been the worst bombing of any city in the entire war. I've never seen anything like it."

"I hate the British," Luther said.

"I don't blame you," the man said. "But I'll tell you who should hate even more?"

"Who?"

"Hate the Americans. They were the ones who bombed us today. I saw the planes. American planes, B-17's. Hundreds of them. I couldn't believe my eyes. I used to have some measure of respect for the Americans. But they're no better. We have no military targets here. Not a single flak gun to defend us. Not even a bomb shelter to protect us. The Brits totally destroyed Dresden last night.

Thousands of people were already killed. Tens of thousands. What purpose could the Americans possibly have sending their bombers here today? There can only be one, to kill the survivors. As if we haven't suffered enough. I thought the Brits were devils, but for the Americans to pour it on like that…they want to kill every last one of us. Every man, woman and child."

"And every mother and sister," Luther added. Tears filled his eyes again. He had all but accepted the fact that Ernst had been killed last night. Now, today, the evil Americans had come, and for absolutely no reason, they had taken Eva and his mother away.

Now he was alone. Completely alone.

Luther looked up, locked eyes with the old soldier. "I will always hate the Americans," he said, "from now until the day I die."

# The
# Present

# 12

Jack had been at the cabin for just over an hour. Mostly getting situated. He'd hung up his button-down shirts, unpacked his suitcase, put the food and drinks he'd brought in the fridge and cabinets. Then he'd spent some time figuring out the best place to set up his laptop for writing. There were two choices: a dinette table near a window with a decent view of the lake or a desk in the loft bedroom. It also had a window but didn't face the lake.

From the outside, Jack couldn't even tell the cabin had a second floor because of the high-pitched roof. The loft was really just an open room with a double bed in one corner and some mismatched upholstered chairs in the other. The desk stood between them under the window. A braided oval throw added some warmth to the scene.

For now, he decided to put his laptop and research materials downstairs on the table. The downstairs bedroom was smaller than the loft, but the bed was softer and you didn't have to duck your head to get into it. Except for the bedroom and bath, the rest of the downstairs was just one big open space. Coming in the front door, the whole right side was the living area. The furniture looked decent but pretty old. There was a portable TV on an aluminum stand, not even plugged in. Jack didn't think cable companies even supported these old analog sets anymore.

But the cabin did have Wi-Fi; he'd confirmed that with the realtor. That was all he cared about.

A stone fireplace centered the living room wall, but the opening was filled by an old wood-burning stove. Functional but unattractive. The stovepipe went right up the chimney flue. The stones under the mantle were all blackened with soot. Jack walked over and rubbed his finger along one of the darkened stones. Nothing came off. The stove hadn't been used in years. The realtor did say the owner hardly ever came out here. Jack stood back and admired the matching dark-wood bookshelves on either side of the fireplace. The shelves were full of books, mostly hardbacks. The bottom shelves were taller, loaded with coffee table books, illustrated history books and what looked like a couple of photo albums squeezed in between.

He was startled by the sound of footsteps on the front porch. He looked over and saw a shadow glide by through the shears in one of the front windows. He opened the door revealing a man just about to knock. Jack was shocked to see the man holding a rifle in the other hand. He wore denim overalls and a T-shirt, a baseball cap and a scraggly beard.

"Whoa," the man said, putting his hand down. He looked Jack up and down. "Guess you don't look like an intruder."

"I'm not," Jack said. "I'm renting the place, just for the month."

"Really? Senator Wagner doesn't normally rent the place out, as a rule."

"Senator Wagner?"

The man's face grew serious. "Maybe you are an intruder then."

"No, I'm really not."

"Then how come you don't know the Senator?"

Jack thought a minute. The name sounded familiar. "Is Senator Wagner…the owner?"

"Now how come you don't know that?"

"Maybe because I have never spoken to the man. I rented this cabin from a realtor who's managing the property for an owner, who I've never met. I'm guessing that's Senator Wagner. But I can assure you, I am not an intruder. I even have the rental agreement. It's probably in my brief bag over there by the table. I'd be happy to show it to you."

The man didn't answer for a moment. Just stood there staring at Jack, sizing things up. He finally said, "Would've been nice if the Senator had a-told me he was gonna start renting the place out."

"I'm not sure he is, Mister…" Jack extended his hand.

"Bass. The name's Bass. Yeah, just like the fish. Gave me all kinds of grief growin' up." He shook Jack's hand.

"I'm Jack, Jack Turner. You can call me Jack. I teach military history at Culpepper."

"You teach at Culpepper? Shouldn't I be calling you Professor?"

Now there was an interesting question, one Jack had wrestled with ever since he'd taken over Professor Thornton's job. That's what the students called him. But it didn't feel right to Jack. He didn't have his PhD yet. That's why he was out here, to work on that. "You can just call me Jack. Would you like to come in a minute, Mr. Bass?"

"You can drop the Mister. Bass is fine. No, I gotta git. I just come over to make sure you're on the up and up. Senator Wagner sends me a check every month to keep an eye on the place. Writes 'Security' in the memo. So I guess you could say I'm a security guard. He's hardly ever out here. Wants to make sure vagrants don't break in and that college kids don't use it for a party."

"So you live out here year round?"

"Been living out here every year since I was about your age."

Jack figured that had to mean at least the last thirty years.

"I been here since old man Wagner owned the place. He came here—what was it, the early nineties? Only lived out here several months of the year back then. Well, not here exactly. There's a shack down the lake a-ways. He lived in that till this cabin was built. Then he lived here all the time near the end. Passed it onto his son when he died, I guess. That's the one that pays me, the son. Old man Wagner wasn't from around here."

"You mean Culpepper?"

"No. I mean this country. Had some kind of accent. You could understand him okay, but it was some kind of European accent. Sounded a bit like that big muscular fella, you know the actor who became a governor?"

"Arnold Schwarzenegger?" Jack said.

"That's the one. Old man Wagner sounded a bit like him when he talked. Of course, he wasn't all muscle-bound like Schwarzenegger. But I gotta tell you, he had his own way of intimidating people, if you know what I mean."

Jack did not.

"Old man Wagner wasn't friendly like his son is. The few times I talked with him, he'd barely say anything in reply. He was a strange one. Had this fierce look in his eyes. I was a younger man then, bigger than I am now. Linebacker in high school if you can believe it. Wasn't afraid-a nothing. But if I'm being honest, I was afraid-a him. Made me feel like he'd snap my neck if I crossed him. So, I pretty much left him alone, and he left me alone. And we got along just fine after that."

"You remember when he died, the old man?" Jack didn't know why he was asking these kinds of questions. It was none of his business.

"Old man Wagner's been dead a good while. Ten, maybe fifteen years. Don't remember exactly when. Had some kind of bad stroke. Almost felt sorry for him, seeing what it did to him there at the end. Killed him slow. He just wasted away, sitting out here all by himself for the most part. The son hired nurses to look after him the last few years. They didn't live out here. Came out most every day there at the end." Bass looked around, then up at the sky. "Anyway, I better move on before I lose all the light. Gotta get home, exchange this rifle for my fishing pole." He smiled. "Fishing's great on this lake, by the way, if you wanna join me some time."

"Maybe," Jack said. "Thanks for the offer." He couldn't remember the last time he'd fished.

"Well, I better git. Glad you weren't an intruder. Would a-hated to have to shoot ya. You need me, just head west through the woods a bit. I'm the next place over." He smiled and walked off the porch the way he came.

Jack closed the door. So…Mr. Bass would become his permanent neighbor if Jack bought the place. Should he put the checkmark for that in the pro or con column? He walked toward the living area, mostly thinking about the things Bass had said about old man Wagner. Had to be some kind of a story there. A moment ago, this cabin was just a cozy little place on a quiet lake. Now, it had some history.

Hmmm. Old man Wagner.

He may have been dead for decades, but Jack was all about history. He loved snooping into stories about interesting old guys who'd been dead for decades.

# 13

The following morning, Jack decided he would head outside and enjoy this fresh air, but first he wanted to improve the quality of the air inside the cabin. Last evening and all the way until bedtime, he'd noticed how musty and stale it felt in here. Another evidence the cabin hadn't been used in a while was the little dust cloud that lifted off the braided, oval throw rug in the living room whenever he walked across it. The same thing happened with the rug upstairs in the loft.

He carefully grabbed both throw rugs, brought them outside and laid them across the wood railing. He'd found a broom in the pantry, brought it out and started whacking them. Kept it up until no more dust came out. The porch quickly filled with a thick gray cloud. He had to step off it every thirty seconds or so to catch his breath. Then he used the broom to break up the dust cloud, get it moving out into the yard. That accomplished, he opened up all the downstairs windows.

Now he could relax. He walked his coffee out to the fire pit facing the lake, sat in one of the adirondack chairs. A few charred logs had been left in it from the last time it had been used. He guessed maybe a year. He didn't notice what time it was, but judging by the lack of mist on the water and the height of the sun, it was after nine. On these writing retreats, he generally ignored bedtimes and wake up alarms. That was part of their charm.

He could get used to this view, that's for sure. The water was a soothing dark blue, a nice contrast to the sky. The properties that bordered this part of the lake were set on rolling hills. Enough trees that he could see only a few traces of the other cabins. Except for the boat docks sticking out here and there, he could feel he had the lake all to himself.

Tapping an icon for a Bible app on his iPad, he spent the next few minutes reading the Proverb for the day. Something he'd done off and on through the years. Most months had thirty to thirty-one days and there were thirty-one chapters in Proverbs. Made it easy to know which one to read.

A singular theme emerged in today's chapter that had to do with the wisdom of listening to others and getting counsel before making decisions. That seemed to confirm something he did last night before turning in. The main reason he was out here was to settle on the topic for his doctoral dissertation. Then to hammer out the basic outline. If possible, maybe even write the first few chapters.

As he'd told Rachel on the phone yesterday, he had narrowed the list down to three choices. She said she'd come out here and see him once he'd narrowed it down to one. Last night, Jack had crafted an email to send out to his students at Culpepper. Not all of them, just the ones who'd taken two or more of his classes the past year.

He'd explained his dilemma and asked for their help. He listed the three topics, wrote an intro paragraph to each and asked them two questions:

1. *Which of these three subjects would interest you the most?*
2. *Which of these three do you know the least about?*

He wasn't looking for them to make the decision for him. He just wanted to see if the majority of students would pick the same topic he was leaning toward already. Setting his coffee mug on the little table in between the chairs, he tapped on the email app to see how many of them had responded.

His inbox was filled with responses already.

Over the next forty-five minutes, he read through them all and tallied up the votes. It wasn't unanimous but something close. A clear majority had selected the Dresden topic as their main choice for both questions. That was the topic he had been leaning toward, too.

So it was official: he would write his doctoral dissertation on the Dresden bombings in World War II. He picked up his coffee, which had now grown cold, and headed back into the cabin to get his cell phone.

When he picked it up from the dinette table, he realized he'd forgotten to eat breakfast. There was the frozen breakfast meal unopened, sitting on the table. The box felt plenty cold, so he popped it in the microwave. Before hitting the start button he decided to call Rachel first.

Walking over to the recliner in the living room, he plopped down and tapped the screen to start the call. It rang three times. "Hey, Rachel. Can't believe I got you, first try."

"Am I that hard to reach?"

"In the mornings you are. Sometimes."

"Well, you know I'll always pick it up if it's you, unless I'm in class. So, how was your first night in the cabin? Anything go bump in the night?"

Jack laughed. "No, but I got spooked by an owl for a few minutes. Till I figured out it was an owl. It is pretty dark out here. I just came in from that fire pit I told you about yesterday. Had a nice time out there. Really beautiful view in the morning."

"Getting any work done on your dissertation?"

"I am. As a matter fact, that's why I'm calling. You said you'd come out once I figured out which topic I was going to do my dissertation on. I just made the decision a few minutes ago."

"Really? That fast? I was thinking it would take a couple of days."

"Well, I was going to go through a detailed analysis, but I've been leaning toward one all along." He explained to her what he did with the email survey of his students, and the results. "That really firmed it up for me."

"Well, I'm glad. You're going to be spending a lot of time on whichever one you picked, so I'm glad you're sure about it."

"I am. So…does that mean you can come out tonight? I can fix you a nice dinner. Then we can take a walk, maybe a sunset canoe ride."

"Jack, that sounds nice. But…"

"But what?"

"It doesn't sound like your mind's too much on this dissertation. That's the main reason you're on this retreat."

"My mind is on the dissertation. It's just not the only thing. I mean, look, I've already picked out the topic. That's huge. Some people take weeks on something like that. I'm just decisive. When I know what I want, I go for it."

"Okay, I guess I can come out there. I just don't want to be a distraction. You getting that dissertation done is a big thing for our future. I know the regents at the school love what you're doing, and this past year your classes have all been full. But having that doctorate is part of the deal, right?"

"Yes, you could say that." Wait, he thought. Did she just say *our future*? She did, didn't she? Jack had definite plans about popping the question to Rachel, but he wasn't quite there yet. He had been dropping hints here and there about his intentions. So far, she hadn't said anything negative when he did. But this was the first time he'd heard her say something like this. Should he say something? Should he point it out?

"Jack?"

"What?"

"Sounded like you had something more to say."

"No. I'm just wanting to see you, Rach. That's all. I didn't rush this decision just for that. Dresden really is the topic I want to work on. And I know how important this dissertation is. This retreat is all about getting that outline done and turned in, not just to the regents but to my publisher. That's my goal before my time out here is through. I won't let anything get in the way of that, I promise."

# 14

Jack had spent the last four hours reacquainting himself with the research materials he'd gathered over the years on the Dresden bombing. He already knew more about Dresden than the average WWII buff, even more than the average military history major, but nowhere near enough to create a detailed outline for a doctoral dissertation.

More than that, Jack had to catch himself up on all of the new things about Dresden that had come to light since he had last studied it in college. There were new books to read, new websites to explore. And some serious controversies to examine. One side claimed the Dresden bombing was totally immoral, actually referred to it as a war crime by the Allies. The other side presented evidence that Dresden was a justifiable military target. Jack would have to get his mind around all of this and navigate around these delicate matters as he sought to make his own mark and offer his own contribution to the historical discussion.

But right now? Right now he needed a break. His brain needed rest, and his body needed some exercise.

He got up from the dinette table and headed outside. When he woke up this morning, knowing at some point he'd do a workout, he'd dressed appropriately. Now seemed like a good time. He walked around the cabin once, mainly to make sure he really did have the whole area to himself. His eyes scanned the woods and perimeter of the lake again. Jack was a little self-conscious about doing his Muay Thai routines out in the open like this. Especially the stretches. Rachel laughed out loud the first time he'd done them in front of her. Confident he was alone, he found some level ground under a shady tree and started.

Jack had begun learning Muay Thai nine months ago, about three months after Nigel Avery had tried to kill him. It had taken that long for Jack's gunshot wound to heal up to where he could work out without pain. During that ordeal, Jack realized how helpless and defenseless he truly was. He'd never thought about owning a gun. And he was 100% sure he couldn't properly defend himself in a fistfight. He'd be knocked out in the first ten seconds.

Neither of those things were true of him now.

In Muay Thai, Jack was still considered a novice, but he felt reasonably sure he already knew enough to adequately defend himself. And with the help of Sergeant Joe Boyd, the police detective who'd saved his life, Jack now owned a 9mm Glock and a concealed weapons permit. The gun made Rachel a little nervous, but considering what they had been through, she completely understood.

Jack finished with his stretches, then moved into his stance and started shadow boxing, working on his footwork then his basic punches. After several minutes, he added in some elbow strikes and knee kicks. It had been awhile since Jack pretended he was whopping on Nigel Avery during his workout. When he'd first started, he imagined beating the crap out of Avery every time. Eventually, the reality that Avery was dead and could never hurt Jack again took hold, and he was able to let it go.

But he knew, he never wanted to feel that helpless again.

After thirty minutes, Jack finished his workout and headed inside for a shower. As he got dressed, he noticed the time. There really wasn't enough time to dig in and do more research. Not with Rachel coming for dinner. Sizing up the kinds of food he had brought with him, sometime in the next hour or so he really needed to head down to the store and buy a few things. He walked over to the dinette table and began carefully placing everything he'd spread out back into the plastic container. They needed to eat on this table in a couple of hours.

The last thing he picked up was the one fiction book he'd brought along, a copy of Kurt Vonnegut's novel, *Slaughterhouse Five*. Jack had read it many years ago but thought, in light of his decision to pursue the Dresden bombing for his dissertation, it might be a good idea to read it again. It wasn't exactly a war novel and not exactly about Dresden. Vonnegut had elected to depict the Dresden bombing, which he experienced firsthand as a POW, in bits and pieces throughout a unique, if not bizarre, sci-fi story about a guy named Billy Pilgrim who gets "unstuck" in time. One of the scenes Pilgrim keeps revisiting is the bombing and aftermath of Dresden.

Jack walked the novel over to the recliner and sat down. It was pretty dog-eared and the pages had yellowed, but it wasn't falling apart. He started to read the back cover when his eyes glanced above the book toward one of the two bookshelves on either side of the fireplace. People's bookshelves had always fascinated him. You could tell a lot about a person by the books they kept in their personal bookcases. Of course with his generation and the ones coming up behind him, it was something of a dying art. Nowadays, people could store several bookcases, even entire libraries on their tablets.

Jack set the novel down on the armrest and stood. His head tilted and his eyes began to roam slowly across the top shelves, taking in the titles. Interesting. As he'd noticed before, most of them were hardbacks. Quite a few books about World War II. Some about the aftermath of the war, the creation of the Iron Curtain and the Cold War era with the Soviets. In some of the middle shelves, Jack noticed several books weren't written in English. Some were in Spanish. Quite a few were in German. Judging by the age of the collection, Jack guessed the books were put here by old man Wagner, not the son.

He was about to pull out a few then paused. The dad had been dead for years, but Jack had no idea what the son was like. The Senator. Was he the kind of guy that would notice if someone had been fiddling with his father's books? Maybe, maybe not. He had rented the place out to Jack. He knew it was for a month. He had plenty of time to come in and take out anything he considered too personal for rental guests to see.

Jack looked down at the bottom shelves. Wasn't that his answer? How much could the son care about privacy if he'd left family photo albums on the shelves? Jack wouldn't even do something like that. And hadn't Mr. Bass said that The Senator hardly ever came out here anymore?

Jack walked back to the dinette table and picked up his phone. Just to be on the safe side, he decided to take pictures of the books in place first. Then he wouldn't have to worry one way or the other about getting them back in their proper place.

After finishing that task, he started thinking more about old man Wagner and his son, the Senator. He suddenly didn't care so much about thumbing through all those first edition hardbacks. Squatting down, he pulled out one of the photo albums. There were just two. Not a matched set. The one he pulled out, judging by its condition, looked to be the oldest.

He straightened up and walked backwards holding it in his hands. Suddenly, his right heel banged into the edge of one of the floorboards. Fortunately, he was shuffling his feet slowly or that could've hurt more than it did. He bent down and rubbed his heel, then looked at the cause of his pain. Sure enough, the floorboard was slightly higher than the ones around it. Looking at it more closely, it seemed a slightly different shade than the other boards, too.

He'd have to watch out for that one, at least until he brought the rug back in from airing out.

He stood, stepped over the board and plopped into the recliner. He was just about to open the photo album when he remembered the time. He still needed to run down to the store and get some things for his dinner with Rachel. Pulling out his phone, he checked the time, then smiled.

He had a good thirty minutes before he needed to leave for the store. Knowing how quickly he could get lost once he opened the album, he tapped his alarm app and hit a thirty minute pre-set button he used quite often.

Then he sat back and carefully opened the first page. The pages were made of thin black paper and so brittle. All the pictures on the first page were very small and all were black and white.

# 15

The first thing Jack noticed about the pictures was that they were all children. They appeared to be elementary school-age. A few girls but mostly boys. The boys' haircuts were short and choppy. The girls wore braided pigtails. They were of differing heights but all looked uniformly thin, gaunt even. None of the children smiled in any of the pictures. If anything, they looked worried. The word pensive came to mind.

The next thing he noticed was how dirty and dingy the scenery was. Granted, the pictures were all black and white, but it was more than that. The roads were grimy and dirty. He saw no trees or bushes, certainly no flowers. There appeared to be no sunshine reflecting on anyone's faces. In every photo gray, cloudless skies.

He wondered when and where they were taken. No obvious clues from the pics themselves. His first guess was the 1940s or 50s. Then again, judging by the apparent poverty, it could be from the 1930s, during the Great Depression.

Carefully turning the page revealed much the same thing on pages two and three. More pictures of children looking poor and disheveled. They weren't playing with games or toys. If anything, they were standing around or else doing chores. In several pictures, some children pulled and others pushed what looked like a handmade wooden wagon filled with scrap metal. One showed two boys sweeping a concrete floor. Another showed four boys filling up burlap bags with rocks—or were they potatoes—picking them up by hand. The odd thing was, Jack didn't see any parents or grandparents in any of the pictures.

Whenever he looked at their old family photo albums, they were mostly filled with adults, posing. Relatives from every branch of the family tree. Kids might be in a few of them, but not every one. If they were, they were smiling. Everybody smiled. Even in pics Jack had seen taken in the black-and-white era.

But no one smiled in these. What had they gone through and what were they still going through when these pictures were taken that could take away all of these children's smiles?

Another thing Jack remembered from his family's old photo albums was that people often wrote things on the back. The pics were usually glued to the paper, the corners tucked into little tabs. But over the years, some would break loose. He turned another page and saw that one had broken free and was tucked into the center crease. He lifted it out and looked at the front.

Finally, an adult. Two in fact. Both women. They were dishing out watery soup from a tall silvery kettle to a line of anxious children all holding little white bowls. A few children in the foreground sat at a wooden table spooning away. Were these the same children that were in the first three pages? Jack wasn't sure.

He turned the photograph over and read the words:

*Das bin ich, das dritte Kind in der Schlange. Ich vergesse , der das Foto nahm. Vielleicht 6 Monate nach der ich eine Waise. Alle in diesem Foto sind Waisen.*

Okay, he didn't expect that. Looked like German, which likely meant the date in the picture wasn't during The Depression, after all. It was more likely in Germany after World War II. Rachel had taken German in college, but he wasn't sure how fluent she was and didn't want to bother her with this. Then he remembered Google Translate. Rachel had told him it wasn't always accurate but you could often get the general idea of something using it.

Bringing the photo to his laptop, he opened the program, selected German and typed the words into the left box exactly as they appeared. As he did, these words appeared on the right box in English:

> *That's me, the third child in line. I forget who took the photo. Maybe 6 months after I become an orphan. All in this photo are orphans.*

Jack turned the photo over and focused on the third child in the soup line. It was hard to tell his age. Maybe eight, maybe ten. He had light brown hair, parted to the side. He wasn't looking into the camera. His eyes focused like lasers on the lady's hand dishing out the soup.

Although there wasn't a name on the picture, now it was something real. Not just a smattering of miscellaneous photos, but someone's collection. Holding the photo in one hand, he browsed through the pages he'd already seen, comparing those pics to the loose photo. The boy wasn't in every picture but in most of them. Jack started to recognize some of the other children, as well. Perhaps they all lived in the same orphanage. As with the loose photo, the little boy never looked into the camera. And he pretty much had the same look on his face in each one. Serious and sad.

Well, that would make sense now, wouldn't it? Considering what he'd just read on the back of the photo. The boy had become an orphan six months earlier. His whole world had been shattered. Not just with the loss of his parents but likely his childhood home. He had probably been relocated to a different city. Jack had read about this situation. There were hundreds and thousands of orphans in Germany after the war. In some ways, the effort to rescue them included a desire to rescue their souls.

All of Europe had just suffered through a Second World War foisted upon mankind by the German people. Everyone agreed…everything that could be done must be done to make sure this never happened again.

It was decided, the minds and hearts of these orphaned children had to be redirected toward a brand new way of thinking, on every level. Germany needed a clean slate, a fresh start. These orphans were seen to be part of that solution, but only if they could be raised with a brand-new set of values. Relocating them to different cities helped accomplish that goal. All ties to the past had to be severed. A new day was dawning for Germany. Or so that was the hope. Judging by the looks on these children's faces, they weren't buying any of it. Not yet anyway.

Something else Jack had noticed in these pictures confirmed another thing he'd read. These German orphans were all mixed together. Whites of Aryan blood bunked together with surviving children from the concentration camps. Poles, Czechs and other Slavic children were also part of the mix. Leading up to the war, the Nazis had tried to create a master Aryan race, whites only need apply. Jack could clearly see the blending together of all these people-groups in the faces of these orphans. And none of them seemed to struggle with each other in the least. They were all bonded together in the simple struggle for survival.

He was so tempted to pull some of the photos off the pages to see what else he could learn from what was written on the back. They would add so much more to this little boy's story.

Maybe there was a way.

What if he took a picture of each page? That way, he'd make sure he glued all the photos back in their proper places. He would only pull off those that came away easily, without tearing the page. It could work.

He was just about to try with the pics on the first page when he realized…he didn't have any glue. Maybe he could pick up some when he went to the store. Just then, the alarm sounded on his phone. He looked at the screen and remembered. Rachel. The store. Dinner.

That's what he should be doing right now, not playing around with this old photo album. He slipped the loose photo back in the crease of the page, got up and slid the photo album back in its place on the shelf.

As he walked toward the dinette table, intending to write out a list of things he needed, his foot caught the edge of that stupid floorboard again. "O-o-w-w," he yelled. He sat on the edge of the couch and took a look at his foot. He'd scratched it but it wasn't bleeding. He wasn't thinking of bringing the throw rugs in from outside just yet, but maybe he should reconsider.

Then he looked down at the floorboard again. No wonder it had lifted up. It wasn't nailed down. He couldn't see if the other end was properly fastened; it was under the recliner. But maybe that's all it needed, a couple of nails. He had seen a toolbox in the pantry when he'd gone looking for the broom. He could probably fix this in a few minutes. Glancing at the clock, he realized he didn't have a few minutes. He'd have to do it later.

Just out of curiosity, he pushed down on the board to see if it would lay flat. It didn't want to go down, but he knew with a couple of nails and a good pounding it'd behave. He also noticed when he pushed down on it, how loose it was. He grabbed the end with his fingertips and lifted.

"Well, look at that," he said aloud. It came right up. The end under the recliner mustn't be nailed down, either. He slid the board out of place and set it on the floorboards beside it. It revealed a long, thin dark hole. Jack knew there wasn't any cellar. The cabin was built a few feet off the ground, had a crawlspace underneath. That's probably what he was seeing.

But why would this one floorboard not be nailed down? And why was it a different shade than all the others? He looked at the clock again. Better worry about this later. On the off chance the owner or Mr. Bass came by while Jack was gone, he quickly set the board back in place.

# 16

Sergeant Joe Boyd responded to the radio call. "I'll get this one, Sandy." He already heard the location of the convenience store and was only half a mile away.

"I thought you were off this afternoon," Sandy replied. "What are you even doing listening to the radio?"

"I'm already out this way. Checking on a cabin out here by Lake Sampson." He got his lights flashing and whipped his unmarked car around. "Thinking of renting one for the family the last two weeks of summer. This a real 2-11?"

"The store owner called it a robbery," she said. "No guns involved. Sounds to me like some college kids are making a ruckus. A little hard to understand him. Some kind of accent, maybe Indian."

"Are they shoplifting?"

"I don't think so. I asked him to stay on the line, but he already hung up. I could hear yelling in the background. Want some back up, just in case?"

"Might as well. It's probably nothing. But send who's ever closest here. Tell them not to kill themselves or anyone else getting here. I'll call in when I get there if anything's urgent."

"Will do."

Boyd knew the guys pretty good by now. Someone would want in on this. He'd been here in Culpepper just over a year now. Except for that one major bit of excitement right in the beginning with that crazy conspiracy-experimental drug-multiple murder-shootout ordeal at the university, things had been relatively quiet. No, make that super-quiet. Too quiet for him. At least compared to his sixteen-plus years in Pittsburgh.

But Kate loved it here. The kids even more. And he had to admit, Boyd's blood pressure liked Culpepper, too. His GPS said the convenience store was right up on the left just around this curve.

And so it was.

As he pulled into the parking lot, he could see the "ruckus" had moved outside. A short dark-skinned man with jet black hair was standing by the doorway—likely the store manager or owner—holding the glass door open with one hand and pointing toward three males in the parking lot with the other. They looked like college kids. Two of them even had "Culpepper" written on their T-shirts. It looked like the one without the T-shirt, the tallest one, had just thrown something in the dumpster. One of the kids with a school T-shirt was capturing everything on his cell phone.

Great, just great, Boyd thought as he got out of his car. Everyone involved looked at him.

"You see? You see what I have to put up with?" the owner yelled. "Arrest him! The tall one. Arrest them all."

"Arrest us?" the tall one yelled back. "You're the one who should be in jail. Selling crap like that in your store."

Boyd walked toward the owner. The three boys came a little closer. The one recording everything took a few steps back, holding his phone up about head high. He kept checking the screen. Boyd guessed to make sure everybody fit in the picture. He'd been seeing a lot more of these smart phones showing up at calls, especially with the college kids. Get it on video, no matter what. Everyone wanted to be the next thing that goes viral. "Could you please put that away?"

"I got a right to do this," he said. "I'm not breaking any law."

The kid was right. Stupid, but right. "Well, keep it out of my face."

"I'm nowhere near your face."

Boyd shifted his focus toward the main issue. "Okay, what's going on here?" The Indian guy and the tall college kid started talking on top of each other. Boyd put up his hand. "Okay stop! One at a time. I'll hear both of you, so don't interrupt. You first," he said to the owner.

The owner took a deep breath. "I'm in my store, minding my own business when these three young men walk in. They don't look like trouble. I smile but they don't smile back. I look outside, see their car, see they have gotten gas. They all go to the cooler, open the doors. They are picking out their drinks. Then they all come to me, set their drinks down on the counter."

"Could we skip to when the trouble starts?" Boyd said.

"I'm getting there. It's the next thing. I ask them, will that be all? The tall one says, no, that will not be all. He points to a jar on the counter filled with little red flags."

"Confederate flags," the tall student said.

"Yes," said the owner. "Little Confederate flags. I ask him if he wants one and tell him the price. He yells at me that he doesn't want one and asks why I'm even selling these in my store. I tell him, some people like them." He looks at Boyd. "What can I say? We are in Georgia. It's the truth. Some people do."

"Well they shouldn't want them, and you shouldn't sell them," the student yelled. "They're racist flags. Everybody knows that now.

Haven't you been paying attention?"

"Wait your turn," Boyd yelled back. "Go ahead, sir. Finish what you were saying."

"See how he talks to me? It was louder than that in the store. He says to me, you of all people should understand what that flag stands for. I'm thinking, what does he mean, *me of all people*? Does he think I am black? Is he that stupid? Can he not see I am from India, or at least somewhere in the Far East? So I tell him, this flag means nothing to me, or to my people. It's just a flag. If he doesn't want it, no one is forcing him to buy it. But that is not enough for him."

"What were his two friends doing while this was going on?" Boyd asked.

"They were just nodding in agreement to everything he said, except this one with the phone. He took it out and starts to record everything."

Boyd started to figure out what was going on.

"The boy, the tall one," the owner continued, "he says, this flag is a racist flag. It offends him and the overwhelming majority of Americans. I tell him, well, obviously not everyone." The store owner smiled. "I make a joke, try to ease the tension. But he gets angry. More angry. Then he looks at his friend taking the video, as if to say, make sure you get this next part."

"That's not what I was doing."

"That's what it looked like to me. Because next, he grabs all the flags and pulls them out of the jar. He knocks the jar off the counter, and it shatters all over the floor."

"That was an accident. I didn't mean to knock the jar over."

"Then he starts walking toward the front door with all the flags in his hands. I yell at him to stop, where are you going? He says he is doing me a favor, since I don't have the courage to do it myself. Then he walks right out the door with the flags, his two friends right behind him. I yell at them to stop, but they keep going. That's when I picked up the phone and dialed 911. I run outside and find him standing there in the parking lot, holding all the flags and giving some kind of speech about racism and injustice."

"To who?" Boyd said.

"To no one. There is no one here at the store but us. He is talking to the phone. He is doing all this for a video."

"Where are the flags now?" Boyd said.

"In the dumpster…where they belong," the student said.

"He threw them in there after he finished his speech. It happened just before you drove up."

"Did they hit you or hurt you in any way?" Boyd said to the owner. He shook his head no. "Did they take anything else besides the flags?" No, again. Boyd looked at the college student. "Let me guess, you didn't pay for these flags, right? You just walked them out the door."

"And right into the dumpster. I wouldn't pay a nickel for that crap."

Boyd looked at the owner. "What's the value of the merchandise he took?"

"There were fifty flags. I'm out a hundred-and-fifty bucks. I don't know what the jar costs."

"Interesting," Boyd said. "And I don't suppose you want the flags back? I mean, we could just take them out of the dumpster."

"No, I don't want them back. They are ruined. The dumpster is full of garbage. We just threw out all our outdated food last night. I can't sell them now."

"I'm assuming you want to press charges."

"Yes, I do."

"That's all I needed to know." He took out his handcuffs, turned to the college student. "Turn around. Put your hands behind your head."

"What, you're arresting me? For what?"

"For shoplifting, for starters."

"I didn't shoplift anything."

"The law says you did. You took this merchandise out of the store without paying for it, and you threw it into the dumpster. And since the value of the merchandise you destroyed is over one hundred dollars, I gotta take you in."

"I can't believe this. This is ridiculous." The student looked at his friend holding the smart phone as he put his hands behind his head. "You getting all this?"

"Every bit."

"This obviously racist cop is arresting me," the student said staring right at the phone, "for simply standing up for the rights of the oppressed. That's all I'm doing here, taking a stand against racism, and this racist symbol this store owner is selling for a profit."

After Boyd finished handcuffing him, he turned toward the kid with the phone. "Okay, videotape this." He looked right into the screen. "My name's Sergeant Joe Boyd. I'm a detective with the Culpepper PD. What I'm arresting this young man for has nothing to do with racism. It has to do with stealing and destroying property that is not his. I'm not a racist now and never have been. I've been a cop for seventeen years. Some of my close friends are African-American. A few have even saved my life. I'm from Pittsburgh, so this Confederate flag has no meaning for me. Far as I'm concerned, the Civil War ended a hundred and fifty years ago. When it was going on, my ancestors didn't even live in America, let alone own slaves. This store owner is from India. Pretty sure he never owned any slaves, either. He has a right to sell this flag, if he chooses. And you all have a right not to buy it."

He turned toward the kid in handcuffs. "You even have a right to share your opinion with the store owner, respectfully. You can even tell him it offends you and that you wish he wouldn't sell it. But that's where your rights end. What you did next is a crime. And if I recall, you could get up to twelve months in jail and pay up to a one-thousand dollar fine, even for a first-offense."

He looked back into the camera. "So, go ahead and keep filming if you want. I doubt this little stunt of yours has a chance of going viral. It's way too boring." He looked up to see two cars entering the parking lot, one of them a patrol car. "Oh look, your chauffer has arrived." The other car was a shiny blue BMW sedan.

It looked familiar.

# 17

Jack enjoyed the way his BMW handled these winding roads. So tight. It was tempting to just let it go, let it drive the way it wanted to. Made him wish this trip was longer than fifteen minutes. His GPS lady informed him his destination was right around the next curve. As Jack pulled into the convenience store, it was obvious a little excitement was underway. There were two police cars, lights flashing. One was unmarked. One man dressed in regular clothes was handing off a college student in handcuffs to a uniformed patrol officer.

Wait a minute, the first guy looked like Boyd, Sergeant Joe Boyd. It was him. Jack pulled into an open parking place and got out. Looked like three kids from the University. One of them was filming everything. The patrolman helped the handcuffed kid get in the backseat of his car. "Sergeant Boyd," Jack called out.

Boyd turned and looked. "Jack, or do I call you Professor now?"

"Jack is fine."

"Then you knock off the Sergeant, how about? I think after all we've been through, you earned the right to call me Joe." He held out his hand, Jack shook it.

Boyd was right. They had been through a lot together. This was the man who had, literally, saved Jack's life last year. "You know, in some cultures I would be indebted to you for the rest of my life."

"I was just doing my job. The guy was shooting up my town. Can't have guys shooting up my town."

"Are we all set?" the uniformed officer asked Boyd.

"We are. You can bring him in, get him booked." He turned to the student's two friends. "You can follow him down to the station, if you want. He's going to be there a few hours, at least."

"What about me?" the storeowner said.

"You can head back into your store for now. We'll need you to come down a little later and sign a criminal complaint. You may be asked to come back to testify if there's a trial. Doubt there will be on something like this. I'll take some pictures of the flags in the dumpster in a few minutes, then come in and chat with you."

"Okay. Thank you, Sergeant." The store owner headed back toward the store.

The patrol car drove off and the two college kids headed toward their car in the parking lot, leaving Jack and Boyd alone.

"This is kind of off the beaten path for you, isn't it Sergeant? I mean, Joe. I'm guessing that was a shoplifting thing?"

"Technically. The college kid was all riled up about the owner selling Confederate flags. Tossed them in a dumpster. I don't usually take calls like that myself, but I was already out here checking out some cabins to rent for our vacation. Speaking of off-the-beaten-path, what are you doing out here? Shouldn't you be teaching a class?"

"In between semesters," Jack said. "I'm out here in one of these lakeside cabins working on a doctoral thing."

"Didn't you inherit that cabin from Thornton? That's way on the other side of the lake, isn't it?"

"It is. But it isn't mine anymore. Sold it to some fishermen. I couldn't relax out there after everything that happened. Too many bad memories."

"So, you bought another one?"

"Thinking about it. Renting one for a month. The owner wants to sell it. Pretty obvious he doesn't use it anymore. You might know who he is. Senator Wagner?"

"Wagner? Yeah, I know him."

The look on Boyd's face was almost sour. "Don't like him?" Jack said.

"Aah, nothing personal. Let's just say he's the kind of guy born to be in politics. Guys like that generally rub me the wrong way."

"I've never actually met him," Jack said. "So far I'm liking his cabin. Might just buy it. Say, when do you need yours?"

"In two weeks," Boyd said.

"Rats," Jack said. "I'll still be renting this one then. But I tell you what, if I do wind up buying this one or another one, you and your family can use it anytime you want, rent-free."

"Well, that's very nice of you, Jack. So, how are you making out now? You all healed up?"

"Pretty much. Even after I healed up from the gunshot wound, kept having nightmares and some mild PTSD symptoms for about another six months. But I'm doing much better now."

"Good to hear. You and that girl Rachel still together?"

"Definitely. In fact, that's why I'm here. She's coming up for dinner at the cabin in a little while."

Boyd got a confused look on his face. He turned around and looked at the convenience store. "And you think they've got something you might want to serve her for dinner…in there? Jack, I stopped in there a few times. We're not talking Wa Wa or even 7-Eleven. We're talking shipped-in food made last week, or maybe last month."

Jack laughed. "I've already got most of what I need for the dinner. Just missing a few things. Thought I'd stop in here, take a chance, see if they had 'em. The nearest supermarket's another fifteen minutes away."

Boyd nodded. "Gotcha. Glad you guys are still together. She's a nice lady."

"She truly is. I'm actually pretty close to popping the question."

"That's great to hear. Congratulations."

"Haven't done it yet."

"Well, when you do, I'm sure she'll say yes."

Jack felt pretty sure too. "How are things around Culpepper from your perspective? Seems pretty quiet. At least, I never hear about anything major on the news."

"Definitely nothing major. Sometimes it's too quiet for me. But I keep reminding myself, that's why we moved down here. Seriously, that thing you went through last year. That was the big leagues. That would've been handled by major crimes in Pittsburgh. Here, it was almost like the apocalypse was going down."

Jack laughed. "Glad to hear it. Truth is, I like quiet. That was way more excitement than I prefer."

"Well," Boyd said. "I better get back in there and finish things up. You stay out of trouble now. Don't need you getting involved in anything that might mess up my vacation? It's just two weeks away."

"I'm a history professor, Joe. What kind of trouble could I be getting into?"

# 18

Jack had dinner all set.

The chicken piccata was ready, in the oven on warm. The angel hair pasta was draining in the strainer. Table set. Chilled bottle of wine in the fridge. He'd asked Rachel to call him once she had started the drive up here, so the dish wouldn't get all dried out. He looked at his watch. She should be here any minute.

That was another nice thing about living in a small, southern college town. No such thing as rush-hour. He didn't know how people who lived in places like Atlanta ever managed to coordinate a dinner time.

He stepped outside onto the porch intending to be there when she got out of the car. Really, just to show off the place a little. Then he saw the two oval throw rugs hanging over the wood rail. He'd forgotten all about bringing them in. He grabbed the one that went upstairs first and headed inside. As he carried it up the stairs, he could already tell it didn't smell near as musty as before. And when he plopped it down on the floor, no dust clouds.

He hurried down the stairs but heard the obvious sounds of a car coming onto the property. Looking through the front window confirmed it was Rachel. He paused a moment and glanced around the room, especially at the dinette table. Everything looked fine. He was sure she'd love it in here. He walked onto the porch, glanced down at the second throw rug and decided to let it wait. Rachel's car pulled in next to his. Walking around the back of her car, he was there to greet her as she opened the door.

"Hey Jack," she said, as she turned and set her feet on the ground. "I like the drive out here from town. Very pleasant. All except for that shack back there. That kind of threw me for a loop."

"Shack?"

"Yeah, you know, the shack?" she said, still sitting in the car. She reached for her purse. "Once you turn in off the main road? Your directions said to stay on the dirt road until it opens up to clearing on the left. I see what you mean now that I'm standing here. But I guess you forgot that dirt driveway on the left, halfway between the main road and here. It kind of looks like a clearing, so I drove down it. It doesn't go very far then it opens up to a clearing of sorts, and there's this old shack facing the water. I thought it was the cabin, and I wondered why you thought it was so nice. Then I realized I didn't see your car, so I thought maybe this wasn't the cabin after all. At least, I was hoping it wasn't. So I backtracked, drove further on the dirt road and came here."

"I forgot all about that shack. I haven't actually seen it. Mr. Bass mentioned it. So did the realtor, so I knew to keep driving past that opening in the road. Sorry, I forgot to tell you."

"Who's Mr. Bass?"

"A neighbor. Apparently, he gets paid to keep an eye on the place." Jack held out his hand and helped her to her feet. As she stood, he leaned toward her for an extended kiss. They hugged, and he kissed her once more.

"Okay, that makes up for it," she said.

"Well, seeing the real thing might make up for it some more.

They held hands and walked around the car, now in full view of the cabin and the lake.

"Wow. That is beautiful." She was looking mostly at the lake. "A way better view than the cabin you inherited last year."

"And it doesn't make me feel creepy," he said.

"You wouldn't say that if you'd seen that old shack," she said, looking at the cabin now. "But *this* is really nice. I like this."

"It's about one-and-a-half times bigger than the one I sold. It's got a loft too, which the other one didn't have. And the best part? No dead guys lying on the bed."

"Another nice feature."

"Speaking of nice features," Jack said, "step over here away from my car and feast your eyes on this." He led her toward the fire pit.

"That is nice. It's just the way you described it."

He put his arm around her shoulder. "Can't you just see us sitting out there some evening a month from now, drinking hot chocolate as the sun's going down? The only sound is the crackling logs in the fire, maybe a few crickets and katydids?"

"I can. But does this glorious scene include mosquitoes? They've been really bad this summer."

"No mosquitoes. They don't come out anymore once it starts getting cold."

Rachel slapped her forearm. "Well, they're out now. Can we go inside?"

"Of course. Dinner's all ready."

"What are we having?"

"Chicken piccata over angel hair pasta. I have a nice bottle of white zinfandel chilling in the fridge."

"I could use a glass of that right now."

"Then you shall have one." He took her by the hand and led her toward the porch.

"Is the shack part of the property?" she said.

"I'm not sure. I'll have to ask the realtor. If it's that creepy, I kinda hope not."

She stopped walking when she saw the braided oval rug on the railing. "That's interesting."

"I've had it airing out all day. It smelled so musty. The whole cabin did. I've had the windows open all day, too. I just closed them a few minutes ago."

"Don't you think you should bring that in? It'll get damp if you leave it out all night."

"I'll bring it in after dinner." He opened the front door and stood to the side to let her in.

As soon as she walked in, she sniffed the air. "Smells wonderful. I love your chicken piccata."

"That's why I made it," he said and closed the door.


They spent the next thirty-five minutes enjoying a romantic dinner for two, getting caught up on what each other had done the last few days. Rachel was really glad to come out here and take a break from her schoolwork. She was taking two classes over this summer semester, but it felt like they were being assigned three times the homework. When the semester ended, she'd be at the halfway point in her Master's program. Like her bachelors, it was in political science.

Jack shared with her some of the progress he had made with the Dresden material, doing his best not to get lost in the weeds and bore her to tears. Although, Rachel could typically hold her own on almost any military history discussion, especially from the World War II era forward. Mainly because, she had taken several courses on it at Culpepper in an effort to get closer to her father, a retired

Air Force general. That's where Jack and Rachel had met last year—well, met again—when she had attended his Pearl Harbor lectures in Professor Thornton's class.

During dinner, the whole time Jack shared his part of the conversation, he kept thinking about that old photo album he'd been looking at before he'd left for the store, wondering if Rachel would be interested in seeing it. For the most part, she seemed to enjoy his interest in historical things and even chatting about it, but he also knew she had a boundary line. The problem was, he didn't. He could go on for hours. The only thing that held that in check was his people skills.

Thankfully, he had some.

Boring others—especially boring others without knowing it—could be an occupational hazard for any professor, especially those who taught history. Lord knows, he'd been bored by a fair share of academics in his occupation over the years. People who lacked the ability to recognize the warning signs when people had completely lost interest in what they were saying.

Jack never wanted to be *that guy*, especially with Rachel.

"Okay, Jack. Where did you go?"

"What? What do you mean?"

"I can tell I lost you, maybe two paragraphs ago. What are you thinking about?"

"It's nothing. Nothing important anyway."

"Most of what we've been talking about throughout dinner is not important," she said. "Since when has that been our standard?"

He smiled and reached for her hand. "See, that's why I love you."

"I love you, too. So what's keeping you from being totally enchanted by what I'm saying?"

He stood, picked up his wineglass and started walking toward the bookshelf on the left side of the fireplace. "Come, and I'll show you."

She stood and followed. "A book? You want to show me a book?"

"Not quite a book," he said. "Here, I'll show you." When he got closer to the bookshelf, he bent down. "How good is your German?"

# 19

"My German? Pretty good I guess. I don't get to speak it very much, so I'm sure I'm rusty. But I can probably read it okay."

Jack slid the old photo album out from its place and stood with it. "I think this belongs to the cabin's owner."

"Senator Wagner?"

"No, his father. But I'm not sure. I haven't seen any names yet. I've only just started to look through it, then I had to stop and get ready for dinner. It's full of photographs, original ones. A bunch of kids, German orphans I think, just after World War II. I'll sit on the couch, so we can both look at it." He sat near the middle and, after setting her wine glass down on the coffee table, she cuddled up beside him.

He turned through the first few pages slowly, the ones he had already looked through, letting her eyes take everything in. Then he pointed out the little boy he now believed to be the focus of the album and showed her how often he appeared in the pictures.

"You're right," she said. "He's in most of them. You said he is an orphan, how'd you know that?"

Jack turned to the third page and pulled the loose photo from the center crease. "Read the back."

She looked at the front for a moment then turned it over. "He tells us himself," she said. "I guess he doesn't have any siblings, either. You don't see any other children in all of the pictures. Or even most of them. I'm thinking if a number of kids from the same family were orphaned together, it would be hard to keep them apart."

"I think you're right. He doesn't mention any other siblings in that picture. But it's only one picture. I'm thinking he probably wrote on the backs of most of these. That's what my family did."

She started flipping through the other pages.

"What are you doing?"

"Seeing if there are any other loose pictures." She stopped after three or four pages. "Wow, you can see he's getting older on the pics on this page."

Jack leaned a little closer. "You sure that's the same kid?"

"Yeah, you can see it in his eyes and cheek bones. But he's more like twelve or thirteen in these." She turned a few more pages. "I can't believe there aren't any more loose ones."

"Maybe that doesn't matter."

"What do you mean?"

"I mean, I think we can still see what's on back. The pictures are just glued onto the black paper. Probably using something like Elmer's. I know in my old photo albums, the pictures pull away with just a little bit of effort."

"But what if they rip? I'm guessing we're doing this without permission?"

"He can't care too much about it, considering he left these albums right there on the shelf for anyone to find. If I was renting a place out, I'd bank on people being totally nosy…"

"Like we're being," she added.

"Yes, like we're being. The point is, I wouldn't leave something out unless I expected people to look through it."

"But you're not talking about just looking through it. Like I said, what if we start pulling these pictures off and the paper rips? Or some of the pics do?"

"We'll be super careful," Jack said. "We'll just lift the top edge a little. Like this." He demonstrated what he was saying. "See, that one doesn't want to give, so I'll just leave it." He tried a few more and found one on the bottom row that popped right off and slid down the page. "There we go." He turned it over. "Well, nothing written on this one. But see, it didn't rip. And I bought some Elmer's glue at the store before dinner. I'll get my phone, take pictures of every page so we make sure we get them all back where they belong. And when we're done, we'll just glue them all back. It'll be fun. Like having a safe, kind-a historical little adventure. I'll even let you be the one to decide which pics are loose enough to come off."

"Okay, but if I think one of these pics is gonna rip, even a little, I'm going to leave it in place."

"That's fine. I'm just thinking it'll be so much more fun if we knew what was going on in some of these pictures. When I read that first one, it's like I wasn't just looking at a bunch of miscellaneous pictures anymore. I was stepping into someone's story."

"That's why you're such a good history teacher, Jack. This stuff comes alive to you."

He leaned over and kissed her and looked down at the album. "Okay, start flicking the pics off the page."

"No, first you go get your phone and take pics of these pages."

"Right." He got up and found his phone. When he came back, they spread the photo album out on the coffee table. She helped him take pics of each page. It only took a couple of minutes. Then they snuggled back on the center of the couch.

After giving up on the next five or six pics, Rachel found one that flicked off easily.

"Bingo," Jack said, looking at the back. Four lines in German, the same handwriting as before. He turned the pic back over a second to see who was in it and what was happening. Two little boys, one of them the main one; the other considerably younger. Both in bare feet standing on a cobblestone road. Behind them, a cracked, broken sidewalk. Behind that, a bullet-scarred wall. They were looking at whoever was taking the photograph with sad yet hopeful eyes. "Doesn't it almost look like someone has just promised them something?" he said. "Like maybe some food, if they stood still for the picture?"

"I don't know," Rachael said. I just can't get over how sad they look, in every picture." She flipped it over and read the words aloud, in German.

*Das bin ich und ein kleiner Junge Ich befreundete . Ich weiß seinen Namen nicht mehr erinnern . Er wurde krank und starb am nächsten Winter. Der Fotograf war gerade bot uns ein kleines Stück Schokolade.*

"You were right, Jack. The photographer had just offered them some candy. How did you know that?"

"I didn't. It's like when I see these old photographs, I put myself there. I just imagine what might be going on."

"You're pretty good at it. She read what it said now in English:

*This is me and a little boy I befriended. I don't remember his name now. He got sick and died the next winter. The photographer had just offered us a small piece of chocolate.*

"It's so sad," she said. "They're standing there in bare feet. Looks like they haven't had a bath in weeks. They're both so skinny. And he can't even remember his friend's name...because he died.'"

"I wonder when he wrote this note," Jack said. "It was obviously many years after the picture was taken. Could have been decades. Whenever it was, it looks like the same time as when he wrote on the other pic. Let's check out some more."

Rachel turned the page. "I have to admit...this really is fun."

They continued doing this for the next hour or so, making their way to the fifth page. Rachel was able to safely extract two or three pics on each page. Of those, about half had writing on the back. Both agreed, the writing was all done by the same hand, using the same ink, probably at the same time.

The story of this young orphan boy's life after the war began to emerge. He definitely had no siblings still alive. He'd said as much on one of the pics. The reason why the backgrounds in the pictures seemed so different was due to how often he'd been moved. Not just to different orphanages but even different towns.

By the seventh page, there was at least some noticeable progress in his situation. He wasn't skinny anymore, and his clothes didn't look so shabby.

On the ninth page, the pictures began to change somewhat dramatically. It looked like the young boy—now grown into a teen—had joined some kind of military youth organization. Jack and Rachel had only looked at the back of one picture on that page, and it had no writing. The boy was standing with two friends in front of a large banner with the letters "FDJ," which sat atop a logo that looked like a sunrise.

"What do you make of that?" Rachel said. "What is FDJ?"

"I have no idea," Jack said. "My East German history after the war is pretty malnourished." But he was definitely intrigued. "I can look it up."

Rachel glanced at her watch. "No, I better go. It's not that late, but I've got some homework I have to do before bed."

"You really have to go?"

"I really do." She set the photo album back on the coffee table. They both stood, and he walked her toward the front door.

Once outside, they kissed several times, as they always did saying goodbye.

"So glad you came," he said. "Hope it wasn't too weird. Doing that photo album thing at the end."

"It wasn't too weird. After reading the first few, I got sucked in, like finding the missing pieces of a puzzle. I wanted to keep finding more of them with writing on the back. But hey, don't you get too sucked in."

"What do you mean?"

"I know how you get. This photo thing might be a nice diversion…like, when you need a little break. Don't let it become an obsession."

"That's not gonna happen."

She gave him that look. They'd only been together a year, but he knew that look. He decided not to argue the point. She waved and smiled again, walked toward her car. "Hey Rach, wait up. I'll follow you in my car down the dirt driveway, till you get to the main road. It's pretty dark and then there's that…."

"Creepy shack?" she said.

"Yeah, that."

# 20

After Rachel left, Jack spent the next half hour cleaning up after dinner. While they were eating, Rachel had offered to help, but Jack refused. He knew she had the homework to do and couldn't stay long. He didn't want their time together eaten up with chores.

Now that the dinette table was clear, he spread all his Dresden research material out the way it was before. He lifted the lid to his laptop and opened the file he had already created. It took some doing, but he was finally able to break free from the old photo album's gravitational pull. He had to get back on this research project. The outline wouldn't write itself.

Within fifteen minutes, he was fully into it again, then spent the next three hours totally immersed in the project, adding five new pages to his outline notes. There were so many more angles to the Dresden bombing than he had ever imagined. A lot more websites, survivor interviews and controversies to explore. The worst part of the controversies were the eyewitness accounts telling of American fighter planes flying down to ground-level to deliberately strafe and kill civilians, who were literally running for their lives. Even Kurt Vonnegut had said this happened.

But there were just as many other accounts—the more official accounts—that denied such a thing ever took place. Was this a case of history being determined by the victors? What was the truth? Jack wasn't sure how he would handle this part of the story. But he was sure he needed to take a break.

Getting up from the table, he poured himself a glass of iced tea. He walked outside for a breath of fresh air. Stepping off the porch, he glanced up at the half-lit moon and starry sky. They provided just enough light to allow him to trace with his eyes the silhouette of the trees as they wrapped around the lake. It was so peaceful and quiet, so soothing. Hard to imagine anyone experiencing the kinds of things he had just been reading about.

Not only during the World War II years, but even now in various parts of the Middle East. Planes were still bombing targets. People were still dying. Only now, the idea of carpet-bombing civilians was unthinkable. This was the age of smart bombs and drone strikes. Military strategists did everything they could to avoid "collateral damage."

Jack wondered how the military leaders during World War II would have fought the war if they'd had these hi-tech weapons at their disposal. How would it have changed things? Would it have changed things? The world was such a different place then. He had read recently that since 2003 almost 6,000 American soldiers had died in the wars in Iraq and Afghanistan. Even with this figure, people today were outraged by such losses.

But during World War II, more Americans died than that in the Battle of Iwo Jima alone. More than double had died in the Battle of Okinawa. More than triple had died in the Battle of the Bulge.

Yes, it was a much different time then.

Jack sighed.

Here he was in this peaceful place with this beautiful scenery, almost overwhelming his senses, and he was thinking about the horrors of war. About battles and statistics. He needed to get his mind on something else, something smaller, more personal. Maybe he should call it a night, pick up the research project in the morning. For light reading, he'd only brought Vonnegut's book, *Slaughterhouse Five*. That didn't seem like the change of pace he needed.

Then he remembered…the old photo album. That might be just the thing.

He was about to head inside when he noticed the oval throw rug still hanging over the wood railing. He'd better bring that in first before it started getting damp. Setting his iced tea down, he shook the rug out a few times, then walked it inside. He needed to move a few things around in the living room to lay it back down properly. One of them was the recliner. As he pulled it back, his eyes zeroed in on that board. The loose floorboard. He could see the whole length of it now. It really was a different shade than the rest. The grain pattern was even different.

It made him wonder…what must have happened to the original floorboard? Did it crack or get destroyed somehow? And why replace it with a new floorboard but not nail the board down? Jack looked at it closely. There weren't even any nail holes. It had only ever been set in place, as if….

As if someone had wanted it to be an easy thing to pull up and put back. Now he really was curious. He got down on his hands and knees and pulled the board up. All the floorboards were pretty wide, maybe ten inches. Once again, he stared down at a dark hole, probably the crawl space under the cabin. A flashlight. Jack had packed one; it was in his backpack.

He hurried to the bedroom, grabbed the flashlight out of his backpack and headed back to the living room. This was probably all for nothing, but what the heck? It was pretty fun and had definitely gotten his mind off of battles and war statistics. He turned the flashlight on and dropped to his hands and knees.

He could see right off the bat, this wasn't nothing.

He was looking at a black box, clearly visible through the floorboard opening. He lay on the floor and reached down to feel it. Hard plastic. With his right hand, he felt around the perimeter, trying to get a sense of its size. Maybe eight inches high, a little over a foot wide and a foot deep. He sat up and shone the flashlight on it some more.

Now he knew what it was. A portable safe.

# 21

Still on his knees, Jack looked at his right hand. It was filthy, just from handling the safe. Clearly, it hadn't been touched in a while. Possibly for years. He shined the flashlight all around the safe again, trying to get an idea of what he was looking at. How did the owner get the safe down there? It didn't look like it could fit through the opening. It was too wide. Did he bring it in through the crawl space? But that didn't make any sense.

Then he figured it out, and felt pretty stupid. The safe was too wide to bring up horizontally, but it was only eight inches high. The opening was at least ten. You could pull it up if you turned it sideways.

So he did.

It came right up through the opening with a little room to spare. He laid it flat on the wood floor. It really was so dusty and dirty. If someone told Jack it had been down there for twenty years, he would've believed it. He shined the flashlight back down through the opening, because something had caught his eye as he lifted the safe through. Now he could see some concrete blocks lying on the dirt. That's what the safe had been sitting on. Which made sense; the blocks would have kept it off the ground in case any moisture or standing water ever gathered there.

Jack was just about to get up and wet some paper towels to clean it off, when he stopped to think about it some more. Was that a good idea? If it was all cleaned up, someone would know somebody else had messed with the safe besides the one who'd put it there. Then Jack realized, he'd already messed up that idea when he felt along the safe's edges with his hand and lifted it through the opening. It not only looked messed with already, his fingerprints were all over it.

Cleaning it up was actually a necessary step now.

It only took a few minutes and the safe looked good as new. Now, the bigger problem became evident. The safe was locked. It wasn't any kind of fancy security system, just a simple opening for a key, which of course Jack didn't have. The crazy thing was, having gotten this far, seeing what was inside the safe had quickly grown from a mild curiosity to something just shy of a quest.

He bent back down and shined the flashlight all around the concrete blocks and the dirt underneath where the safe had been. No key. Nothing even shiny or metallic. He got up and sat on the edge of the recliner. This thought involuntarily ran through his head: *If I were the owner, and I wanted to hide a key in this cabin, where would I hide it?*

He stood and spent the next thirty minutes going room to room, and spot to spot, trying to answer that question. But no luck. He located one hopeful drawer in a dresser in the loft upstairs. It was filled with odds and ends: spare buttons, old combs, tie tacks, nail clippers, some old coins, and even some keys. All of them, however, too big to fit in the safe opening.

After another fifteen minutes of searching, which included a number of locations on the porch, Jack finally gave up. The key was probably on a keychain somewhere, possibly, probably…in the possession of the Senator, who now owned the cabin and all its contents. But if that was true, it seemed pretty clear the Senator had forgotten all about it. Which also probably meant, whatever its contents, they couldn't be worth very much.

Which meant that Jack was wasting his time. But really, did that matter? He had all kinds of time at the moment. He wasn't taking time away from his research. He'd already quit for the day. This was free time.

Speaking of time, what time was it anyway? He glanced at the clock. Almost 1AM. But see, that wasn't a problem. He could stay up until two if he wanted. Wake up in the morning whenever his body was done sleeping. Jack sat and leaned back in the recliner. It was likely true the key to the safe was on a keychain somewhere. But these store-bought safes came with two keys. He had one sitting in his master bedroom closet at home. These weren't the kind of keys you kept on the keychain you used every day. Jack didn't keep either of his safe keys on a keychain. He kept one in a dresser drawer, the other taped to a shelf in the closet. You wanted a key, at least one of them, near the safe. In case you lost the key or forgot where you put it.

It was worth a try.

Jack got back on his hands and knees near the opening and started feeling around the underside of the boards with his hand. About two boards in from the opening, Jack felt a bump. He explored the bump until he was sure he was feeling duct tape, then continued scratching until he found an end. He peeled it back carefully making sure whatever was causing the bump didn't fall to the ground. He felt something metal, small and metal. After pulling the rest of the tape off, he pulled his arm up through the opening.

"There you are," he said aloud.

The key was the perfect size. Had to be it. He carried the safe over to the dinette table. He stuck the key in, turned and it opened right up. Okay, what was this? Two notebooks, or journals. Both black, slightly different sizes. He lifted them out and set them aside. That's it? There was nothing else in the safe? He didn't know what to expect, but he was hoping for something more than this.

He walked the two notebooks back over to the recliner and sat. Opening the first, he saw it was a journal filled with handwritten pages. They all looked to be in German. Since he didn't read German, and it would be an impossible task to look all this up in Google Translate, he set it aside. The other one appeared to be a small scrapbook filled with newspaper articles, all cut out and pasted to the pages. He scanned through the articles and didn't notice anything remarkable other than that they appeared to be obituaries, all written in English. The pictures of some of the deceased were fairly old men. Others showed black-and-white pictures of much younger men in military uniforms.

Jack quickly picked out the ages of the men from the text. All were in their seventies when they died and all appeared to be military veterans, at least at one time. So what was this, a scrapbook filled with the obituaries of old war buddies? Not very intriguing. He yawned as he set the scrapbook down on top of the journal. This was a total waste of time. There wasn't anything here. The only question now was, should he put this mess back together now or in the morning?

He yawned again. In the morning then.

He stood and stretched, then a thought popped into his head. Really an image, then a second image. The German handwriting in the journal. The German handwriting on the back of the old photographs. Were they written by the same hand? He stepped over to the bookshelf and pulled out the photo album then sat with both on his lap.

Glancing back and forth between the two, it didn't take long to see. They were both written by the same person.

The little orphan boy in these photographs had written everything in this journal, which had been tucked away in a safe, hidden under the floorboards of the cabin.

Now, this had possibilities.

# 22

Jack yawned again.

As interesting as this was, it was still all written in German, which Jack didn't speak. Rachael wasn't here and based on her concerns that he'd become obsessed with this, he wasn't likely to get her back here to read this in the next day or two. Using Google Translate was okay for a few sentences, maybe even a paragraph. But it was way too inaccurate to use for an entire notebook.

He got up with both books and walked back to the dinette table. After setting the notebook back in the safe, he was just about to lay the scrapbook with the obituaries on top of it when an earlier thought percolated upward. When he'd glanced through it the first time and noticed all the dead guys were military vets, he'd dismissed it completely, thinking it was just a scrapbook filled with *the obituaries of old war buddies.*

Then he realized…if the person who'd written on the back of the pictures was the same one who'd written the notebook, he was almost certainly a natural-born German, not an American. Since all the obituaries were of *American* servicemen, they couldn't possibly have been war buddies. And there was this: the pictures showed he was a little boy during the war, not old enough to be friends with any of these Americans.

There was no way these were obituaries of war buddies. That being so, why would someone paste these obituaries into a scrapbook and consider it important enough to save for all these years, hidden away in a safe stashed under the floorboards?

Jack took the notebook out of the safe and walked back to the recliner with it and the scrapbook. He set the notebook on an end table, yawned and stretched then sat with the scrapbook. There was something here, something to discover. He was sure of it. As he flipped through the pages again, he confirmed that all the dead men were World War II veterans. He also noticed something else…some of the articles had handwritten notes in some of the margins that also looked to be in German.

Holding the scrapbook in his lap with his right hand, he reached for the notebook with his left and opened it. The handwriting in both looked identical. So, all three things were written by the same person. And who was this man? Jack's gut told him it was Senator Wagner's father, *the old man* according to Bass.

Bass had said the old man talked with an accent, similar to Arnold Schwarzenegger. Schwarzenegger was Austrian. But they spoke German there, so that added up. And Bass had said the son had inherited the cabin from his father when the old man died. The words on the backs of the album pics, those in the notebook, and the notes written in the margins of the obituaries were likely, then, all written by the old man. He'd left them here in the cabin for his son. Some of them hidden in a safe under the floorboards.

And for some reason, his son didn't know or didn't care. Why else were they still here?

So many questions were gently knocking on the door but would have to wait. His body would no longer follow where his mind wanted to go. He had to get some sleep. The only question that remained: should he leave everything out for tomorrow or put it all back where it belonged?

Jack awoke the next morning and as he went through his morning routine, did his best to ignore the budding mystery that beckoned in the living room. That was the compromise he'd made with himself last night. He didn't put everything away, just moved it all into the living room, then he'd spread out all his Dresden research back on the dinette table.

As he sat now at that table drinking his second cup of coffee, he had to keep reminding himself...*this* is why I'm here. Not *that*. That stuff in the living room was for breaks and free time only. Still, it held a ridiculous amount of interest for him. By now, Jack knew how he was wired. Part of his success as an author and as a history teacher was his ability to make history come alive for his audience. That wasn't his self-assessment; it's what magazine and blog reviewers had said about his books over and over again. What his students had said about his lectures in countless emails.

Jack knew what made that possible. He had always followed after things that stirred him, things that lit him up inside. If something stoked his curiosity, he'd keep pulling on those threads and running down those rabbit trails wherever they led. It was an offbeat approach to the learning process. Some might even call it undisciplined.

But it was hard to argue with the results.

Following those same instincts had led Jack to pursue this Dresden project for his doctoral dissertation. He still believed it was the right direction to go. But right now, in the face of this unfolding mystery in the living room, its luster had faded. All he wanted to do was get up from the table, head over to the living room and give himself to this new pursuit.

He turned in his chair, as if to free his legs from their hold beneath the table, when Rachel's parting words to him last night came to mind. *"I know how you get. This photo thing might be a nice diversion right now…like, when you need a little break. Don't let it become an obsession."*

Then a reminder of his own reply: *"That's not gonna happen."*

Here it was happening, the very thing.

Jack knew what he had to do. He stood, walked to a closet, pulled out a blanket, walked into the living room and tossed it over the whole mess. Covered the notebooks, the open floorboard…even the recliner.

He walked back to the dinette table and his Dresden research, confident he had freed himself from the pull of this distraction. If not for good, at least until his morning break.

# 23

Jack spent the next three hours listening to online interviews from Dresden survivors, taking notes and cross-checking things they'd said with known facts. The stories were sufficiently gripping to easily hold his interest. Before long, the project in the living room had faded and was no longer distracting him. The Dresden story really was an amazing chapter in World War II history and Jack was again glad he'd picked this topic for his research.

At the moment, he was watching a video of an elderly woman with a thick accent speaking to a library group somewhere in the US. She had been born in Dresden and was a teenager during the firebombing. It took her a while to get to the relevant part of her story but, once she did, Jack was riveted by what she said. So much so, he almost didn't see his cell phone ringing. He had shut the ringer off but left the phone in plain view.

When he saw Rachel's beautiful face on the screen, he grabbed it. "Rachel?"

"Hi, Jack. It rang so much, I thought it was going to be your voicemail."

"I'm sorry. About an hour ago, I got several phone calls from the school, so I shut the ringer off."

"I didn't mean to interrupt your work," she said. "Got a few extra minutes before my next class, thought I'd give you a try."

"I'm glad you did. You're my favorite distraction."

"So, the research is going well?"

"Definitely. And as always, where would I be without the internet? I know it was around when I studied for my bachelor's, but it wasn't anything like this. Between Google and YouTube…it's crazy to be able to listen and watch videos on almost any topic you can think of in a matter of seconds. It almost seems unfair how much easier it is to study for a doctorate now than it was twenty or thirty years ago."

"That's true," she said, "but you're still the one doing all the work and the one who's going to have to write that big paper. Oh, before I forget, I had a brief chat with my dad on my drive to school this morning. He said to say hi, by the way."

Jack still wasn't used to being on such familiar terms with Rachel's dad, a retired Air Force general. Especially a man he had served under many years ago.

"He called just to touch base," she said, "nothing special. I was telling him about our little adventure last night. You know, that photo album you found with all the little German children. Of course, he wasn't in the military during World War II. Vietnam was his era. But he told me something I didn't know about his story. He was stationed in Berlin for a few years, was there when the wall went up."

"Really? That's pretty cool."

"Isn't it? I thought I knew his whole story. Anyway, I asked him about those last few pictures we saw when the little boy was a little older. Remember that one when he was standing under a big banner with those big letters?"

"FDJ?" Jack said.

"That's the one. My dad knew what that was. I thought you'd find this interesting."

"What's it stand for?"

"The exact German translation is *Freie Deutsche Jugend.* In English it means, *Free German Youth.* My dad said he always found that to be an ironic title for a group of young people who were anything but free."

"What do you mean?"

"They were in East Germany, Jack. It's a communist youth group. Apparently, that little boy in the photo album grew up on the other side of the Iron Curtain."

"Really?"

"That's what he said. FDJ was a huge communist youth organization. He said it reminded him of the Hitler Youth the Nazis had set up. It was all about indoctrinating young people in the communist ideology from the ground up. He said it was especially big among the thousands of orphans raised in East Germany after the war ended. It became like their family. I bet you if you kept looking at the rest of that album, you'd see a lot more pictures of life in East Germany before the Wall came down."

As he listened, Jack stood and walked over toward the living room. He pulled the blanket back exposing the end table and recliner. He was looking right at the photo album, but also at the scrapbook with all the obituaries of the American pilots. He wanted to tell her all about it but wasn't sure that was a good idea.

"Jack?"

"What?"

"You didn't answer. Usually that means you're distracted. What are you thinking about?"

Women's intuition was a scary thing. "I'm wondering if you want me to hold off looking at the rest of the album until you get over here and we can do it together."

"I'd love to come back, but I don't want to get in the way of what you are supposed to be doing."

"You won't be in the way. I can't do my research day and night. My head would explode. You could come after dinner, after I quit working for the day."

"I suppose I could do that."

"Of course, you can. Let's plan on it. I'll finish up, let's say, around six thirty."

"How much time will you need for dinner?"

"That includes dinner. I'm going to work through it. I just bought some of those frozen dinners. I'll pop one in the microwave and eat while I'm working."

"Okay," she said. "I'll do it. I'll be over there sometime just after six thirty."

"Great."

"Well, I better go. Can't wait to see you."

They both said "Love you" and hung up.

Jack was standing behind the recliner now. He looked at his watch. The phone call had only lasted five minutes. Really, not much of a break when you think about it. She really did interrupt the flow of his concentration, in a good way. Maybe he should just go with the flow and take his lunch break a little early.

Yes, that made sense. And while he was eating, he could spend a little more time on this project. Eat on the couch, as he looked over the scrapbook with the obituaries.

He'd save the photo album for this evening, when Rachel came over.

# 24

Jack sat in the recliner with a fresh cup coffee, the scrapbook lying open in his lap. As intrigued as he was by the photo album, he had quickly become even more so with this. A photo album made sense. A collection of one's pictures over time. This did not. Unless it was a collection of obituaries from deceased family members, which this was not. Jack had already concluded it wasn't a collection of old war buddies, either. So, what was it? What was the point of cutting out various obituaries from a local newspaper—of people who were not relatives—and pasting them into a scrapbook?

Jack slowly turned the pages and quickly realized…none of these obituaries were from the local newspaper. None were even from the same newspaper. He read them aloud. "*The Florida Times-Union, The Miami Herald, The Sarasota Herald-Tribune, The Post and Courier from Charleston, The Daily Sentinel in Texas, The Houston Chronicle, The Roanoke Times* and *The Kansas City Star.*"

Eight in all.

Jack noticed something else, something he hadn't realized before but should have. All these obituaries were written in the 1990s. He had assumed they were newer than that. But given that the ages of the dead men represented were all in their seventies, the articles would have to be that old. World War II veterans dying now were in their nineties. He quickly thumbed through them and confirmed something else: the obituaries had been pasted in chronological order. In other words, the first article was about a man who'd died in February, 1993; the last one died in April, 1998.

Eight men in five years.

He flipped back to the first article and began to read:

### WWII Pilot Dies in Accidental House Fire

William James Hanover, son of Tom and Madilyn Hanover, died in his home on Sunday, May 13, the likely cause was smoke inhalation. He was 71 years old. An investigation of the fire is still underway but authorities do not suspect foul play. Hanover was known to be an avid smoker. He appears to have died while taking a nap on the living room sofa, a fire department spokesman said. Results of an autopsy are still pending.

When the fire department arrived, one whole side of Hanover's house was fully engulfed in flames. He was a widower and lived alone.

Hanover was a long-time Tampa resident, having moved here in 1952 with his bride, Mary Gleason from Vermont. The couple had been married since 1945, shortly after Hanover came home from the war.

Hanover served in the U.S. Air Force during World War II. He was a First Lieutenant, captain and pilot of a B-17 bomber in the 379th Bombardment Group. His crew successfully flew 35 missions over Germany from Kimbolton airfield in England. Hanover won the Distinguished Flying Cross after one harrowing mission to Cologne, where he managed to bring his bomber home with only one remaining engine.

Jack continued reading a few more paragraphs, but the article shifted to things like what Hanover had done after the war and listed the names of his surviving children and their spouses.

He carefully turned the black scrapbook page and began to read the second obituary. It was from the Miami Herald, dated about six months later. This man's name was Franklin Hodges, who died at age 74. Like Hanover, he had also died in his home but Hodges was killed from what appeared to be an explosion. Fire department officials suspected a ruptured gas line. Once again, no foul play suspected.

Jack read down a bit until he found the paragraph describing Hodges' World War II involvement. Again, like Hanover, Hodges had flown B-17s in the war. The article didn't mention which bombardment group Hodges flew for, but it did say he was based in Kimbolton, England. Jack was pretty sure that meant Hodges must've also flown for the 379th. He set the scrapbook aside for a moment, went over to his laptop at the dinette table and googled it. Sure enough, Kimbolton was where the 379th had been based.

Hmmm. What were the chances?

He brought the laptop back over to the living room and set it on the coffee table, in case he had any more details to look up. Picking up the scrapbook, he went on to read the third obituary, dated five months after the second.

Okay, this was becoming ridiculous. The headline itself grabbed Jack's attention:

### Former World War II Bomber Pilot Dies in Fire

Before reading any further, Jack read the headlines and first few sentences of all the other obituaries. Every single man, in one way or another, had died at home in some kind of fire-related accident. He spent the next thirty minutes reading through each article, only this time he took notes.

Besides the fact that they were all killed in some kind of fire in their homes, none of the fires appeared to be listed as arson. All of them were cited as accidental deaths. No foul play suspected. If not plainly stated, that was the implication.

The other astounding coincidence? All of the men had flown B-17 bombers during the war and all but the last one mentioned either Kimbolton airfield or that they had flown for the 379th bombardment group. The last one didn't mention any bomb group affiliation, but Jack was certain if he looked it up he'd find this pilot had flown for the 379th, as well.

This was crazy.

Jack set the scrapbook down on the coffee table next to his laptop and sat back on the recliner. The implications of what he'd discovered began to set in. A scrapbook of former bomber pilots, all from the same bomb group, all killed in their homes over a period of five years in fire-related accidents.

And no one suspected a thing.

Why would they? The deaths took place in different cities across several different states. The internet was alive then but in its infant stage compared to now. Most local police departments had no way of comparing data with other police departments, let alone different law enforcement agencies.

If someone had a mind to kill these men this way, and make it look like an accident, Jack saw how they could easily get away with it. Just then, part of that first conversation he'd had with Mr. Bass played through his mind. They had been standing out on the porch. Bass had been talking about "old man Wagner."

*He was a strange one. Had this fierce look in his eyes. I was a younger man then, bigger than I am now. Linebacker in high school if you can believe it. Wasn't afraid of nothing. But if I'm being honest, I was afraid-a him. Made me feel like he'd snap my neck if I crossed him.*

Jack shuddered. He was certain he was holding a scrapbook old man Wagner had put together himself. Jack had no idea why just yet, but what else made any sense? These obituaries were his trophies. Men, who for some reason, Wagner had killed in house-related fires made to look like accidents.

And Jack was holding in his hand the only thing that tied them all together.

# 25

It was another gorgeous afternoon in downtown Culpepper. Burkhart Wagner—called Burke by friends, Senator Wagner by the rest—stood by the thick burgundy drapes in his plush sixth-floor office peering out at the sight. He was looking down at the array of historic shops and buildings that surrounded the manicured city square.

Wagner had paid some serious dues for this view and liked to catch it whenever he could. Right now his eyes focused on the County Courthouse Annex. He could see it clearly from his office. It was a place he knew well—from the inside. As exciting as it was arguing live cases before a jury, these days Wagner preferred to avoid courtrooms. Too much work for the money. Of course, it was his ability to sway juries in those same courtrooms during some high profile cases ten years ago that secured the leverage he now enjoyed, as he hammered out far more lucrative financial schemes behind the scenes.

Those victories had earned Wagner something of an intimidating reputation. No one wanted to fight him in court. The threat of it alone tended to make folks settle out of court fairly quickly. The following year, that same public exposure had secured an upset victory for Wagner in the district's state Senate seat, held by a retiring Democrat. Since then, Burke Wagner had become one of the state's rising Republican stars. He found it amazing how much attention people paid to someone who could talk well.

Over the next few years, Wagner found it just as easy to sway folks on the Senate Chamber floor as he had in the jury box. Of course, it helped if you didn't mind bending the truth here and there to make your points. Burke Wagner wasn't a true conservative, either morally or politically. But he didn't consider that much of a handicap. As he'd confided to one of his closest friends, "I could certainly play one on TV."

The talk was now that Wagner was in line to become the leader of the Republican majority in the Georgia senate, which would make him one of the state's most influential power brokers. In that office, he'd have a strong voice in shaping every major bill that came before the Georgia General Assembly. He'd be among a handful of people who made the final decisions on which programs were funded in the state budget.

Now…a position like that would mean some real money.

Wagner smiled as he thought about it. What would his father think if he could see him now? The old man certainly had his virtues, but his methods in dealing with people had been archaic, even brutal. Burke could never get him to see it. The game was all about leverage. One could whack people with a stick or use that same stick to set a massive boulder rolling downhill.

Wagner turned from his view of the city below and sat in his stuffed leather chair. It squeaked slightly as he leaned back. He loosened his silk tie and shifted his neck from side to side, working out a kink. He took a final sip of his Cafe Amaretto and thumbed quietly through the pages of some contract negotiations, prepping for a meeting with his young aide, Harold Vandergraf.

Being a state senator was a part-time job for Wagner. Had to be, considering the senate only convened the first few months of each year. The rest of the time, Wagner practiced law as a senior partner in the firm of Wagner and Reynolds. But Wagner had already set his sights on bigger things. Either the Attorney General's office or winning a Senate seat in Washington.

The intercom chimed. Wagner leaned forward. "Yes, Jane?

"Harold's here."

"Okay. Send him in."

The sleek black door opened admitting a lean, impeccably dressed, young man in his mid-twenties. "Afternoon, Senator."

Wagner hadn't insisted Vandergraf call him that, but he didn't mind. He nodded. "Got a mission for you, Harold. Come on in, have a seat.

"What is it?" Vandergraf sat in an upholstered office chair.

"It's a piece of cake. Can I get you anything? Coffee, a drink?"

"No, I'm fine."

"I need you to pay someone a visit."

"Anyone I know?"

"Maybe. He has been in here a few times last month, and I think you were with me when we visited his office once. Mr. David Herndon, owns Herndon Real Estate Group. His firm is looking to buy a huge tract of land on the edge of town, out where that new on-ramp is scheduled to connect State Road 19 to the highway."

"Is that official?" Vandergraf said. "I thought it was still just talk."

"It's not official, but it's more than talk. I'm in a position to change that, but I'm also in a position to shut it down, or else delay it so long it might as well be. I communicated that to Mr. Herndon. He's been weighing his options about a decision I've asked him to make a few days ago. The problem is, I didn't give him a few days. I gave him one day. I need you to visit him and remind him of that discrepancy."

Vandergraf smiled. He didn't need to ask why Wagner didn't just send Herndon an email or give him a call. Most of the tasks Wagner gave him were handled this way. In person. No paper trail, no recordings, no digital fingerprints.

"What incentive do you want me to offer Mr. Herndon, to induce him to get back with you right away?"

Wagner sat forward in his chair. "Since this is just a first warning, simply suggest that I'm leaning toward delaying this improvement project until next year…unless he can give me a good enough reason to speed things up. He'll know what you mean." Wagner picked up a plain vanilla folder and handed it to Vandergraf. "But just to make sure, here's a file to look over. It's Herndon's personal information. Names and addresses of his wife, kids, what school his grandkids attend. Things like that. I'll let you decide what to do with it."

Vandergraf looked down at the folder, opened it, glanced at it for a second then closed it. "I understand. I'm guessing by the urgency in your tone, you'd like this done soon?"

"Very," Wagner said. "Like this afternoon." He got up and walked to the wet bar, popped open the glass top to a crystal carafe half-filled with scotch, poured himself a drink.

"No problem. I can do that. Is there anything else you need me to do?"

"Not at the moment. But there will be if I don't hear back from him today." He held up his glass of scotch. "One for the road?"

Vandergraf stood. "No, thank you. I'll get right on this, sir."

"Good, you do that," Wagner said.

# 26

Harold Vandergraf rode alone in the elevator, watched the digital numbers rise in the only other building in downtown Culpepper taller than five floors. It was owned by the Herndon Real Estate Group, which occupied the entire top floor. As the elevator climbed, Vandergraf thought through his strategy, how to best convey to Mr. Herndon the Senator's concern.

If there was one thing Vandergraf had learned from the Senator, it was that words had power, so choose them carefully. A few sticks of dynamite properly placed can blow the side off a mountain. One's eyes were another effective tool but they worked more like lasers, fierce and precise. Together, Vandergraf had found they enabled him to manipulate soft, pudgy men in expensive suits with relative ease.

He let go of the polished brass handrail as the stainless steel elevator doors opened. As he stepped into the lobby, he digested the scene of Herndon's world: plush tan carpet, walls paneled in marble and mahogany, a petite brunette sitting behind a large colonial reception desk.

The receptionist noticed Vandergraf standing there. She looked and gave him more than a courteous smile. "Can I help you?"

Vandergraf walked up confidently. "I sure hope so."

"Me, too," she said, then laughed.

"I'm here to see Mr. Herndon."

She glanced at the computer screen. "Do you have an appointment?"

"I don't."

"I didn't think so. I didn't have any scheduled on his calendar."

"But I'm pretty sure he'll see me, if you'll just let him know I'm here."

"And you are?"

"Harold Vandergraf. I'm Senator Wagner's aide."

"I thought you looked familiar. You were here before, a few weeks ago, right?"

"Good memory. That's true, I was. You could tell him I will only take a few minutes of his time."

She clicked a few buttons then spoke into her headset. She listened a few moments, looked up and said, "Mr. Herndon said you could come right in. Do you remember where his office is?"

"I think so, but maybe you should escort me, just to make sure." Vandergraf took a few steps, intentionally in the wrong direction.

"Wrong way," she said, taking the bait.

He followed her down a wide hallway. Her walk suggested she'd spent time on the runway.

"Right in there," she said. "Through the big wooden door. Mr. Herndon's executive secretary is out today. Just pass her desk through the second set of doors."

"Thank you very much, Miss...."

"Just call me, Julie," she said, holding out her hand.

First name. Very good. "Thank you very much, Julie." He let his grasp linger. Julie did not resist.

"Right in there," Julie repeated, gently pulling her hand away.

"See you later," Vandergraf said.

"I hope so." She gave him another interested smile as she turned to walk away. He stepped into Herndon's roomy outer office, noticed the empty secretary desk and the second set of doors.

As he opened the one with a door knob, he heard, "Come in Harold. I've been expecting you." Herndon spun around in his overstuffed chair to face Vandergraf, but did not get up.

"You have?"

"Well, I figured the Senator preferred to handle matters like this in person. Considering how busy he is, didn't figure he'd come himself."

"I assume then you know why I'm here?"

"Let me guess?" Herndon said. "I'm late."

Vandergraf nodded.

"Care to have a seat?"

"I don't plan on being here long enough."

"Suit yourself."

"Have you made a decision?" Vandergraf said.

Herndon didn't answer. He inhaled deeply, then exhaled a sigh. "See, the thing is—"

Vandergraf held up his hand. "I don't want to hear what the thing is. I'm not here to discuss the matter with you. I don't even know enough details to do so."

"What do you know?" Herndon said.

Vandergraf needed to be careful. He quickly scanned the room looking for any obvious signs of a video camera. He didn't see any, but they could be well-hidden. "I know it has something to do with a large tract of land your company wants to buy, if you can get certain…assurances. I know that Senator Wagner is inclined to recommend delaying any activity along those lines, at least in the current fiscal year."

"Is that what he said? He's planning on delaying the project?"

"I think the phrase I used was...*inclined to recommend.* But I understand he gave you some things to consider. Specifically, a decision to make."

Herndon sat back in his chair, sighed again.

"I've come for your reply. And as you said, you are...late."

Herndon sat up. "It's not as simple as you make it sound."

Vandergraf shot him a menacing look. "I'm afraid it is." He noticed Herndon's office had a balcony. "Shall we finish our discussion out there?"

Herndon glanced at the glass door. "Why?"

Vandergraf walked toward it. He realized by the look of fear on Herndon's face. He was thinking Vandergraf was planning to assault him, maybe even throw him over the side. He wasn't. Not for a first warning. But it certainly didn't hurt for Herndon's mind to go there. "It's a beautiful view. I like fresh air. Take your pick." The real reason was, he couldn't be certain Herndon wasn't recording the conversation. On the balcony, he could speak freely. When he got to the glass door, he unlocked it and slid it open. "You coming?"

Herndon stood up but didn't move. "Why can't we talk in here?"

"Come on," Vandergraf said, more like an order than an invitation. "This won't take a minute."

Herndon sat back down. "I don't...I'd rather..."

Vandergraf stepped out onto the balcony, left the door open for Herndon. He waited a few moments. Finally, Herndon appeared.

"I've made my decision," he said, still standing on the carpet. "Tell the Senator I accept his proposal."

"As is?" Vandergraf said.

"As is."

"Good. I'm glad to hear it."

"The Senator said if I did, it might give him enough reason to change his mind and get fully behind this project."

"He did?" Vandergraf said. "Well, if he said it, I'm sure he meant it. The Senator is a man of his word."

They stood there looking at each other a few moments. "You sure you don't want to come out here, Mr. Herndon? It's really very nice."

# 27

All afternoon, Jack did his best to stay plugged into his doctoral research project, but he was having the hardest time. Whenever his mind was free for even a few moments, it instantly drifted back to the scrapbook with the obituaries. In the hours since making the discovery, he was only more certain he'd found something very dark and sinister.

The implication was stunning: old man Wagner was a killer. Not just a killer, but a serial killer who, for some reason, had stalked these eight elderly World War II pilots over a period of five years and systematically executed them. Nothing else made any sense.

But why these eight men? Were there more than eight? Was there another scrapbook somewhere, or were there others he had killed but didn't save the obituaries?

He got up from the dinette table and walked into the living room, picked up the scrapbook again. This wasn't just innocent or idle information; it was evidence of a crime, a series of premeditated murders. Jack knew by itself, it wasn't proof. At least, not enough to gain a conviction, but it seemed like enough evidence to launch an investigation.

He picked up the journal, thumbed through all the handwritten pages. This had been in the safe with the scrapbook. And it was written by the old man. Maybe there was more evidence inside, incriminating statements that could link him to these murdered pilots. Maybe even a confession. He couldn't read a word of it. But Rachel could. He had to call her. She had to see this. He set the books down on the coffee table and pulled out his phone.

The phone rang four times. "Hey Jack, I was just thinking about you."

He so loved the sound of her voice. "Hi Rachel, that's nice to hear. Obviously, I was thinking about you. Actually, I was thinking about how much I wished I could see you."

"That's funny," she said. "That's exactly what I was thinking about."

"Actually, the reason I want to see is probably a little different. I mean, I'd love to see you anytime. But something's come up. Something pretty serious, I could really use your help with it."

"Uh-oh, that doesn't sound good. Are you okay?"

"Yeah, I'm fine. It's not me, it's something I found here at the cabin."

"Something in the photo album?"

"No, something else. It's connected, but it's something else. Something a lot more serious. Is there any chance you could come out here?"

"I'm sure I could. What time are you thinking?"

"How about…right now?"

"Now? Okay, I guess it is pretty serious then."

"It really is."

"Can you tell me anything else?"

"I'd really rather just show you. After you see it, we can talk."

She paused a moment. "Do you see the time?"

He glanced at his watch. "It's getting pretty close to dinner."

"That's what I was thinking. Want me to bring something up with me?"

"Sure, that would be good. Maybe some Chinese, or some other kind of takeout. You decide. You know what I like."

"Okay," she said, "then that's what we'll do. I can be up there in about forty-five minutes."

"Great. See you then. Love you."

"Love you, too."


Jack was straightening up the cabin when he heard Rachel's car pull up outside. He had decided to leave the living room, as is. The recliner moved out of the way, the floorboard exposed, the scrapbook and journal laid out on the coffee table. His cleaning efforts were mainly about getting all his research material put away, so they could eat on the table. That and making his bed, putting his dirty clothes in a laundry bushel.

He hurried to the front door and opened it just as she stepped onto the porch. "Chinese! I was hoping it was going to be Chinese."

"I figured you were." She leaned forward, and they kissed. She handed him two little white boxes. "These are yours. Szechuan pork and pork fried rice."

"And yours is…orange chicken with white rice."

"Of course."

Jack had never seen her order any other kind of Chinese food since their first date. They walked back into the cabin toward the dinette table, but Jack noticed Rachel's eyes instantly lock onto the mess in the living room. Especially down at the opening in the floorboards.

"Jack, what have you been doing? Did you tear that up?"

They set their boxes down on the dinette table. "No, the board wasn't nailed down. It lifted right up."

"How would you even know it was loose?"

Jack laughed. He realized how odd the scene must look now viewing it through her eyes. "I kept banging my foot on it. Since it wasn't nailed down, I guess over time it warped a little, which made it raise up a little from the rest. After the second time, I looked down and noticed, it wasn't only not nailed down, it didn't even have any nail-holes in it. It never had been nailed down."

Rachel gave Jack a puzzled look.

"What?"

"I don't know, the things you notice. Who would ever see such a thing and, if they did, would feel compelled to investigate it further?"

"It wasn't only that. I could also see that this one floorboard was a different shade than all the others. It even has different grain marks. Here, let me show you." Jack walked over and picked it up. He bent down and laid it on the floor. "See? Not even close."

"She walked over. Okay, I see that. But still…"

"Okay, I can see how that still seems a little weird. But it just made me wonder, why would they just replace one floorboard? If you had water damage or bug damage, it wouldn't limit itself to one board. And even if it did, why wouldn't you nail down the replacement board. It made me wonder if he didn't do it on purpose. So he could have easy access to something under the floor."

"You said *he*. Who's *he*?"

"Old man Wagner."

"Senator Wagner? The man who owns this cabin? He doesn't seem that old."

"No, I'm talking about his father. Senator Wagner inherited this from his father. I'm about ninety-five percent positive the pictures in that photo album we were looking at last night were his. When he was a kid. Mr. Bass—he's the next-door neighbor I met shortly after I got here—he told me all this. And, that old man Wagner lived here in the early nineties. He's dead now. Died of a stroke quite a few years ago. Mr. Bass also said he was afraid of him. Now I know why."

"Why?"

"That's why I wanted to see you. I found something really disturbing. Do you want to see it now or after we eat?"

Rachel glanced over at the Chinese food on the table. "I want to see it now. We can heat the food up in the microwave after if it gets cold."

# 28

Jack and Rachel sat close together on the couch. He pulled the coffee table closer so they could easily see the scrapbook and journal.

"So what are we looking at?" Rachel said.

"I think we're looking at a collection of trophies. You know how serial killers collect trophies? That's what this is. I can't think of any other conclusion that makes sense. Senator Wagner's father was some kind of cold-blooded killer. I'm not sure why yet, but he had it in for World War II pilots, especially B-17 pilots. That's what all these obituaries have in common. But it's more than that. They actually all flew in the same bomb group, at the same airbase in England. I haven't figured out the significance of that yet."

"You've read them all?"

Jack nodded. "Several times, and I made some notes."

Rachel turned to the second one.

"You can read them, if you want. I'm in no hurry."

"No, I know how thorough you are. I believe you."

"They all died in fire-related accidents," Jack said. "Well, that's what they were called. But I think every single one of those fires was deliberately set...by the old man."

"And he's dead?"

"For over ten years."

Rachel released an obvious sigh of relief. "Do you have any idea why? Why old man Wagner would want to kill all these pilots, and why he waited till they were so old?"

"I haven't gotten that far into this yet. But can you think of any other reason why someone would collect a bunch of obituaries like this?"

Rachel turned a few more pages, glanced at the headlines. "It's definitely very strange. More than strange, it's downright creepy. So I guess that makes these, like, cold case files."

"I guess," Jack said. "But they're not even that yet, if you think about it. No one even knows these were murders. To this day, the family members all think their loved ones died in accidental fires. For that matter, it happened so long ago, I doubt they even think of these men very much anymore. Not even the police who served in the cities at the time know these men were killed intentionally. They wouldn't even have cold case files opened on them. I mean, why would they?"

She kept turning the pages, slowly, until she came to the last one. "You know what I think this is? I bet they're revenge killings. Why else would someone track down all these pilots, men who all flew the same planes from the same airbase? And then kill them all either in a fire or an explosion?"

"Yes! That's what I was thinking," Jack said. "But I wanted to see what you'd say." He loved the look in her eyes. She was into this. He had half-wondered if she'd be upset with him for spending so much time on it. "We already know," he continued, "old man Wagner was an orphan. Maybe this tells us why."

"Do you know what missions the—what is it?" She glanced down at one of the articles. "—the 379th bombardment group flew on? I'll bet one of the towns they bombed was his hometown. Maybe the bombs killed his family."

"I haven't had time to check, but I'm sure I can find out. From my book research, I've spent lots of time on World War II websites. You'd be amazed at the volume of details people have put on the internet. I bet with some digging, I can find out not only which cities the 379th bombed, but what missions all eight men have in common. Obviously, if these are revenge killings, then these guys all flew in the same mission that killed old man Wagner's family. But we don't have to do all that now. I can look into it after you leave."

Rachel sat back. "This is really something, Jack. What are you going to do with it? I mean, with this information? Everyone involved is already dead. Even the killer."

"I haven't thought through that part, either. But it seems like way too big a thing to ignore. Seems like the families have a right to know." They both just looked each other a few moments, as the implications involved began to settle in.

Rachel spoke first. "I just thought of a scary thing."

"What?"

"Do you think the son knew anything about it, or maybe was involved in some way?"

Jack thought about it. "Well, it happened in the nineties, and I'm guessing the Senator is in his early-forties now, wouldn't you say?" Rachel nodded. "These killings happened over five years, so that puts him in his late teens, maybe early twenties."

"College-age," Rachel added.

"Right. He certainly could have known, but there's no proof he definitely did."

"His dad might've done all this while he was away at college," she said. "What's that?" she pointed to the journal sitting beside him.

"Oh, I'm glad you reminded me. Maybe the answers we need are in here. Problem is, I can't read it. It was in the safe with the scrapbook. I'm almost certain it's the same handwriting that's on the

141

back of the photographs. I was wondering if you could take a look at it. Maybe translate some of it. At least enough to let us know what it's about, see if it's connected to the murders." He handed it to her.

"Why don't you pull out some of the loose photos from the photo album," she said. "Let me take a look at them."

Jack did and handed them to her.

She opened to the first page of the journal, set the back of one of the photos right beside the page. A few moments later, "Definitely the same handwriting."

"What's the first page say, in the journal?"

Rachel read for a few minutes, then turned through several of the pages. "I'd say this is definitely connected."

"Really?"

"Let me read some more."

Jack waited, tried to be patient. A few long minutes went by. "Well…?"

She looked up. "I think old Mr. Wagner was pretty clever."

"Why?"

"I would say these are notes, things he was thinking about, plans he was sketching out as he set up each of these murders."

"That's perfect then. It proves what we're thinking?"

"Not exactly. I need to read a lot more, see if he slips up anywhere."

"What do you mean, slips up?"

"That's just it. I realized, as I read a little more, he never really admits anything. It's almost as if he's writing in code."

"Why did you think it was connected, when you first started reading?"

"I still think it is connected, totally connected. But I realized that's just because I already know what the obituaries mean. If you read the words here, at face value, I'm not seeing anything that you could say definitely ties into these murders. But let me take this home. I'll translate the whole thing. It might take me a few days to work it into my schedule, if that's okay."

"Sure. We're in no hurry. This case has sat in silence for twenty years. What's a few days?"

"Like I said," she continued, "maybe he'll say something more specific in one of these entries, or slip up in some way."

"I hope he does. Thanks for doing this. I know how busy you are."

"I am, but this is kind of fun. Like solving a mystery. I don't know where all this is going, but I definitely want to find out more."

"While you're doing that—in my spare time and not in any way that's even close to obsessive—I'll start seeing what I can find on the internet about the 379th bomb group connection."

She closed the journal and Jack closed the scrapbook. "Now, I definitely am hungry. Let's heat up the Chinese."

They stood. Jack looked at the disheveled state of the living room. "Maybe I should put this all back the way it's supposed to be. I doubt anyone would ever come in here besides me, but both Mr. Bass and the Senator have keys."

"You probably should, but how about we do it just before I go? After we eat, I'd still like to look over that old photo album together."

"Well, I found that on the bookshelf. We can still look at it even if I put this room back together. But if anyone walked in on this, it would be pretty hard to explain."

"Okay, you put the living room back together, and I'll heat the Chinese."

Jack didn't really think Bass or the Senator would come in here. But Rachel suggesting that the son might know about these murders, or somehow be involved, made him tense up.

# 29

Jack and Rachel enjoyed their Chinese take-out. All the conversation centered on this unraveling mystery in the living room. By the time they had finished eating, both realized what a big thing this really was.

Rachel got up from the table and started cleaning the after-dinner mess. Jack had protested, but she insisted. "Do you want me to save this?" She pointed to Jack's half-empty boxes.

"Sure. Can't let food that good go to waste. There's plenty of room in that little fridge."

"I'll definitely bring mine home," she said. "I love cold Chinese food for breakfast."

"I can't even imagine that." He got up from the table to help.

"The more I think about this, the crazier it feels," she said. "It's almost like being in the middle of one of those true-crime TV shows. Like Cold Case Files. Even the way you stumbled into this, finding all this stuff in a hidden safe under some floorboards. There could have been anything in that safe, but it turns out to be evidence of a decades-old series of unsolved, horrific murders."

"That part of it's starting to get to me," Jack said. "When I think about how these men were killed, the brutality of it. I mean, these poor men were war heroes. They deserved to die peaceful, natural deaths. Honorable deaths. And considering how long so many World War II veterans have lived, these guys all had many more years left to live on this earth. Instead, old man Wagner decides to hunt them down, one by one, and end their lives suddenly in this violent and, probably, very painful way."

"Yeah, I've thought about that, too." Rachel brought a washcloth over and started wiping down the table. "If these truly were revenge killings, I can just imagine the Senator's father feeling the need to confront these men, so he could pour out his hatred in person before setting in motion whatever fiery death he had planned."

"That's a horrible thought," Jack said. "Your last moments alive on earth having to deal with something like that, some*one* like that."

She stopped wiping the table and said, "Jack...do you think it could be possible old man Wagner came from Dresden?"

"That would be wild, if he did." No one said anything for a moment. "Even if that were true," Jack said, "knowing the awful things that happened in those bombing raids in Dresden...it's not like these pilots could have done anything about it. Every mission they flew was under orders. They didn't have the option of saying no. Certainly had no say in what cities or targets were picked for bombing."

He slid the chairs back under the dinette table. "I was reading through one interview in my Dresden research. One of the British pilots who bombed the city, talking years later. He said how terrible he felt when he heard the target was Dresden. He'd visited there with his parents as a teenager. Said it was one of the most beautiful towns he'd ever seen. He flew on the second raid. By the time his squadron flew over the city, most of it was already on fire. He couldn't believe the sight. Said it reminded him of what the Lake of Fire in the Bible must be like. And he knew, it wasn't a military town. With most of his missions, he at least knew they were bombing things that supported the Nazi war effort. But Dresden didn't have anything like that. He said he cried when he heard about the tens of thousands of civilians they had killed."

Rachel didn't answer right away. Then she said, "War is so horrible. I'll bet those bomber pilots old man Wagner killed felt the same way. They probably tried to explain that to him when he came there to kill them. And I'm equally sure it didn't make any difference to him. It's so senseless."

The kitchen was all back together. Jack reached for her hand. "C'mon, let's head outside for a little while before we finish looking through that old photo album. It's so nice out right now. Think we could both use some fresh air."

She took his hand. They walked past the porch into the clearing. "Want to take a walk?" she said. "Or want to sit on those nice chairs by the fire pit?"

Jack could tell her preference easily. "How about the chairs? A walk would be nice, but the only paths I found so far are all pretty much through the trees. You don't get any view of the lake."

"You're leading the way." She smiled.

They headed for the adirondack chairs. Jack took the one on the left. It was funny. Neither had ever done anything intentionally, but Rachel always ended up on Jack's right side, whether sitting or taking a walk. The chairs were just wide enough apart to comfortably hold hands.

"This is so nice," she said. "I hope it works out for you to get this cabin. I could really get used to this."

Jack wanted to say, *me too*. He hadn't said anything to her yet, but the discovery under the floorboards was giving him second thoughts about making an offer on this place. Talk about being creeped out. Professor Thornton's cabin had only involved one murder. This one turned out to be the hideout for a serial killer. "What do you think I ought to do about all this? I mean, about the scrapbook and journal? About them being criminal evidence?"

He heard her sigh. She was trying to change the topic. He had spoiled the moment.

She turned to look at him. "Are you saying, do I think you ought to go to the police?"

He nodded. "I don't see how I can avoid it. Do you?"

"I don't know. It's definitely a big deal. I get that. But who would you go to? From what we know so far, none of the murders took place here in Culpepper. Most were in different states. This might be an FBI situation. Don't they handle cases that cross state lines?"

"I hadn't thought about that. But you might be right. Of course, we might find out more incriminating info after you translate that journal into English."

"Like whether or not the son was involved in what his father was doing."

"Even if he wasn't directly involved," Jack said, "I think it matters even if he knew about it and didn't say anything. If he spoke up, he could have stopped his father's madness. If that turns out to be true, that could be a huge deal. I mean the guy's a State Senator. He's in the local news all the time. I've heard reporters ask him about whether he plans to run for anything bigger, like the U.S. Senate or maybe Attorney General."

"What does he say?" she asked.

"He doesn't say. At least, I've never heard him give a straight answer. But he always gives this coy smile, and you can tell that's his goal. If not something bigger."

"You mean like being President some day?"

Jack nodded. "He's an ambitious guy."

"He's also not a native born American," she said. "That shuts the door on becoming President. That's why Arnold Schwarzenegger could never go any higher than being Governor of California."

"Okay, Governor them. Either way, like I said, he's an ambitious man. Guys like that care about their reputations. Bigtime. He's not going to want any of this to come out." Jack shuddered as he thought about it. In fact, he didn't want to think about it anymore.

"Maybe you should just talk with Joe about it," Rachel said. "You know, Joe Boyd."

He liked the idea. "Yeah. I think that's exactly what I'm going to do."

# 30

The following day, Jack sat in his car in the Culpepper Police Department parking lot, wrestling about whether or not he should go inside. Last night, it was a settled issue. Rachel had agreed this was too big a thing to ignore. As they'd sat together on the couch looking over more photos from old man Wagner's youth, they'd talked about how different it was seeing these pictures now than it had been just the day before.

The first day, their hearts were full of sympathy for this poor orphan boy, growing up all alone in a dark and dreary communist land. Last night, it was more like watching the formative years of a soon-to-be serial killer unfold. Picking up from where they'd left off, it was apparent that as a young man Wagner had joined some kind of para-military organization. From about the age of fifteen onward, he mostly wore a uniform.

They also remarked at how much his facial expressions had changed as he grew from a child into a young man. Gone were the innocent, almost fearful glances toward the camera; the look of a child longing to be loved and cared for. As a teenager, Wagner's face looked stern and hard in almost every photograph. Always serious. Rachel pointed out his eyes. She'd even used the word *fierce* when describing them. Jack had instantly remembered Mr. Bass' words:

*Had this fierce look in his eyes.*

As it turned out, Bass had feared old man Wagner with good reason. He wondered what Bass would think when he learned the truth about what had really been going on during that time, and the true nature of the man who'd been living next door all those years.

*The truth.*

That's what this was really all about. And that's why Jack felt a duty to see Joe Boyd now. Jack had always been a defender of the truth. He didn't know exactly why. Could be his upbringing. His parents had raised him in the church. He had memorized the Ten Commandments, word for word, by the time he was six years old. Some of his most significant childhood punishments weren't for doing something wrong, but for lying about it.

Defending the truth was really at the core of the way he'd studied and taught history. He knew the old saying: *History is written by the victors.* And he knew what it meant: since those who'd won the battles got to tell the battle stories, the "historical" version of an event might not always be the truth. Which is why Jack felt it was the nature of a true historian to go beyond the victor's accounting of things and, like a detective, investigate a matter fully, exploring every side until you uncovered the true history of an event.

That's what drove him to pursue the Dresden firebombing for his doctoral dissertation. And that was probably why he was sitting there in his car, holding an old scrapbook he'd found under some floorboards in a hidden safe.

He got out of the car with the scrapbook under his arm and headed across the parking lot.

Joe Boyd looked up from his computer screen. Hank Jensen had just walked in. Hank was unofficially Boyd's partner. Unofficially, because technically Hank was still a patrolman, not a detective. Boyd was trying to get that changed.

"You got a minute, Joe?"

Hank was about the only guy in this building Joe didn't mind being interrupted by. But Hank had this look on his face. "Sure, Hank. I'm just rereading this report I wrote before I forward it to the DA…for the umpteenth time." Boyd was a lousy writer, and he knew it. Always had been.

"You're not gonna believe who's out in the lobby."

"Okay, you got me. Who?"

"Jack Turner. You remember the history teacher whose butt you saved last year in that shootout at the college?"

"Jack? Yeah, I remember him. I just bumped into him at that convenience store mess the other day when I was out by the lake checking out cabins."

"Well, I don't think this one's a social visit. He's wanting to know if he could speak with you…about something important. I asked him what, but he said it's complicated. The thing is, he's got that same expression on his face he did last year. Remember when he came in here with that whole conspiracy deal?"

Boyd did. He also remembered totally blowing Jack off, and then everything turned out to be true. "Wonder what in the world it could be? He seemed totally fine when I chatted with him the other day."

"Well, something must have turned up. He doesn't look very fine to me."

"Then sure, send him on back. Let's hear what he has to say."

Hank headed down the hall. If it had been anyone else, Boyd would have figured they were probably making something out of nothing. But Hank had decent instincts. Boyd slid his chair over a few inches, centered himself behind the desk. Through the glass in his partition wall, he saw Hank escorting Jack back this way.

Jack looked up, saw Boyd, smiled and nodded. But it was clearly a forced a smile. Boyd could see it in his eyes; something was bothering Jack bigtime.

Jack stepped through the doorway. Hank turned to leave. "I don't mind if you stay, Hank." Jack said, "If it's okay with Sergeant Boyd."

"It's okay with me," Boyd said.

"Appreciate it," Hank said, "but I'm working on something that's kind of urgent. But if you need me here, Joe…"

"No, you go on then. Let me hear what Jack has to say. I'll call you if I need you." Hank headed back the way he came. Boyd looked at Jack. "Come on in. Have a seat." He was holding some kind of ragged-looking notebook under his arm.

"I really appreciate you seeing me like this. I know you're a busy guy." Jack sat, then set what looked like a scrapbook on the edge of Boyd's desk.

"No problem. So what's going on? Hank said you seemed pretty serious. Have something to do with this?" Boyd pointed to the scrapbook.

"It has everything to do with this."

"He also said you told him that it's complicated."

"It kind of is. What I really meant was, it's not something I can summarize in a few sentences. And I didn't really want to talk about this out in the lobby."

"Okay. Then I guess you better get to it. What's going on?" Jack leaned forward in his chair and was just about to speak, when Boyd said in a lighthearted manner, "First, tell me this…nobody's trying to kill you, right?" Last year, that's what was happening when Jack had come in to see him.

Jack didn't pick up on Boyd's attempt at humor. "No, it's nothing like that." He didn't even smile. "And I sure hope it stays that way."

# 31

Boyd couldn't tell if Jack was serious. Was he really in some kind of trouble again?

Jack opened the scrapbook to the first page and spun it around so that it faced Boyd. "This is why I'm here. And before I get too far into this, thought you should know…I've run this whole thing by Rachel, and she totally agrees that there's really something here. Something potentially pretty serious."

Boyd pulled the scrapbook closer and glanced down. Some kind of newspaper clipping. The headline spoke of a World War II veteran dying in a fire. "Is this something that just came up? Because you seemed totally fine, even relaxed, when I bumped into you at the convenience store."

"This is brand new. I didn't know about this then."

Boyd turned the page. Two more newspaper articles, one on each page. The headlines both talked about the same thing. World War II veterans dying in some kind of fire. "These look like obituaries."

"They are," Jack said. "There's eight of them in there. All from different newspapers, from several different states. I've spent some time digging into this. The men died over a five-year period, between 1993 and '98."

"Okay," Boyd said, "I'm getting curious. But why would you be collecting obituaries from dead World War II pilots? I know you teach military history over at the college. This have something to do with that?"

"No. This isn't my scrapbook. It's something I found."

"Where?"

"The cabin where I'm staying." Jack looked as if he had more to say but wasn't sure if he should. "Look, I know this is a strange thing, me coming here like this. I've been sitting in the parking lot for almost a half hour arguing with myself about getting you involved. I remember what happened last year and how crazy that all sounded at first."

"Jack, it's okay. I gave you a pretty hard time last year when came in with that whole conspiracy thing involving that professor. You gotta admit, it was really out there."

"But all of it turned out to be true." Jack was getting a little defensive.

"I agree. That's my point. I was wrong to blow you off last time. I didn't take you seriously until the whole thing started spinning out of control. If I recall, though, I apologized to you after it was all over."

"You did."

"So I'm saying you don't need to be on edge here. I know you're not a whack job or some kind of conspiracy freak. If you're telling me this situation, whatever it is, is potentially serious, I'm inclined to give you the benefit of the doubt. So take a deep breath, relax, and tell me what this is all about."

Jack sat back in his chair, his shoulders slumped slightly. His facial expression lightened up, just a tad. "Thanks Sergeant—I mean, Joe. I really appreciate that. I hope you still feel that way after I'm through." This time, he did smile.

Boyd turned another page. Like Jack said, more obituaries. Similar headlines. "Okay, so you got this at a cabin. Do you know who put these together and why? What am I looking at here?"

"It's the cabin I told you about the other day. The one I'm renting, the one I might buy if I like it."

"I remember."

"That's not all I found. There was an old handwritten journal with it. Problem is, it's written in German, which I can't read. Rachel does. She took it home to translate over the next few days. I also found an old photo album filled with pictures that has an indirect connection to all of this. But I'm getting ahead of myself. I'll just cut to the chase and tell you what my research, and my gut instinct is telling me. That…" Jack pointed at the scrapbook. "…is a collection of trophies compiled by a serial killer."

Whoa. Boyd didn't see that coming. He tensed up. "You think the owner of your cabin is a serial killer?"

"No. But his father is. I mean…*was*. He's dead now, for over ten years."

"That's a relief. So nobody's in any danger, right? Not you, not Rachel? We're talking about a potential cold case situation, correct?"

Jack nodded. "The thing is, the killer got away with it. At least in this life. And these aren't exactly cold case files, because no one even knows these men were murdered. I stayed up last night and did some checking on the internet. In the weeks and months after each of these men died, there's nothing in the news that indicated any further investigations were ever conducted. What it says in those obituaries is the last word on each of these cases."

Boyd wanted to read a few. "How about you go get a cup of coffee and let me check a few of these out? You know where the coffee pot is, right? There's a stack of foam cups right beside it. Don't worry about the sign reminding you to put fifty cents in the can. My treat."

Jack agreed and left the office. Boyd started reading. He'd gone through three of them by the time Jack returned. They all read like standard obituaries, with a few extra paragraphs, given that each of these men had been former World War II pilots. That's when he picked up on something. He quickly flipped through the other articles, scanning them for the paragraphs about the men's war records. "Each of these guys flew B-17s."

Jack sat, put his cup of coffee on the edge of Boyd's desk. "They did."

"And it looks like most of them flew in the same bomber squadron," Boyd said, "and out of the same airfield in England."

"You got that right, too. Actually, all of them did."

"That can't be a coincidence."

"Nope."

"And they all died in accidental house fires," Boyd said.

"Or explosions," Jack added, "like from a ruptured gas line. In any event, they were all fire-related deaths."

"And someone paid enough attention to these...*accidents*...to collect each of these obituaries and paste them into this scrapbook."

"Yep," Jack said. "But there's more. Remember that old photo album I mentioned a moment ago? It is full of black-and-white pictures of orphans whose parents were all killed during World War II. One orphan in particular shows up in every photo."

"Let me guess," Boyd said, "You think these kids were made orphans by these B-17 bomber pilots."

"I'm certain that's the case," Jack said. "At least with this one orphan. But I haven't confirmed that fact yet. I think with a few more hours' research, I can nail that down. But the evidence points solidly in that direction. I'm thinking that these eight bomber pilots all flew on the same mission, and that that mission wound up killing the killer's family. So, decades later, he killed these pilots in revenge.

Made them all die a fiery death, just like his family did."

Boyd looked down at the obituaries in front of him, specifically looking for the date. Then he remembered, Jack had said the men had died in the mid-90s. "Why do you think he waited so long? If he became an orphan during World War II, he would have been an adult by, say…the late 1950s. Why wait forty years to avenge your family's death?"

"Because," Jack said, "the pictures in that old photo album I mentioned confirmed that the killer spent the rest of his childhood in East Germany, behind the Iron Curtain. He wouldn't have been free to travel to the US until the Soviet Union fell apart and the Berlin wall came down. That happened at the end of 1989, the beginning of 1990. The first B-17 pilot was killed in early 1993. Maybe it took a few years for him to get over here and get set up."

Darn if this thing wasn't making some sense. "I hate to say it, but I think you might be onto something here, Jack. I mean, who collects obituaries of dead pilots? Especially ones who all flew the same kind of plane, from the same bomber group and from the same airfield in England?"

"Who all died in fiery deaths ruled as accidental?" Jack said. "And the internet wasn't what it is now in the mid-90s. How would someone even know where to find these obituaries in the first place? They were spread all over, in different states, several months apart. All printed in local newspapers. None of these incidents made the national news. Who would even know to connect them all together?"

"Unless they were the one making things happen," Boyd added. He sat back in his chair. "I guess it's a good thing this guy's been dead for ten years."

"I agree," Jack said. "Does that mean you don't think we should do anything about this?"

"I don't know, Jack. It's a whole lot to take in. I might need some time to digest this." He sipped his coffee, now almost cold. "But hey, I guess since this thing's been sitting around so long, there's no great hurry here. Not like there's any tie-in to the present."

Jack's face got real serious.

"It doesn't, right? All this stuff happened twenty years ago."

Jack was shaking his head.

"What's the matter? What are you thinking?"

"Are you forgetting who owns the cabin?" Jack said. "The identity of this serial killer?"

Wait a minute. Jack had said it at the convenience store. It was....

"Senator Burke Wagner," Jack said. "The serial killer is his father."

"Oh, crap."

"Right." Jack continued. "And remember I said I found this handwritten journal with this scrapbook? Written in German, the one Rachel's translating? I don't know if he'll be implicated by anything in the journal, but by our calculations, Senator Wagner was in his college years during the time his father was committing these murders, going to school here at Culpepper. What if he knew about it, or was involved somehow?"

"Oh crap," Boyd said again. He wanted to say something worse, but he'd been working hard on his language to make Kate happy. He leaned forward, picked up his phone, looked at Jack. "You mind going through all of this one more time?" Jack shook his head no. "Good." He pushed the button for Hank's desk.

Hank picked up. "What's up, Joe?"

"Can you come in here for a few minutes? There's something I'd like you to hear."

# 32

Jack didn't expect this. Boyd was taking him seriously. He offered a silent prayer of thanks. The Bible verses he'd meditated on after his workout this morning talked about trusting God no matter what. All that anxiety out in the car had been for nothing. Officer Hank Jensen had just walked in and sat in the other chair.

Boyd spun the scrapbook around and slid it over to Hank. "Take a look at that. The reason why will become clear as Jack explains some things." He looked at Jack. "Tell Hank everything you just told me."

So Jack did, took about ten minutes. Would've taken longer except Boyd jumped in at several places. Jack couldn't tell if he was sharing too many details, or if Boyd was just really into this.

As they talked, Hank flipped slowly through the scrapbook pages. He never said a word until they were through. Then he said, "Wow, that might be the craziest story I've ever heard. This is for real, right?"

"Totally," Jack said. "There's still some details to nail down, some facts to check on the internet. But I can't think of any other conclusion that makes sense."

"Can you?" Boyd asked Hank.

"Not off the top of my head." He looked at Jack, then got a look on his face Jack couldn't read. "I can see why your classes are always full, Professor. You're one heckuva storyteller."

"Just call me Jack. But this is not a story."

"I'm not saying it is, or that I don't believe you, it's just the way you lay things out…you'd make a great attorney. Don't you think, Joe? That was like listening to some A-plus closing argument."

"I get what you're saying," Boyd said.

Jack didn't. Was Hank saying something nice or insulting him? His confusion must have been obvious based on what Boyd said next.

"Hank means no offense. He's just pointing out the gap we deal with all the time in this business."

"The gap?" Jack said.

"Between what we think happened and what we can prove," Hank said. "Between the facts and our hunches." He looked at Boyd. "You remember that Tomlin case, Joe. What was that, four months ago? Remember how angry the DA got when all that crap hit the fan, and the judge overturned Tomlin's conviction?"

The Tomlin case had made the national news. Jack had a vague memory of it. Some guy one county over had been in jail for ten years. He got a new trial and a jury wound up overturning his conviction. "I don't see the connection," Jack said.

"It was a major humiliation for the DA who tried the case," Boyd said, "and the entire police department who'd arrested him ten years back. The whole case was built on weak circumstantial evidence, you ask me. Probably should've never gone to trial in the first place. The point is, our DA made it real clear to us—"

"Don't even think about bringing a circumstantial case to me unless it's rock solid, front to back," Hank said, repeating it like a quote.

The picture was becoming a little clearer. "I think there's way more than just my hunches going on here," Jack said. "What other explanation about this obituary scrapbook makes any sense? I'm wide open if you have anything to offer?"

"I don't have one, Jack," Hank said. "Not at the moment. This could all be exactly what you said. I'm just saying that, right now, all you really got is a scrapbook filled with old newspaper clippings. Everything else is you connecting up the dots for us. Very skillfully I might add. But I'm not seeing anything we could act on here. Are you, Joe?"

"You mean like arrest someone?" Boyd said. "No, we're not even close to that. Besides, the guy who did this has been dead for a decade. But I do think there's some real substance here. My gut tells me this is for real. Jack is on to something."

"I'm not saying he's not. But even if it's all true, what can we do about it? It's not just that the killer's already dead, but from what Jack said, all of these killings took place somewhere else. Not even in Culpepper. Not even in Georgia. So, we don't even have jurisdiction over any of it."

"Not about the original killings." Boyd looked at Jack. "You didn't tell him who owns the cabin, or about the journal Rachel's translating."

"The cabin belongs to Senator Burke Wagner," Jack said, "which means the killer is his father."

"Senator Wagner? You're kidding?"

Jack shook his head. "I'm staying at the cabin now, renting it for the month."

"Tell him about the journal," Boyd said.

"I found a handwritten journal with the scrapbook. It's in German, which I don't speak. Remember Rachel? She speaks it fluently. She took it home last night to translate. She should be done in a few days. Nothing may come of it, or it could be full of things that implicate Senator Wagner. He was attending college here during the years his father committed these murders. Maybe he helped his father, or at the very least, knew what he was up to and did nothing to stop him. That would be a big deal, don't you think?"

Hank's expression totally changed. "That would be a huge deal. Wagner's become more than a local bigwig. He's a bigwig on a state level. But even so, unless he was directly involved, like he actually helped his father pull these killings off somehow, I'm not sure the DA would go after him for something his father did twenty years ago. Especially with cases that were never even opened. It could certainly hurt him politically, but I'm not sure there's a crime here. And we gotta think about this...if the DA's drawing such a hardline over some average guy like Tomlin, he's gonna be triple that way if we try to bring him some case against a prominent state senator like Wagner."

"I don't know," Boyd said. "I guess it depends on what turns up, if anything, when Rachel translates that journal. But no one's talking about going to the DA, not yet anyway. I agree, to go after someone with the clout of Senator Wagner, we'd have to have rock-solid evidence, and plenty of it. And like you said..." He looked at Hank. "We might not even have any jurisdiction here. A good part of the case, if not most of it, would belong to the FBI."

Jack had to admit: they made some good points. Some things neither he nor Rachel had thought about yet. But still, how could it possibly be right to do nothing at all with this? "So are you men suggesting I just drop this whole thing? Put everything back in the safe and pretend I never saw it?"

"Put everything back where?" Hank said.

Suddenly, Jack realized how bad that sounded. "In the safe. That's where I found these things."

"What?" Hank said, "you broke into the guy's safe?"

"No, I didn't break into anything." How could he say this without making it worse? He almost felt like he should plead the fifth. "I found the key."

"So where was the safe, exactly? In the wall?"

"No." There was just no good way to say this. "I found it in the crawl space under a floorboard in the living room."

"Jack," Boyd said, "tell me you weren't prying up floorboards in this guy's cabin."

"I wasn't prying up floorboards in this guy's cabin. There was only one floorboard involved, and I didn't pry it up. It was never nailed down. That's what got my attention. I stubbed my toe on it. Then I noticed it wasn't laid flat like all the others, which were nailed down. And it was even a different shade of wood. So, I got curious. What can I say? I'm a curious guy. I bent down to look at it and realized, it didn't even have any nail-holes. It lifted up pretty easily, which made me think it was put down that way on purpose, which made me wonder why. I lifted it up, and there it was. The safe, staring right back at me. The other significant thing I recall is that it was caked in dust. It hadn't been opened in years. Clearly, it was something being hidden. And now we know why."

"Jack, no need to get upset," Boyd said.

"Do I sound upset?"

"A little bit."

"Then I apologize." Jack no longer enjoyed the feeling that he was being taken seriously. He was starting to regret ever coming here at all. "Can we at least wait and see what Rachel turns up when she translates that journal? What if it directly implicates Senator Wagner?"

"If it does," Boyd said. "You get on the phone and give me a call."

# 33

Located down the hall just one door from Boyd's office was the men's restroom. Officer Tony Campbell just happened to be coming out of the restroom five minutes ago. He had planned on just walking past Boyd's office back to his desk. That is, until he'd heard someone mention the Senator Wagner's name. His ears perked right up like a dog hearing the dinner bell.

Campbell stood still, very still, and listened to what the men were saying. It was Boyd talking with Hank Jensen, Boyd's pet. There was a third man who was clearly the one stirring up all this talk. Campbell recognized him from that big shootout case that happened last year out at the college. Jack something. He didn't remember his last name. An easy problem to solve.

He didn't really understand everything they were saying. Something to do with the Senator's father. Campbell had never met the old man. But for the last two years, Campbell had been receiving a steady monthly check from the Senator for what they had agreed to call "private security services." It was easy money. So far, he'd just wanted Campbell to alert him to any conversations about him that took place at the police station, or anything that concerned him, his law office, or his dealings as a state senator—no matter how small.

This certainly qualified.

He hadn't had anything to report for about six weeks, so he was actually glad he'd stumbled into this. Wouldn't want to give the Senator any reason to cancel this lucrative arrangement. Campbell was making his bass boat payment with it.

When he got back to his desk, he spent some time digging through the online reports until he found those related to the college shootout last year. He didn't have to read long before he found the name he'd been looking for. He'd remembered the guy had been wounded. Sergeant Boyd had actually received a commendation for saving the man's life.

His name was Jack Turner. Back when this whole thing went down, he'd been a guest lecturer at Culpepper. Campbell had heard something about him teaching there full time now. He pulled out his personal cell phone, looked up the number the Senator had given him for Harold Vandergraf, the Senator's aide. He was instructed to always call Vandergraf first. Vandergraf would decide when, or if, Campbell's information needed to be passed up the ladder.

Campbell got up from his desk, pulled out his cigarette pack and showed it to one of the guys as he headed outside. "Smoke break." He pushed the send button.

After a few rings, Vandergraf answered the phone. "Officer Campbell, been a while since I've heard from you. I was wondering if you'd forgotten about us."

"No, nothing like that. Just nothing worthwhile to report. Guess no news is good news, though, right?"

"I suppose that could be true," Vandergraf said. "You calling must mean you have something worthwhile now..."

"Potentially," Campbell said. He lit his cigarette. "Overheard a conversation just now in Sergeant Boyd's office. He was talking with another officer and a professor at the college, who'd come in to see him."

"And this is significant because…."

"I heard them mention Senator Wagner's name. A few times, in fact. Couldn't hear everything they said, because the door was half closed. I was out in the hallway. Piecing together the parts I did hear, it seemed this college professor had come in to talk about something to do with the Senator's father. Like maybe he was trying to push them toward looking into something he thought the father might have done years ago."

"You don't say."

"I didn't hear anything specific, but I did hear somebody use the phrase *implicate Senator Wagner*. That sounded pretty significant to me."

"Hmmm. I'd have to agree with you on that. Did it sound like this professor was persuading the officers to pursue this, whatever it is?"

"No, I'd say it was just the opposite. Sounded like they were trying to talk him out of it…whatever it is."

"Well, that's good to hear. Maybe this will be the end of it then. Whatever it is. Between you and me, I know very little about the Senator's father. From what I understand, they weren't all that close. I do know he's been dead for ten years and that anything he might have done while he was alive is likely irrelevant and would likely be of no interest to the Senator."

"So you want me to drop this then? Not pass on anything else I hear?"

"On the contrary, you've done well to call. By all means, call again if you learn anything more or anything new."

"Great. I'll do that. You have a good rest of the day, Mr. Vandergraf."

"You, too, Officer Campbell."

Vandergraf put his phone back in his suit coat pocket then quickly took it out again. Contrary to what he had told Campbell, the Senator had confided in him some information about his father. Though he got the clear impression what he'd been told was just a fraction of the story. He knew enough to know the Senator would not take kindly to the news that somebody was digging into his father's past. And it's never a good thing to hear the word *implicate* spoken by police officers in a police station.

He sat back in his office chair, swiveled around until he faced the picture window behind his desk. A plan was already beginning to take shape in his mind. No need to overreact at this point. It certainly could be nothing at all. And he was glad to hear that the two officers involved in the conversation were discouraging the professor from pursuing this matter any further.

Vandergraf had just thought of a way to ensure that the good professor did just that…and follow their advice. He hit the button to call Campbell back. Campbell answered almost immediately.

"Hello, Mr. Vandergraf." He was almost whispering.

Vandergraf knew that meant he must be inside the police station.

"Something I can help you with?"

"Has that professor left the station yet?"

"He just walked by my desk toward the front door, not two minutes ago."

"Could you quickly get up and watch him get into his car. Find out the make, model and color and call me right back?"

"I can do that. I can even get you the number on his license plate if that'll help."

# 34

The atmosphere inside the arcade was perfect, just how Jack remembered it. He hadn't planned on coming here but as he'd driven by, it almost seemed to call out his name. He'd spent so many hours here years ago as a student at Culpepper. Used to be his favorite way to unwind. It was also a much cheaper hobby for a student on a tight budget than something like golf, or even fishing. After the meeting he just had with Joe, he could use a little unwinding time.

He was surprised to find the arcade still in business. These days, gamers could find ten times the sophistication and better graphics on their Xbox and PlayStation consoles. Really, even on their smart phones and tablets. When he had been in college, arcade games were the cutting edge.

Jack, however, wasn't into hi-tech. Just lo-tech pinball.

To his great surprise, one of his favorite pinball tables was still here, in good working order, occupying the same spot it had so long ago. He decided to blow a few dollars' worth of tokens then head back to the cabin and dive into his Dresden research.

Within five minutes, he had recovered his old rhythm with the flippers, had the bells and lights ringing and was running up the score.

"Aren't you a little old for pinball?" a male voice said over Jack's shoulder. Jack thought the words were directed at him but ignored them, hoping he was wrong.

"Didn't you hear me? I'm talking to you," the same voice said a little louder.

Jack turned to look for just a second. Two guys, college-age. One short and well-built, Hispanic, baseball cap on backwards, baggy jeans. On his left stood a much bigger and taller guy, thick-necked with a shaved head. Had a dumb look on his face, like someone with a room temperature IQ. Something about the way he looked reminded Jack of a big toe. Were they there to rob him? "I heard you," Jack said, "but I'm kinda busy trying to keep this little silver ball alive. Why do you care anyway?" He tried sounding tougher than he felt.

The ball slid between the flippers. Jack turned to face them. Gave a quick glance at their hands. No weapons. Mentally, he readied himself in case either one reached behind them for a gun stuffed in their pants.

"I didn't hear him ask if he could play our pinball table, Paco," Big Toe said to the shorter guy.

"I didn't know it was your machine," Jack said. "So, this is your place?"

"Not really," Paco said. "We just look after it sometimes. And when we do, people gotta pay a little extra. Like a cover charge. For you, I'd say fifty bucks should about do it."

Jack looked around the arcade, hoping to locate a security guard. At least somebody who worked here.

"There's nobody else here," Paco said. "We checked."

Jack couldn't think of anything clever to say. He had no plan. But he felt surprisingly calm. Was it the grace of God or the fact that he knew how to take care of himself a little better now? He'd never had to test those skills and hoped he'd never have to but, if it came to that…"Well gentlemen," he said. "I think it'd it be a good idea if you both just turn around and head back the way you came. Or, put some tokens in one of these machines. Either way, this isn't your establishment, and I have no intention of giving either one of you a dime."

Paco and Big Toe took a step forward at Jack's remarks. Big Toe's expression stayed the same, but Jack saw a tinge of fear in the shorter man's eyes. Paco wasn't used to being opposed.

"Maybe we should tell him the real reason we're here," Big Toe said. "Cause in a minute he won't be able to understand a thing either one of us say."

"Maybe you're right," Paco said. "We hear you been digging into somebody else's business. Putting your nose where it don't belong. Asking questions and stirring up trouble. We're here as a friendly warning. It's time for you to butt out."

What were they talking about? Jack thought. This couldn't be about his conversation with Joe and Hank, could it? That seemed impossible.

"He's acting like he doesn't know what you mean," Big Toe said. "He knows."

"But we don't even know," Big Toe said.

"Shut up," Paco said. "Doesn't matter. I was told he'd know, and that's enough." He looked back at Jack. "You do know what I'm talking about, don't you? And now, you've been warned. Walk away from it."

Paco pretended to turn around, then quickly came back at Jack with an overhand right, aimed right at Jack's face. Jack deflected it easily with his left forearm, then counter-punched with a right, straight into Paco's exposed temple. A reflex reaction. Paco was off balance when the blow came and fell to the floor. Jack drop-kicked him full-on in the ribs. Paco moaned loudly.

"You're dead, Mister," Big Toe said, lunging forward.

Jack took two quick steps back. Big Toe grabbed for Jack and got a square yard of thin air. Jack sent two fast chops into his gut, bending him in half, then brought his knee up, hard, into his face. The big man dropped to the floor and grabbed his face. Blood began to flow between his fingers. He swore then yelled, "You broke my nose."

Jack looked down at Paco, who was still holding his stomach, then at Big Toe. He grabbed the bigger man by his shirt collar and lifted him slightly. "What's your name?"

"What?" he asked.

"Your name?" Jack repeated.

"Jeff."

"Okay Jeff, this didn't exactly go the way you guys planned, you agree?"

"Yes."

"I've got some more things I could do right now, but I'm willing to stop. You guys said someone sent you here to warn me. I want to know who, and why?"

"I don't know," Jeff said, through his hands. "That's Paco's department."

"Hey, Paco, are you listening?" Jack said.

Paco began to sit up. Jack saw him grab for his jean pocket. He was pulling out a knife. Jack quickly stomped on his forearm. Paco screamed. Jack bent over and slid out the knife. He pushed a button on the handle, and the blade snapped to attention. Jack continued to apply pressure to Paco's forearm with his foot. "Paco, that wasn't smart."

"You're gonna break my arm," he shouted.

"No, I'm not. But I could. It wouldn't be that hard to do at this point. You obviously haven't learned your lesson. I'm not wanting to hurt you. I came in here to relax, play some pinball. You two came in here after me. Now I want to know who sent you here, and what this is all about."

"I can't tell you."

"Can't, or won't?"

"Can't," Paco said. "No matter how many times you hit me. I tell you anything, and I'm dead."

What in the world was he talking about? This didn't make any sense. What kind of people were these guys involved with, and why would people like that want anything to do with Jack? "Well, the two of you get up and walk right out of here, now, while I decide whether or not to call the cops." He lifted his foot off Paco's forearm.

Paco stood up, so did Jeff. "Do I get my blade back?" Paco said.

Jack shot him a look. The two young men walked down the aisle toward the double glass doors. Paco looked back at Jack, just once, confusion on his face.

Jack put the knife into his pocket and walked back to his favorite pinball table. He still had two games left, but he wasn't in the mood anymore. He went into the restroom and splashed cold water on his face. Then headed toward the parking lot. He had no category for what just happened.

Ten minutes later, as he drove out of the downtown area and over the Chambers Road Bridge, Jack tossed Paco's switchblade out the window into the river. He didn't need it. His Glock had been sitting all along in its holster under his seat. He had a permit that allowed him to carry it with him.

Would he have to start doing that now?

# 35

Jack drove along the winding, hilly roads back to the cabin. A drive that normally relaxed him. Not this time. He felt all keyed up inside. Some of it was likely the adrenaline rush receding to its proper tide. His mind kept involuntarily replaying the incident over and over in his mind. It had all happened so fast, and none of it made any sense.

He had just gone into that arcade maybe twenty minutes after his meeting with Joe Boyd and Hank. He hadn't told anyone he was going there. It was just a spontaneous whim. So how did these two guys know to find him there, and who could have sent them…and why?

He thought about calling Rachel, then thought again. She'd be so upset and worried if she found out what happened, even though Jack had made it through unscathed. Just the idea that two guys had jumped him like that, clearly intent on beating him to a pulp. A year ago, before Jack had started taking the Muay Thai classes, that's exactly what would have occurred. He wouldn't be driving leisurely back to the cabin; medics would be rushing him to the hospital in the back of an ambulance. He managed a smile as he thought about that.

He'd just taken out two thugs, barehanded, and pretty handily at that.

He might tell Rachel about it later, but not now. Instead, he waited until he pulled into the clearing beside the cabin, got out and called the Culpepper PD, the non-emergency number. The woman answering the phone said that Detective Boyd was interviewing someone and couldn't come to the phone. "Is Hank Jensen available by any chance?"

"Hank? Yeah, I think Hank is still here. I'll put you through."

"Officer Hank Jensen, how can I help you?"

"Hank, this is Jack. Jack Turner."

"Jack…what, did you forget something?"

"No." Jack sighed. "I just got jumped by two thugs at the Fun Spot Arcade."

"What?"

"You know the one on Franklin Street?"

"Yeah, I know it. Are you okay? Maybe you should be calling 911."

"I'm okay. Actually, neither one laid a hand on me. I've been taking Muay Thai classes the last year. They came in pretty handy just now. Think I may have cracked one guy's ribs and broken the other guy's nose."

"Whoa, Jack. For real?"

"Yep. The one guy was even going for a knife. I got it off him before he could do anything."

"Jack, where are these guys? We need to pick them up."

"They took off. I don't know where. I've never seen either one of them before. I don't think they're students at Culpepper."

"Were they trying to rob you?"

Jack walked over to the fire pit by the lake, sat in one of the adirondack chairs. "I thought so at first, but that's not what this was about. It's kind of crazy. Before they attacked me, one of them told me why they were there. From what he said, they were there to see me, specifically."

"I'm not following you. This wasn't random? They were targeting you?"

"Yeah, apparently." Jack told Hank exactly what they had said.

"Someone had sent them there to warn you? Who?"

"I don't know. I tried to make them tell me. The big guy didn't know, and the shorter one—he's the one seemed to be in charge—said if he told me anything they would kill him."

"Kill him? You're kidding."

"I wish I was. That's what he said. See, this doesn't make any sense to me. First, they tell me that I'm butting into somebody else's business, stirring up all kinds of trouble, then say they were sent there to warn me I better stop. I had just come from my meeting with you guys, talking all about Senator Wagner's father and this old cold case murder idea. I'm wondering, how they could possibly know about that?"

"There's no way they could know," Hank said. "It was just you, me and Joe in that office. I haven't told anyone, and Joe and I didn't even get a chance to talk about it. Right after you left, he had to interview a witness about some car theft case we're working on. He's still in there with the witness now."

"Can you see why I'm a little spooked?" Jack said.

"Sure, I can. But this has to be some kind of a mistaken identity deal. They must have thought you were somebody else. Did either one of them ever use your name?"

Jack thought a moment. "No, I don't think they did."

"Well, see? They weren't targeting you. They must have had you mixed up with someone else. Maybe some other guy was supposed to be there at that arcade right then and by some crazy coincidence, you popped in instead. Wrong place, wrong time."

Jack so wanted to believe what Hank was saying.

"Nothing else makes any sense," Hank continued. "Even so,

these are some nasty characters hanging around town. Sounds like you dished out your own measure of well-deserved justice, but I'd still like to get hold of these guys and lock 'em up. Think you could come down here and go through some photo books. There's a good chance guys like that have been arrested before."

"I suppose I could," Jack said. "But first, maybe you could check with the owner of the arcade, see if they've got some surveillance cameras that picked all this up as it went down."

"Oh, they've got cameras at the Fun Spot all right. None of them work. I've had some dealings with that place. Usually, kids trying to break into the machines. I noticed the cameras and asked the owner about it. He said they haven't worked for years, and he doesn't have the money to repair them. So, you're pretty much all I've got."

"When would you like me to come down?"

"The sooner the better. If we know what these guys look like, we might be able to pick them up right away. You didn't see what kind of car they drove in?"

"No." Jack really didn't want to do this. That's not how this afternoon was supposed to go.

"So, whatta you say, Jack. What time can you be down here? I'll make sure I'm here then."

"Give me an hour?"

"That'll work."

The truth was, Jack wasn't sure he wanted to tangle with these guys a second time. If it was a case of mistaken identity, and he left it alone, it might just go away. Did he really want to get mixed up with them, on any level, and take a chance that whoever sent them might now have a reason to come after him on purpose?

# 36

Senator Burke Wagner looked at his watch as his frustration mounted. It was 1:06pm. Where was Vandergraf? Their lunch appointment had been set for 1pm.

He looked through the glass window of the *Chez Bruchez*, eyeing the montage of walking legs just visible at street level. Then realized how absurd it was, as if he'd recognize Vandergraf's shoes. *Chez Bruchez* was the only high-end French restaurant in Culpepper. Here, patrons got to pay twenty-plus dollars for a half-empty plateful of something they couldn't pronounce correctly. But they earned the privilege of telling others they had eaten lunch at the *Chez Bruchez*.

Wagner leaned back in his chair and looked at himself in the mirrored wall. Two decades in a sedentary job hadn't gotten the better of him. Look at that waistline. He worked out two days a week, played racquetball on a third. Still had all of his light brown hair. Well, almost all.

"Sorry, I'm late," said a voice over his right shoulder. Wagner turned in time to see Vandergraf take his seat, then unfold a linen napkin across his knee.

"Drove in from outside of town, got stuck behind an old man on a tractor. You know how that is. Single lane, curvy roads, no place to pass."

Wagner did know how that was, which was why he always allowed five to ten extra minutes when his route involved the country roads outside of town. "Is that the first slow farmer you've come across since moving here to Culpepper?"

"Well, no…" Vandergraf looked into his eyes. He got the message.

"Ever eaten here before?" Wagner had never met his young aide here. He wondered if Vandergraf might need help to place his order.

"No, actually, I haven't, but—"

"Can I help you, Messieurs? Are we ready?" asked a tall, thin waiter with a thick French accent.

Wagner wasn't convinced it was authentic. "We'll probably need a minute, Jacques. My aide here has been running a little late."

"That's okay, Jacques. If you're ready, Senator, go ahead. I think I know what I want. Let me just take a look here and see if they have it." Vandergraf's eyes scanned the surface of the menu.

"Right, Jacques, well, I'll have…"

"The usual, Monsieur Wagner?" Jacques smiled.

Wagner had only ever tried three items on the menu and had only really liked one. "Sure, Jacques. I'll have that. And a glass of Chablis? Pick a good year."

"Very good," Jacques said.

"Certainement, Jacques," Vandergraf said. "Je voudrais … hmmm … je voudrais *La Canard a l'Orange*, s'il vous plait. Avec Chablis."

"Tres bien, Monsieur," Jacques replied.

"And, Jacques, non presse."

"Very good, Monsieur. I understand." Jacques gave Vandergraf a satisfied grin, wrote down his order, turned and walked away.

Clearly, Vandergraf didn't need his help. Wagner had never learned French. Back in college, he'd thought about taking it, but his father hated the French.

"I spent two high school summers in Paris," Vandergraf said. "Come here often?"

"Every now and then," Wagner said. "Did you get my voicemail?"

"The one about Mr. Herndon coming through with flying colors? I did. I can't say I'm surprised. The way I left him after our meeting, he seemed pretty persuaded. So, I'm glad to hear it."

"You mentioned in your text," Wagner said, "that something fairly urgent had come up. Something we shouldn't talk about on the phone."

Vandergraf looked at his watch. "They should have gotten back to me by now."

"They? Who are they?" Wagner said.

"Earlier today, I gave a pretty urgent assignment to two young men I hire for very specialized kind of work. I've used them before a few times, and they've always come through. They're not very bright, but then, these assignments are never very complicated."

"Anything I should know about?"

"I'm not sure, that's why I wanted to meet in person. This has to do with your instructions regarding plausible deniability. I certainly understand the concept of not sharing certain details of my work with you, to protect your reputation and your ability to remain detached from any activity that might damage it. You pay me very well to exercise good judgment. But the situation I've just become aware of crosses into territory we haven't covered before. It has to do with your father."

"My father?" Wagner said. "What kind of situation would come up that might involve my father? He's been dead for over ten years."

"I remembered that, sir. Nevertheless, it has. I have no idea what it's about, and very few details to offer. I do know how rigidly you guard any information that has to do with your family's past, and I perfectly understand that." He looked at his phone. "I had hoped these men would have called me before we met, so I could include how the situation was resolved as part of my update. They should be getting back with me any minute."

"You do know," Wagner said, "I still have no idea what you're talking about."

"I do," Vandergraf said. "And that's intentional on my part. Seems like the very concept of plausible deniability suggests that I play it safe, and err on the side of telling you too little, not too much."

Vandergraf had a point. But he had also piqued Wagner's curiosity.

"Maybe I could handle it this way," Vandergraf said, "if you learned that someone was asking questions about your father with a police detective, would that be of little concern to you, or would you want me to do whatever I had to do to make it stop?"

Wagner's heart skipped a beat. This wasn't good, not good at all. No matter what it was. He did his best not to let his depth of concern alter a single feature on his face. "I'm leaning toward you doing whatever you have to do to make it stop. Within reason, of course." Wagner knew he had better set some boundaries.

Vandergraf picked up on this in his reply. "Perhaps I over-spoke. When I said doing whatever I had to do, I wasn't referring to—to use an old German metaphor—the final solution. Although, that might be necessary in any assignment as a last resort. But I do feel better hearing your reply. It lets me know I probably handled this in a way that would meet with your approval. If you knew the whole story. Happily, we can leave it at that."

"So, the situation is handled then?" Wagner said.

Vandergraf picked up his phone again. "Hopefully. I believe it should be."

Just then Jacques walked up with their glasses of wine. "Your lunches will be out shortly, gentlemen," he said and walked away.

Vandergraf's phone began to vibrate. He picked it up. "Finally." He looked at Wagner. "I better take this outside."

Wagner nodded.

"Hold on, Paco. I'll be right with you."

Wagner watched Vandergraf navigate quickly through the tables and chairs toward the steps, then up the steps and out the front door.

Out on the sidewalk, Vandergraf un-muted the phone. "Okay, Paco. Please tell me you're calling to say mission accomplished."

A long pause. "I wish I was."

His voice seemed shaky. "What happened? You didn't get caught?"

"No."

"You made sure there were no people, no one recording things on their phones?"

"Yes."

"Then…what? What went wrong?"

"I don't know how to say this. The target, this Professor, he was not like I expected."

"What do you mean?"

"He looked like I expected, but he didn't act like I expected."

"What are you saying? Stop dragging this out. What happened? Just tell me."

"Basically? He kicked the crap out of us. Both of us."

"What?"

"He didn't look like nothing. Like I could have whupped him without Jeff even being there. I warned him like you said. He didn't seem to even know what we were talking about. I didn't really know what we were talking about, so it's not like I could ask him. I figured, maybe he's just playing stupid cause he knew what we were about to do. You know, act innocent and maybe we would go away. So it was time for the beat down, only he suddenly becomes Jason Bourne, and we're the ones getting the beat down, me and Jeff. I can hardly breathe without pain. Man, I think it's my ribs. Jeff's nose is broke. His eyes are all swelled up. You didn't pay us near enough for this."

Vandergraf couldn't believe it. Stupid idiots. This thing was supposed to be quick and easy, over and done. "So, you think he didn't understand the warning? Is that what you said?"

"That's what it seemed like. But like I said, he could've just been acting. All I know is, I don't want to get around that guy anymore unless we go in there with guns. He even took my blade. I've had that thing for six years."

Vandergraf had looked up this guy Jack Turner at the university's website. He looked very average, definitely not like somebody who could go "Jason Bourne" on someone. "All right, Paco. Don't worry about it. I'll put Plan B into action."

"What's Plan B?"

"Don't worry about it. It doesn't involve you. You got your money, right?"

"Yeah, but don't call us for a little while. We need some time to heal up."

Vandergraf hung up the phone, put it back in his coat pocket. He headed down into the restaurant to face the Senator. Just as he reached their table, Jacques came up and set their lunches down on a stand. Vandergraf sat. Both men eyed each other dubiously as he set their plates before them.

"Enjoy," he said.

After he left, Wagner said, "So…is it handled? Everything the way it needs to be?"

"Not quite, sir. My guys dropped the ball. But don't worry. It's just time to implement Plan B." The problem was, Vandergraf had no plan B. He better come up with one pretty quick.

# 37

Officer Tony Campbell was surprised to see that history professor, Jack Turner, back at the station. Twice in one day. Vandergraf wouldn't be happy about that. Of course, Campbell was happy to have some action, anything to keep himself relevant so they'd keep sending that monthly check. But he couldn't call Vandergraf back unless he had something substantial to say.

Turner walked straight to Hank Jensen's desk. Campbell wanted to listen in but another officer kept pestering him and he missed most of the conversation. Hank and the professor headed over to Boyd's office, just long enough to duck their heads in for a chat. Then Hank escorted the young professor down the hall to one of the interview rooms.

Campbell noticed a thick notebook under Hank's arm and realized what it was. The mugshot book. So that's what this was about. Hank had asked him to come in and look at potential suspects. But why? It's not like the Senator's father would be in that book. He had to find out what was going on.

He decided to head back to his desk but keep an eye on the interview room. It wasn't far from the coffee pot. When the two men came out, Campbell would suddenly feel the need to refresh his coffee mug. He was just about to sit when he heard the interview room door open. Hank walked out, closed the door and headed back toward his desk.

Maybe he should get that coffee now. He waited till Hank sat in his chair, then got up. "Hey Hank, isn't that the college professor involved in that shootout last year? The one Sergeant Boyd saved?"

"That's him." Hank started tapping the keys on his keyboard.

"Wasn't he just in here a couple hours ago?"

"He was." Hank didn't look at him, just kept on typing.

Campbell got the distinct impression Hank didn't like him very much. Or maybe it was just Hank getting all hoity-toity now that he was Sergeant Boyd's boy. "What's going on?"

Hank stopped, turned and gave him a look that suggested he wanted to say, "None of your business." Instead, he said, "He was in here a little while ago to talk about something with Sergeant Boyd. A private matter. On his way home, he stopped in at the Fun Spot Arcade for a few minutes and got jumped by two thugs."

"Really? I didn't see a mark on him."

"That's because he whupped them. Both of them. Apparently, he's got some Muay Thai skills. Anyway, I left him in there to see if he can pick either one of them out. Why do you care anyway?"

"I don't. Just passing time. Working on something pretty boring. I remember that situation last year got pretty exciting. The most action I've seen since I started to work here."

Hank turned back to his screen, started tapping the keys again. "Well, sorry to disappoint you. But I don't think this is anything like that."

"Oh well, you know me…always looking for a little excitement."

Hank didn't answer. Just kept tapping away.

Campbell backed out of the space, turned and found the nearest exit. Once outside, he tapped the button on his personal cell for Vandergraf.

After a few rings, Vandergraf said, "Officer Campbell. Twice in one day. I'm kind of busy. Can we make this quick?"

"Sure. I'm pretty busy too. Just thought I'd let you know, that history professor, Jack Turner, came back to the police station again. He's here right now."

"Really? Do you know why?"

"I do. Apparently, after he left here the first time he stopped in at a local arcade, where two thugs jumped him. Unfortunately for them, he's something of a martial arts guy, and they were the ones who got beat up. I didn't see a mark on him. He must have reported it. I guess we called him back to look through our mugshots, see if he can spot the perps. He's in our interview room right now doing that very thing. I don't know if this has any relationship to what I called you about earlier, but thought you'd want to know."

"I'm glad. I definitely do want to know things like this. Let me know if you hear anything more, especially if Mr. Turner IDs anyone in that mug book."

"Will do."

Campbell hung up and headed back inside. He wasn't so sure he liked what just went down. Judging from his reaction, Vandergraf obviously had something to do with those thugs who'd attempted to attack Professor Turner.

They didn't succeed, but it hadn't been for a lack of trying.


Vandergraf hung up, put his phone back in his coat pocket. This wasn't good. He was sure the next time he and the Senator met, he would be asked one question: *Is the situation handled?* The answer needed to be yes.

He took a deep breath and reminded himself to keep the big picture in mind here. He was relatively sure Paco and his big friend would not be in the Culpepper Police Station mug book. They lived two counties away and Paco had assured him that neither of them had ever been arrested in this town, or even in this county. Paco would know better than to lie to him on something like that.

The bigger concern was whether or not Professor Turner would drop this effort to find out any more information about the Senator's father. He was sure now Officer Campbell would alert him if that happened.

Just to be on the safe side, Vandergraf looked up the contact information on the man he'd have to call, should that become necessary. The man's name was Rob Strickland.

Rob Strickland had just become Plan B.

# 38

Jack had spent the last hour going over mugshots. A few of them bore some resemblance to the thugs who jumped him, but his guys were definitely not in that book. He was surprised to see just how many young felons lived in Culpepper. He'd always found it to be a pretty safe place. Other than the ordeal he and Rachel had endured last year, this confrontation at the arcade had been his first run-in with anything violent or criminal.

He closed the lid on the thick notebook and slid his chair out from under the table. Time to get Hank. As Jack entered the hallway, Hank happened to be coming this way.

"Well?"

"No luck. The guys who attacked me are either not from around here, or they've been very successful at never getting caught."

"Do you want to meet with our sketch artist? She's pretty good."

"I don't think so, Hank. I might feel differently if they'd actually hurt me, but I'm thinking of just letting this go. I really need to get back to the cabin, get back to work on my research project. But if these guys wind up attacking anyone else in town, and you catch them, feel free to call me back and I'll see if I can identify them."

"I understand," Hank said. "I'll do that." They shook hands and Jack headed toward the lobby.

Once in the car, he felt a ping in his conscience that he should call Rachel, let her know what happened. He'd certainly want to know if anything like this had happened to her. He found her number and hit the phone icon. If he had timed it right, she should be in between classes.

"Hi, Jack. So good to hear your voice."

"Glad I got you."

"Taking a break from your research?"

"Wish I was."

"Oh? What are you doing instead?"

"I'm just leaving the police station. Spent the last hour or so looking at a bunch of ugly guys in a mugshot book."

"What? Why? What's going on?"

"Nothing to worry about. Wasn't even sure I should call you. Then I started feeling guilty about not calling you, so I knew I should. Now, before I tell you what happened, you need to know I'm fine. I wasn't hurt, and the whole situation is over with."

"Jack, if you're saying all this to reassure me, it's not working. What in the world are you talking about? What happened?"

He spent the rest of his time driving through downtown Culpepper filling her in. He finished just about the time he'd turned onto the country road that led toward the cabin.

Her first comments were, "Well, I'm very glad you've been taking those Muay Thai classes."

"You and me both."

"And Hank's sure these guys weren't targeting you?"

"He is, and the more I thought about it, the more I think he's right. They couldn't have known I'd be at that arcade playing pinball when I did. I only decided to do it on the spur of the moment.

Haven't visited that place for years before today. I don't know who they thought I was, I'm just glad it wasn't me. And really, I'm fine. Not a scratch on me."

"Well, I'm glad. While I have you on the phone, thought you'd like to hear this, one of my morning classes canceled. Between last night and today, I've been making quite a dent translating that German notebook into English."

"Really? Come across anything profound yet? Anything even close to a smoking gun?"

"Not really. More like totally bizarre. Especially now that I know what this is. Most of it has been running like what I said at the cabin. Notes the killer took while he was scoping out the various places where these B-17 pilots lived."

"That sounds significant. If what he wrote connects these obituaries to the journal."

"I'd say they definitely do. But I'm not so sure Sergeant Boyd would agree. The killer's very clever. So far, I haven't found any of the names of the men who died. I'm pretty sure he made little codenames for them. When you know what happened and what he was up to, it's pretty clear what's going on. He's casing them. Writing down all their habits and patterns. Every now and then his hatred for them slips out by some little thing he says. He also occasionally justifies what he's doing and why. At the end of each one, he says 'Justice served.'"

"Well, that sounds like a pretty solid connection."

"To you and me it does. But I've gone back and re-read some of these things after I translated them, trying to see them through the lens of someone who had no prior knowledge. That's where the cleverness stands out. You can tell he's writing something that sounds ominous and sinister, but he always falls short of saying anything specific. I don't know. I haven't finished it yet. There's a chance I could finish it tonight. Maybe something more obvious or blatant will surface. You want to plan on me coming back to the cabin tomorrow night, so we can go over this together?

"Definitely. But maybe you could do something while everything is fresh in your mind."

"Like what?"

"Go back over your translated copy and highlight in yellow all of these kinds of things you just mentioned. The things that give you pause, or make you think are significant. And especially highlight anything he says about his son, if he ever shows up in the parts you haven't finished yet."

"Sure, I can do that. Well, I better go. I'm at the door for my last class of the day."

Jack spent the rest of the car ride to the cabin going over the things Rachel had said. It was a little disappointing. He'd hoped there would be glaringly obvious statements directly connecting the journal to the obituaries. They could still come from the pages she hadn't translated. But he also realized, someone as meticulous and thorough as old man Wagner was proving to be, wasn't likely to make such an obvious error.

Jack thought about another possible angle to pursue. During some of his World War II research for his other books, he had learned about the codebreakers at Bletchley Park. Many of them were mathematical geniuses. Total nerds but brilliant. The FBI and CIA still employed people with these skills. People with deductive reasoning powers like Sherlock Holmes, who could take something that everyone else skips right over and see all kinds of patterns and subtle routines emerge.

Of course, right now they weren't dealing with the FBI or the CIA. They were dealing with the Culpepper PD.

He drove his BMW over the winding pathway cut through the

trees until he reached the clearing. As he put the car in park, he remembered what Joe and Hank had said about the DA not wanting to see any cases—especially circumstantial cases—that weren't backed by rock-solid evidence.

From what Rachel had said so far, they were still miles away from that.

# 39

Jack stepped onto the porch, the obituaries scrapbook under his arm. He unlocked the cabin door and walked inside. The day was mostly shot. There were only a few hours left before dinner. He wasn't in the mood to start digging out his Dresden research materials. He set the scrapbook on the dinette table, stared at it for a few moments.

After his meeting that morning with Joe and Hank, and his phone conversation with Rachel, he realized…this is what he wanted to do. Work on this.

As he looked down at the scrapbook, Hank's words played over in his mind: *This could all be exactly what you said. I'm just saying that, right now, all you really got is a scrapbook filled with old newspaper clippings. Everything else is you connecting up the dots for us.*

For Jack, this was more than a bunch of loosely connected dots. He wasn't some kind of overly-passionate guy driven by emotions. He hated the thought that somehow he'd given Hank this impression. Even Jack's books were known for "their meticulous commitment to historical details." His rational mind and even his gut instincts told him…this scrapbook was exactly what they'd said it was—a trophy book for a serial killer.

But he also understood what Joe and Hank were saying. They

needed proof. Unswerving, unwavering proof. Of course, it would be circumstantial. It would have to be. There was no DNA involved. No video. No murder weapon. But he knew a little bit about how circumstantial cases could be made when circumstantial evidence was the only kind available, and done so in a way it would hold up in court.

Back in college, he had done a paper about the circumstantial evidence used in the O.J. Simpson trial. That case, of course, had ended with Simpson being found not guilty. But Jack had cited many cases in his essay where defendants had been found guilty on nothing but circumstantial evidence. For circumstantial evidence to be effective, it must not only implicate a defendant's guilt, there must also be no other explanation for the evidence that could be shown that supported his innocence.

Jack sat in a dinette chair and opened up the scrapbook. This scrapbook, all by itself, seemed to undeniably support old man Wagner's guilt and rule out any notion of innocence. What other explanation could be offered to suggest a man would innocently gather together a collection of obituaries like this? Wagner didn't know any of the men, wasn't related to any of the men. They had all lived in different cities, some in different states. The only thing that linked the pilots together was that they had all had flown in the same bomb group during World War II.

Wagner was not a B-17 pilot. He was not even an American. Not even an adult. He was a little boy, orphaned by the actions of men like these pilots. That goes right to motive. Wagner had a motive to be angry at these men, especially if Jack could prove these men flew in the bomb group that dropped the bombs over the city where Wagner lived, and that these bombs had actually killed his family.

This information was knowable. This information could be substantiated.

Jack got his laptop and sat with it in the recliner. He opened it to the file of notes he had already begun in Word. Next, he opened Google and began searching through a number of World War II aviation sites. Sites he had already found related to the 379th bombing group. For the next hour, he scoured through the sites and some others pulling on threads and following new leads. He made a list of the pilots then added to that list all the missions they had flown, what cities they had bombed. Most of them occurred in 1944 and the early months of 1945.

He went back and forth between the eight pilots and the cities they had bombed, looking for connections. Quite a few had flown together in some missions, but not in all. After checking and crosschecking the list several times he finally discovered one city, one mission that all eight pilots had flown on together.

When he realized what city, he was stunned. "Unbelievable," he said aloud. It was exactly what Rachel had guessed.

The mission was Dresden. February 14th, 1945.

These eight men had all flown in the third bombing raid. The first two raids had taken place the night before, conducted by the British. Those were the raids that had created the horrific firestorm that had totally consumed the beautiful historic town. Mission three had taken place the following day. From his research, Jack knew the controversy surrounding this mission had been enormous.

Why had American generals agreed to participate in this mission in the first place? For almost the entire war, the Americans had resisted the urge to carpet bomb German cities or conduct any missions that primarily targeted German civilians. But not this time. This time we said yes to the British. Dresden had already been completely annihilated the night before. Coming in for the attack the following day represented the worst kind of piling on. We were killing the survivors, those who had somehow managed to make it through the firestorm. Men, women and children. The elderly. Emergency workers. Those trying to save the wounded and dying.

Those were the people being killed in the third raid.

The American raid.

And very likely, old man Wagner's family. Only he wasn't an old man then. Just a scared little boy.

A scared little boy who grew up hating those who had destroyed the people he loved. A little boy who vowed one day to exact his vengeance.

Talk about motive, Jack thought.


Jack sat at the dinette table finishing up his gourmet chicken pot pie. Well, the box said it was gourmet. In frozen food language, gourmet must mean three or four additional chunks of chicken. He still couldn't get over the information he'd uncovered in his internet search.

Especially, the irony of the thing.

Dozens of German cities had been bombed. Hundreds of bombing missions had been flown. What were the odds that he would pick the one town, the same town, for his doctoral dissertation that old man Wagner had lived in, had been orphaned in, as a little boy? And of all the cabins along the banks of the various lakes surrounding Culpepper, what were the odds Jack would pick this one for his retreat?

And...that this would be the cabin that had served as the refuge and hideout of a serial killer taking revenge on elderly B-17 pilots because they had flown on the same mission over the same city that Jack had picked to study some seventy years later?

This revelation wasn't exactly the proof he needed to convince Hank or Joe to investigate this case, but it certainly had to matter. It had to help the cause. It meant that old man Wagner had come from Dresden, that he was a Dresden survivor. What else could it mean? Why else would he stalk and pursue these pilots?

His phone rang. It was Rachel.

He picked it up. "Hi, Rachel. Didn't expect to hear from you so soon."

"Well, something pretty cool happened. I just had to call. I thought about waiting until tomorrow when I come over, but this couldn't wait."

"That's funny. Something pretty cool happened over here. But you go first."

"Okay, I was going to keep working on this translation project during dinner. When I pulled the notebook out of my purse, that's when I noticed it."

"Noticed what?"

"The loose page."

"What loose page?"

"In the back of the journal. I didn't see it before. I guess it moved around inside my purse."

"What did it say?"

"I'm getting there. So I opened it up and pulled the page out. That's when I realized, it didn't belong in the back of the book. It was just stuck there. It came out of the front. I think it's the title page."

"Okay, so what did it say?" Obviously, it was a big deal since she'd stopped everything to call him.

"You're not going to believe this."

After what he'd uncovered this afternoon, he wasn't so sure of that. "Okay…I'm ready."

"It said, in the same handwriting as the rest of journal: *Erinneringen an Dresden.*"

"Dresden? You're kidding."

"I am not."

"What's the first part mean?"

"The complete phrase, or the way we'd probably say it is…*Remembering Dresden* or *Memories of Dresden*. Isn't that crazy? That must be where old man Wagner came from. What else could it be?"

Jack shook his head in disbelief. "We were right. You were right. It's almost too surreal to comprehend. But he had to come from there."

"Isn't that crazy? That it's the same place you're studying for your doctoral dissertation."

"I know," he said. "You're not going to believe what I have to tell you."

# 40

Harold Vandergraf had just locked his desk drawer and was ready to close the lid on his laptop and head home. As he pulled away from the desk, his cell phone rang. It was Campbell calling from the Culpepper PD, a call Vandergraf had been waiting for. "Officer Campbell. Nice of you to call back."

"Sorry I'm late," Campbell said. "Got sucked into something. But I did find out that info you were looking for. That professor, Turner, wasn't able to find your guys in our book. Looks like he's dropping it. I asked a gal who does our sketches for suspects to make sure. She said Hank told her the professor didn't want to pursue this any further."

"Well, that is good news. Who's Hank?"

"The officer who was showing him the mugshots."

"Does it look like he's going to drop it, too?"

"Seems so. Unless something else stirs it back up."

"That wouldn't be good."

"Well, I'll let you know if it does."

They said goodbye and hung up. Vandergraf was relieved, but not completely. It bothered him that this thing had come up in the first place. Why would it? What triggered it? He had done a little snooping in the past few hours. This fellow, Turner, was clearly a very popular teacher at the school. And he was something of an accomplished author. Had his own website. Wrote books on military history. Had two published so far, both on World War II. The first one had made the New York Times bestseller list.

Was that the connection? Was Turner doing research for another book? Vandergraf didn't know many of the details about the Senator's father, but he did know he had become an orphan during one of the bombings in World War II. But what could have unfolded to cause Turner's interest in World War II to intersect with the Senator's father? He couldn't begin to imagine.

There was just one thread left to pull.

His source at the University had mentioned Turner wasn't teaching any classes at the moment. He was on some kind of study retreat. Vandergraf knew the Senator had a property on Lake Sampson, a cabin. Cabins were often used for little getaways and retreats. Vandergraf had some conversations in the past with an old man who lived next door, Mr. Bass. He was actually on the payroll, if Vandergraf remembered correctly. Looked after the place from time to time, got it ready if ever the Senator wanted to use it.

Vandergraf scanned through his contacts until he found Mr. Bass' number. Hit the button and waited through several rings.

"Hello?"

"Mr. Bass?"

"That's me. Who's this?"

"It's Harold, Harold Vandergraf. I'm Senator Wagner's aide. I believe we've met a few times. I know I've called you on the phone a few more, but it's been a while."

"I remember you, Mr. Vandergraf. That what I should call you or would you prefer I call you Harold?"

"Mr. Vandergraf is fine. The reason I'm calling…just double

checking something. Is anyone renting the Senator's cabin right now?"

"Why, yes. There is. The realtor brought a fellow by, a young professor teaches over at the college there. Met him when he first came in. What was his name? Thurman? Herman?"

"Was it Professor Turner?"

"That's it, Turner. Yeah, that's his name. Seems like a nice fellow."

Mystery solved, thought Vandergraf. "That's all I needed. Just to confirm that little detail. Appreciate your time, sir."

"Sure there's nothing else? Any message you want me to give him?"

"No, no message." Then he thought of something. "But just out of curiosity, have you and the professor ever talked about the Senator's father?"

"His father? I don't think so. Well, wait a minute. We did ever so briefly that first afternoon he arrived. He was just a little curious about the cabin's history. Guess that's normal, seeing he's a history professor. Of course, there's not that much to tell."

"Can you remember what you did tell him? Not word for word, just the gist."

"Hmmm. I mentioned how he lived here off and on in the 90s. Then he got that stroke. Lived here a few more years after that till he died. Pretty sure that's about all."

Vandergraf couldn't see how that could possibly have led to anything that would get Turner showing up at the police station. Was there something left at the cabin that Turner had gotten into? People who write books, especially history books, tend to be the curious type. The kind who like to dig up stories. Whatever it was, Vandergraf needed to sort this out. "Say, Mr. Bass. Any idea how long this professor plans on renting the cabin?"

"I don't recall if he told me."

"That's okay. I can call the property management people on that. Sorry to bother you."

"No trouble at all."

They hung up. He probably wouldn't be out there at the cabin too long. The Fall semester started back up in a few weeks. Maybe nothing more would come of this.

The problem was, his instincts said otherwise.

He had this unsettled feeling he often got when something wasn't right or didn't add up. He had that feeling now. Vandergraf had learned in his short span of years to trust that instinct. It had protected him more times than he could count. He'd been thinking of making that call to Rob Strickland.

Might be good to get him on retainer just in case.

A few minutes later, he had Strickland on the phone. "So Rob, where are you presently?" Strickland was a trucker by trade, had his own rig. Gave him the freedom to come and go as he pleased. As a rule, he stayed within the southeast, so he was never too far away.

"I am riding down an interstate in the fine state of Alabama. Good to hear your voice Mr. Vandergraf. Usually means something good might be coming my way."

"Are you on your way out somewhere or heading back in?"

"Back in. Should be arriving sometime tomorrow morning. Why, you need me?"

"I might. Fifty-fifty chance right now. But when you get back, I'd like you to hang loose near Culpepper at least for a few days, until I get this situation sorted out. If I need you, it'll probably be on short notice."

"By hang loose, I assume you mean at my usual daily fee. Even if nothing comes of this here situation."

"That is exactly what I mean. Keep your cell phone handy and all charged up. I will get back in touch with you with the details if that becomes necessary."

"I can do that. Is there anything else?"

"No, that should about do it."

"A pleasure doing business with you, as always." Strickland hung up.

Vandergraf slipped his cell phone into his suit coat pocket and headed to the elevator. They paid Strickland well on those occasions when his skills were called for. Vandergraf hoped this time would prove to be a false alarm. But it was nice to know Strickland would be close by and ready to go should the need arise.

# 41

It was hard, but the following day Jack had done his best to focus on his doctoral research. There really wasn't much more he could do about the growing mystery surrounding old man Wagner until Rachel came over. Late in the afternoon, Rachel had texted him to say she would be coming over after dinner around six-thirty, that she had finished translating the journal and that she definitely had some new information to share with him.

He couldn't wait to see it. He glanced at his watch. She could be arriving any minute. After clearing the dinette table, he put his research material into two clear plastic containers then stacked the containers against the wall

Even though this mystery had temporarily overshadowed his interest in the Dresden research, he did find the research more stimulating and intriguing, knowing the connection to the murder case. He was particularly more interested in the stories of survivors and how they processed their anger and grief over the ordeal. Such a wide range of reactions.

Some fixed the blame entirely on Hitler and the Nazi regime for leading their country, once again, into a major world war. Clearly, the Nazis had started it all and had aggressively pursued the wholesale destruction of their neighbors, not to mention the annihilation of the Jewish people. They viewed the Allied bombing campaign as mere payback, the Germans reaping what they had sown.

Another group, though agreeing with the first view in part, believed the Allies had gone way too far in the way they had prosecuted the war. In short, the punishment did not fit the crime. There was a point, particularly at the beginning of 1945, when it was clear the Germans had been defeated and the capture of Berlin was a foregone conclusion. But to this group, the Allies continued their incessant bombing campaign, picking out defenseless targets like Wurzburg and Dresden, pummeling them mercilessly into total ruin. In the process, they killed tens of thousands of civilians. Mostly defenseless women, children and the elderly.

This group felt the Allied generals who were responsible for these pile-on attacks should have been tried as war criminals, just like the Nazi leaders were at Nuremberg.

Now Jack realized there was a third group of Dresden survivors. A group that included at least, and possibly only, one member. An orphan boy who grew up and decided to pay back, not the generals who ordered the raids but the actual men who had flown the planes responsible for killing his family. And to pay these men back in the most personal of ways, one by one.

Jack heard the sound of a car outside pulling into the clearing, then the engine turn off. He got up to greet Rachel. They hugged and kissed at the halfway point, then walked back together hand-in-hand. In Rachel's other hand, she held the journal and a manila folder.

Jack pointed to it. "I'm guessing that's the translation?"

"It is. Can't wait to show it to you."

"So…do we have a smoking gun?"

"I'd say so. It's not as strong a link as it could be, but I think it's strong enough. There's also something of a glitch mixed in, too. At first, I thought it might be a deal breaker. But as I thought about it more, I think it has the potential to break this whole thing wide open."

They stepped onto the porch. "Okay. Two quick questions. What is the glitch and how does it go from deal breaker to saving the day?"

"You'll see inside."

Jack steered them to the dinette table. "You can put your stuff on the table. I made half a pot of decaf. Would you like a cup?"

"Definitely. You know how I like it."

"I do." After getting it just right, he brought the mugs back and set them on the table, then took a seat beside her. She had already opened the manila folder. Several pages were flipped over.

"I thought we'd start off where the new and juicy stuff begins. All these turned-over pages are the ones I talked to you about last night."

"The notes he made while he was casing the men at the different locations?"

She nodded. "That's most of what's in here. But then toward the end, after the notes on the eighth victim, things began to change. He gets more philosophical, like he's trying to justify what he's done. Why it's not really revenge he's pursuing, but justice."

"Wait a minute, he tries to justify what he's done? Does that mean he gets specific about what he did? Does he admit to anything?"

"Not plainly. He's still talking in code or using very generalized terms. But to me, anyone with a brain in their head could, if they've been reading from the beginning, understand what he's really talking about. Especially if you have the scrapbook with the obituaries on hand to use as a comparison. But I'm not through yet. There's more."

She laid her index finger on the page, trace down a few lines. "Start reading here, at this paragraph. It's starts getting very personal."

Jack leaned over. "You mean, read out loud?"

"Yes, out loud."

Jack did.

*So you see, my son, this great work I have begun. It is an important work, a just work.*

Jack stopped. "Whoa, my son?"

"I thought that would get your attention."

"That has to be Senator Wagner. And what does he mean saying, the *work I have begun*? Didn't you say this comes after the eighth and final victim?"

"Keep reading, it'll make more sense."

*I'm beginning to realize that I cannot do this work alone. Two things have convinced me. The first is, there are still so many more who participated in this crime against humanity.*

"He says that phrase quite often," Rachel said. "I'm convinced it's the code phrase he uses when referring to the death of his family and probably the entire town of Dresden. But he slipped up a few times here toward the end. I can show you later. He actually said *crime against my family* a few times instead of this phrase. Keep reading."

*When I consider how many months and years it has taken me to execute justice on these war criminals, and how many more of them are still alive, I'm convinced, my son, that I will need your help if I am to finish this work.*

*The second reason is more serious. My health is not what it once was. It is not just my age that is slowing me down. I have been experiencing certain symptoms. A doctor has informed me they are the early warning signs of a stroke. I know you have always seen me as strong and fit. On the outside, I appear to be. But the stress of this task these past five years, multiplied by so many years working for the Stasi, have taken their toll on me.*

"The Stasi? Rachel, do you know who the Stasi are?"

"The East German secret police. I learned about them when I was studying German."

"Those guys were like the KGB. I'm guessing these B-17 pilots were not the first men this guy had killed."

"Didn't you pick up on the other thing he just said?" Rachel pointed to it on the page. "He's talking about the early warning signs of a stroke. Didn't you say old man Wagner had a severe stroke and died a few years later from the complications?"

"That's right."

"Keep reading. You're almost at the part I was talking about, the deal breaking glitch."

Jack glanced back at the page and began to read again.

*So you see, my beloved Ernst, why I need your help. I know this will be hard for you. You are enjoying your life as an American, your new life at the University. But you must not forget your duty. You must not forget who you really are, and why we came to this country in the first place. You are Ernst Hausen, first and foremost. You are my son. We are here to execute justice on behalf of the uncle for which you've been named, for your aunt, and for the grandmother you never had the chance to meet. And on behalf of all of the other innocents who were mercilessly killed by these criminals long before you were born.*

"Wow," Jack said. "Guess we don't have to wonder about the motive anymore. This pretty much just says it, flat out. But I see what you mean about the glitch. You're talking about the name, right?"

Rachel nodded. "He identifies the son as Ernst Hausen, not Burkhart Wagner."

"Which must mean his last name is Hausen also."

"You've got the same look on your face I did when I first read this," Rachael said. "It would seem like instead of connecting it directly to old man Wagner and his son, he severs the connection completely. But after I had some time to think about it, I started to wonder. What if this isn't what it seems? He just admitted he was part of the Stasi for many years, the East German KGB. The Stasi were very bad men. After the Soviet Union fell, quite a few of them were prosecuted for crimes they'd committed during the communist years. I looked it up. You said it yourself, this man had probably killed many people before these B-17 pilots. What if—"

Jack instantly saw where she was going. "What if Mr. Hausen was actually Mr. Wagner, who changed his name when he came here to close the door on his past as a former Stasi agent?"

Rachel smiled, "Which would also mean he'd have to change the name of his son."

"Ernst Hausen becomes Burke Wagner," Jack said.

Rachel nodded. "We're just speculating now, but if they did change their names legally, there'd be a record of that. And if we could confirm that, it would be undeniable proof this scrapbook and journal were written by old man Wagner."

"And," Jack added, "that his son—now the Senator—had to have known what his father had been up to all along."

# 42

Boyd glanced at his watch. This wasn't exactly how he wanted to spend his lunch break. But Jack Turner had said he really needed to meet. Apparently, his girlfriend Rachel had finished translating the journal yesterday. They'd met last night and had some big things to go over with him. Jack wanted Rachel there in case Boyd and Hank had any questions. She could only come during her lunch hour.

He'd better round up Hank, make sure he could join them. He glanced at his watch again. They'd be here any minute. Getting out of his chair, he headed down the hallway, stopped at Hank's cubicle. Thankfully, he was at his desk, though Boyd had to wait for him to finish a phone call. "Say Hank, Jack Turner is on his way here with his girlfriend, Rachel."

"He's coming back again?"

"Looks like it. Remember he said she was translating that journal? I told him to give us a call when she finished, if it turned up anything relevant."

"Guess it did then."

"Guess so. Can you keep an eye out for them? Should be here any minute."

"Sure thing, Joe. I'll bring them back as soon as they get here."

Boyd headed back to his office. He'd already stopped what he'd been doing. Maybe he could wolf down a few bites of that turkey and swiss sandwich Kate had packed for him before they arrived.

Jack held Rachel's hand as they walked across the parking lot toward the police station. He glanced down to see she was holding both the journal and the manila folder containing a marked up copy of her translation.

"What do you think Sergeant Boyd will do once he hears all this?" she said.

Jack sighed. "I hope he'll take it seriously. Hope he doesn't think we're wasting his time."

"You said the last time you guys met he went out of his way to make you feel this wasn't going to go the way things went last year, when he blew you off completely."

"I know, he did say that. But then Hank came in and, next thing you know, I'm heading toward the front door feeling like a kid who got spanked." They reached the glass door. He opened it for her then followed behind her.

She squeezed his hand and whispered, "I don't think that'll happen this time. With this—" she held up the notebook and folder "—we're no longer dealing with speculation."

They reached the receptionist sitting behind the counter. "Hi, I'm Jack Turner. This is Rachel. Sergeant Boyd is expecting us."

The receptionist looked up. "I remember you. Just a minute." She was already wearing a headset. She pushed a button on her phone. "Hey Hank, that couple you asked me about is here. Okay, I'll tell them." She looked back up at them. "Hank will be right here to get you."

Jack tensed up a little. He liked Hank. He reminded himself that Hank was a nice guy and a good cop.

"There he is," Rachel said. She waved.

Jack saw him walking down the hall toward them. He waved back to her and smiled. "Well, here goes."

She squeezed his hand, then whispered. "You'll do fine."

"Hi guys," Hank said, "good to see you. Joe's expecting you. Follow me." As they walked down the hall, he said, "Is that the journal you translated?"

"It is," Rachel said.

"This should be interesting."

"I think you'll think so after we go over it with you."

He led them past an area of half walls and cubicles straight to Boyd's office. When they walked in, Boyd was finishing up a sandwich. He motioned with his hand for all of them to take a seat. Rachel set the two items on his desk.

When Boyd finished chewing, he said, "That the journal?"

Rachel said, "It is."

"Can I see it?" She handed it to him. He opened it, looked at the first few pages. "Definitely written in German. I thought the pages would be more yellow."

Jack spoke up. "It's old, but it was only written in the 90s, or sometime after that."

"That's right, I thought it was written during World War II." He flipped through a few more pages. Handed it back to Jack. "So Rachel, you speak fluent German? How did that happen?"

"Well, for my degree I had to pick a language. It's kind of a long story, but the short version is...my father is a retired Air Force general."

"I think I remembered that, somehow," Boyd said.

"We were stationed in Germany a few years. My dad was the commander of a base there. That's actually where I first met Jack. He was my father's driver, off and on. Of course, he barely remembered me."

"There's a reason," Jack added.

"I was only fourteen at the time. Anyway, I picked up some German while we lived there, though we mostly stayed on base. When I got to college, it seemed like the right language to pick, since I already had a head start."

"That makes sense," Boyd said. "Well, there are a lot of pages in that journal. Can you just summarize the parts that matter? The parts you want to show us?" Joe looked at Hank. "Hank, you close that door?"

Hank got up.

Rachel picked up the journal. She pinched the first three-fourths of it between her fingers. "This whole section here is pretty much the killer taking notes as he is stalking, I guess you could say, the B-17 pilots."

"Is that what he calls them?" Hank said. "Does he name them?"

"No. I should say up front, this man is very clever. He uses codenames and code phrases for all the names and places. But he uses the same codenames for the same people, and the same phrases for the places. You don't need to be an expert code breaker to put it together. Really, just having the scrapbook with the obituaries, I could easily make the connections myself."

"I suppose if this came down to a situation that wound up in court," Boyd said, "the DA could come up with an expert who could officially make the connections. Go on."

"He really could," Jack said. "I spent a little time going over what Rachel did, with the scrapbook right beside it. I spent just enough time to connect up the things he'd written with the first two obituaries. It was very easy. To me, it's so clear, he could just as well have skipped all this codename mumbo-jumbo and talked plainly."

Boyd looked at Rachel. "Go on."

"Things really get interesting in this last section," she said. She read and explained all about the things old man Wagner had said to his son, about how he couldn't kill everyone who needed to be punished by himself, how he needed his son's help and why. She explained his health issues and how they directly correlate with what happened to old man Wagner before he died. For now, she left out the part about the name change. She and Jack had talked about this before they'd arrived, thinking they should go over that separately at the end.

Hank interjected at that point. "But is there any evidence his son knew what his father was doing? Couldn't he just say, my father was a nutcase? I had no idea he was doing these things?"

"I don't think so," Jack said. He looked at Rachel, "Do you mind?" She shook her head no. He picked up a few of the sheets she had translated and found the part he wanted to read. "Look at what he says here: *I know this will be hard for you. You are enjoying your life as an American, your new life at the University. But you must not forget your duty. You must not forget who you really are, and why we came to this country in the first place.*"

Jack skipped over the line where he calls out his son's real name. *"You are my son. We are here to execute justice on behalf of the uncle for which you've been named, for your aunt, and for the grandmother you never had the chance to meet. And on behalf of all of the other innocents who were mercilessly killed by these criminals long before you were born."* He looked at Joe, then at Hank. "It's crystal clear by what he says here, his son knew what his father's purpose was for even coming to the US in the first place. The father isn't informing him. He's *reminding* him…of his duty."

"And remember the timeline?" Rachel added. "Old man Wagner killed these pilots between 1993 and 1998. Senator Wagner was in college during that time. Right here, at Culpepper. I looked it up. Everything connects. I didn't find anything that suggests the Senator actually helped his father kill anyone. But I think it defies logic and common sense to think he had no idea what his father was up to."

"Do you know if any more B-17 pilots were killed after the eighth one?" Hank asked. He was looking at Rachel. "Seems pretty obvious he was planning to kill several more."

Jack jumped in. "I don't think so. I was able to come up with a list of pilots in that same bomb group who had flown on the Dresden mission. I googled about fifteen of them, so far. None of them had died in any kind of accidental fire-related death." Jack restrained a smile. It just dawned on him, what Hank had just said. He was starting to buy into this.

"We're thinking," Rachel said, "since this part of the journal was written near the end, he must have had his big stroke before killing anyone else. And, for some reason, his son decided not to fulfill his father's legacy. But like I said, he had to have known what was going on."

For a few moments, no one said anything. Then Boyd said, "I think there's really something here. I think you guys have stumbled onto something pretty significant. What do you think, Hank?"

"Yeah, I have to agree. This doesn't look very good for Senator Wagner."

Jack looked at Rachel, and nodded. It was time to tell them about the name change.

# 43

"There's something else Jack and I need to make you aware of," Rachel said. "Something pretty important."

"What's that?" Boyd said.

She looked at Jack. "Want me to tell them, or would you like to?"

"You go ahead."

Rachel flipped to the page where the killer mentions his son's name and read the paragraph aloud.

"Ernst Hausen," Hank said after. "Who's that?"

"Sounds like this whole theory just fell apart," Boyd said. "If the son's last name is Hausen, then it must be the father's last name, too. Which means it's not Wagner. Which means this thing was written by somebody other than the Senator's father."

"Not exactly," Jack said. "It could mean that, but we think it could also be the evidence we need that proves both the Senator and his father are totally involved."

"How so?" Hank said.

"We think the Wagner's changed their name. We think their real last name *is* Hausen, and that Ernst is actually Burke Wagner."

"Guys," Hank said, "I think you're really reaching here."

"We're really not," Rachel said. She reminded them about old man Wagner's admission to being part of the East German Stasi and, for Hank's sake, explained who they were and why it mattered. "So see, he would have a high degree of motivation to change his name after moving to the states."

"She makes a good point, Hank," Boyd said.

"But what if they're wrong?" Hank said.

"If we're wrong, we're wrong," Jack said. "Then this whole thing really does fall apart, and we're prepared to accept that. But this name-change thing is something that can be proved or disproved legally. I'm thinking with Burke Wagner seeking admission to a university like Culpepper and having strong political ambitions, he would've wanted to change his name legally. I don't know where to look for that kind of information, but I'm guessing you can find out definitively if someone legally changed their name."

"You can," Boyd said. "All you really need is the county they were living in when they requested the name change. It would be part of the county record. You know if that's here?"

"We don't," Rachel said. "But that would be easy enough to find out. After translating this part of the journal, I got curious and went on Senator Wagner's website. I don't remember which city it is now, but I remember reading his biography page. It definitely mentioned the city they first moved to when they came to the United States."

"Well, there you go," Boyd said. "Figure that one out, and we'll know once and for all who wrote this journal, and whether Senator Burke has any personal involvement in this case."

"And if we find out that the Wagner's last name is really Hausen?" Rachel asked. "Will you guys be willing to pursue this case?"

"Definitely," Boyd said. "It's still a totally circumstantial case, but that might just be the smoking gun a DA would be looking for.

I can't guarantee he would take the case, but I would certainly be willing to go to bat for it if you guys can confirm this."

"And we'd probably need to get the FBI involved, too," Hank said, "since all the murders took place in different states."

Jack and Rachel looked at each other, smiled. Jack stood, so Rachel did, too. "Great. Then we'll go find that out and get back to you when we have the proof, regardless of where it takes us. Thank you for your time, gentlemen."

They shook hands. Jack gathered up the materials, and they turned to leave.


Officer Tony Campbell was sure Vandergraf would want an update on what he'd just observed. Whatever was going on with this history professor, things seemed to be heating up.

He got up and walked over toward the receptionist. "That was that history professor who's been in here the last few days, wasn't it?"

"It was," she said.

"You know who that lady was with him?"

"I think it was his girlfriend. I didn't see a ring, but they were holding hands and they looked at each other like people do when they're in love. Anything else you want to know? I could tell you the color of their eyes."

"No, that's plenty. Thank you." He knew she had been taking some night courses at the college on criminal justice, trying to improve her chances for a promotion.

"Why do you care anyway?" she asked.

"Just curious. You know, nothing ever happens around here. But that's the third time he's been in here this week, now bringing his girlfriend."

"Well, I'm afraid I can't scratch your curiosity itch any further. I have no idea what's going on."

He pulled out his pack of cigarettes. "I'm gonna go grab a smoke."

"Those things are gonna kill you."

"I'm counting on it." He smiled and headed for the side door.

Once outside, he lit up and got a call started to Vandergraf on his private cell.

"Officer Campbell," Vandergraf said. "Nothing from you in weeks. Now you're calling me all the time."

"I know. But something definitely seems to be heating up over here."

"You mean with that history professor?"

"Yeah, Jack Turner. He was here again to see Sergeant Boyd and Hank Jensen. They just left, he and his girlfriend."

"His girlfriend?"

"Yeah. But I don't know her name."

"Were you in on this meeting with your Sergeant?"

"No, he doesn't consult me very much. But I picked up some information before the meeting started. Some stuff I think you will care about."

There was a pause. "Okay, what is it?" Vandergraf sounded serious all of a sudden.

"A few minutes before they came, the sergeant came out to Hank Jensen's desk. He's the cop that works with Boyd the most. Unfortunately, I was on the phone with someone and couldn't hear everything they said. But I did hear him mention that Turner was coming here any minute, and something about this girl having translated some journal."

"A journal?"

"At least, that's what it sounded like. I think they were coming in to discuss some things they'd discovered in it. Then a few minutes later,

Turner and this attractive brunette walk in. I looked and noticed she was carrying two things. That old raggedy notebook Turner had brought in with him the other day when he was here alone, and a little worn-out-looking leather book that looked very much like a journal. Jensen met them and brought them back to Boyd's office. I waited a minute then went to refill my coffee. The pot's within earshot of Boyd's office. But this time they closed the door."

"So you have no idea what they were talking about?"

"I wouldn't say, no idea. I think they were discussing whatever was in that journal, which she must have translated. Although I have no idea from what into what."

"What was everyone's demeanor after the meeting ended?" Vandergraf said. "Last time, you said it was obvious that Turner looked frustrated and you said the officers seemed to be discouraging him from pursuing this…whatever this is."

"Well, that wasn't their demeanor this time. Everyone was shaking hands and all smiles."

Another long pause. "Really?"

"Really," Campbell said. "Before they headed out the front door, I heard Turner say to Hank something like, *we'll dig up that information real soon and get back with you.* Hank said something like, *you do that.* You have any idea what this is all about?"

Once again, a pause. "I might," Vandergraf said. "But I can't be sure just yet. In any case, thanks for calling promptly. You're definitely earning your keep lately."

"I'm trying."

"By all means, continue to call me if anything else develops. Anything at all."

"I will."

Vandergraf set his cell phone down on his desk. He spent the next few minutes pacing back and forth. This new information, coupled with what had already transpired, caused him great concern. He wished the Senator had given him a fuller understanding of what had occurred between him and his dead father, the shadowy history that the Senator wanted to keep hidden at all costs. Then he would know exactly how to proceed. Without that information, he was afraid to act at all on his own initiative.

He paced back and forth some more. It seemed he had no other alternative.

He would have to call the Senator and brief him on these new developments.

# 44

After escorting Jack and Rachel toward the lobby, Hank returned to Boyd's office and took a seat.

"If you want to chat more about the reason they were in here," Boyd said, "close the door. This thing with the Senator, if this is real we need to tread very carefully. He's become quite a powerful man in a fairly short period of time."

Hank pushed it till it latched. "I don't trust him."

"You mean Jack or the Senator?"

"The Senator. I didn't trust him before Jack stirred all this up. He seems like a total phony to me. Every time I hear him on TV, I find myself not believing a thing he says."

"So it's not hard for you to believe this could be true?"

Hank took a seat. "Not at all. It still might be the craziest story I've ever heard. This time, though, it felt a little more real, thinking through all the things they dug out of that journal. Add them all together, combine them with that scrapbook of obituaries…I'm thinking there really could be something to this."

Boyd leaned forward on his desk. "We might really have to act on this, they come back with proof of that name change."

"Are we going to have a problem," Hank said, "with this stuff

Jack found being admitted into evidence? I mean, he's just renting that cabin. And it's not like the owner gave him permission to bring that stuff to us. Couldn't that get everything thrown out?"

"I've been thinking about that. We might be in the clear here. We didn't come by this information through any illegal search or seizure. It came to us independent of any effort on our part. Jack being in that cabin as a renter gives him a legal right to be there. He found the information, recognized that it involved criminal activity, so he did his civic duty and brought it to the police. Don't you think? You know, see something, say something. This isn't terrorist-related, but same idea."

"Yeah, that sounds right to me," Hank said. "Still think there might be a problem if it comes out that he found it hidden under the floorboards in a locked safe."

Boyd had thought about that. "You could be right. But it's not like Jack broke into the safe. The key was right there on the premises." That part still was a little sticky. "We'll just let the DA decide what to do about that one."

"He might just tell Jack not to volunteer the part about the safe," Hank said.

"Could be. Or, he could just say the best part of this case belongs to the FBI and not want to even deal with the Senator's involvement, since he was a college kid when it all went down."

"In any event," Hank said as he stood, "I have a feeling Jack will be back pretty soon with the proof about the name change, if there is any. He's gonna stay on this till it's solved, one way or the other. My gut tells me this really is going to turn out to be just the way Jack and Rachel said."

"I think so, too," Boyd said. "That happens, then this thing could suddenly grow from nothing to huge in a couple of days. Because of that, let's keep this between us for now."

"Agreed. Well," Hank said. "Better get back to my paperwork."

After he left, Boyd thought about the last thing they'd talked about. He picked up his phone and called Jack's cell.

Jack picked up pretty quick. "Hey Joe, what's up? I'm just in town here grabbing something to eat with Rachel before I head back to the cabin."

"I was just thinking about something. Hank and me been going over this thing since you left. You guys get the confirmation on that name change, and this thing could become something big pretty quick. For that reason, we're both thinking you and Rachel should probably not talk about this to anybody but us. The Senator's a pretty popular guy around here with a pretty good reach, you follow me?"

"I do," Jack said. "I think that's wise advice."

"What's wise advice?" Rachel asked.

Jack really didn't want to say. They picked up their food and walked back to the table. "That was Joe."

"I figured that. What was he calling about?"

"I guess he and Hank were pretty impressed with your work, translating that journal, and the conclusions we came to. He's talking like this might be for real."

"Why, what did he say?"

Jack paused. How should he respond to this question? He knew her well enough by now to know she would worry, big time, if he simply told her what Boyd said. Especially after everything they went through last year. But he also knew it would be much worse if he lied to her. Maybe there was a way to say it without raising any red flags. "He just said if it turned out that we found proof of the name change, we should just bring that info back to either him or Hank."

"Why would he call you to say that? That sounds pretty obvious."

Okay, he needed to say more. "I guess he meant Culpepper is such a small town, and the Senator's kind of a big deal. I guess he doesn't want this info showing up in the news, which could happen if we talked about it to other people."

"I can see that," she said. "I don't have a problem with that."

"I guess media attention could make it hard for them to do their investigation." Which was true, although it wasn't what Joe had said. Jack was pretty sure the message behind the Sergeant's warning wasn't aimed at keeping the media away from the case, although he was sure that was true.

Sergeant Boyd didn't want the Senator to get wind of this for Jack and Rachel's sake.

But why? Did he think they were in any danger?

# 45

When Jack and Rachel had finished eating and the waitress had cleared the table, Rachel pulled out her iPad. "This place has free Wi-Fi." She began tapping and swiping the screen. "Why don't we do a little research before you head back to the cabin?"

"I'm for anything that keeps you with me longer," Jack said. "What are you looking up?"

"Senator Wagner's bio info. The Sergeant said if we knew the county Wagner applied to for his name change, we could contact them and find out his real name. That part of his story is on his website." A few more taps and swipes. "Here it is." Another tap.

Jack slid closer, so he could see. They both started to read silently several paragraphs to the left of a photo of a much younger Burke Wagner. Jack guessed he was in his late twenties.

Rachel found it first. She pointed to the paragraph as she read aloud. "Burke moved here from Germany with his father in 1992. They lived in Columbia, South Carolina for a year then moved to Culpepper, Georgia, so Burke could start attending Culpepper University." She looked at Jack. "You think he changed his name here or in Columbia?"

"I'm guessing Columbia. They were there for a year, and I'm

thinking he would've wanted the name changed as soon as possible. Certainly before he started applying to attend college anywhere."

She went back out to Google and searched some more. "This probably won't work. But I thought we could check and see if you can find out that information online. Sometimes, it's crazy the information you can get from these government websites."

Jack watched a few minutes until they both stared at the same information on screen. He read it aloud. "You have to apply at the courthouse in person."

"That's too bad."

"Columbia's not that far," Jack said. "I can be there and back the same day."

"You thinking about going there tomorrow?"

"Yeah. Wouldn't you like to get this thing resolved?"

"Yes. It's just…I can't go with you tomorrow. I've got a major test."

"I'd really love for you to go with me. It would be fun getting away on a day trip, driving my BMW through all those winding, country roads."

"You're making it worse. I can't skip this test."

"Is that the only reason you wouldn't want to go?"

"Yeah, why?"

Should he even mention it? "Nothing. I'm glad."

"Why? What are you thinking?"

"I don't know. It's just…I wondered if you might be thinking this thing is starting to take up too much time."

She thought a moment. See, he shouldn't have said anything.

"Well, it is a distraction. I mean, all the time we're spending on this is time you could be spending on your dissertation. But it kind of feels like we're too far gone at this point, don't you think?"

"I do. I'd hate to have to pull out of this when it seems like we're so close to the bottom." He leaned over and kissed her on the cheek.

"What was that for?"

"For being you. For getting sucked into things like this with me, rather than getting mad at me for getting off track."

"Well, in a way, it's not totally off track. Your doctoral dissertation is on the bombing of Dresden. This whole mystery thing is rooted in the Dresden bombing. All of these B-17 pilots were killed because they flew on that bombing mission." She thought a moment. "You know what this kind of reminds me of? It's like those urban construction projects when they're digging down for the foundation, and they uncover some archaeological artifact. They've got to stop everything they're doing and figure out what this thing is. It's a shame we can't think of a way you could work this whole thing into your dissertation project."

That would be nice. But it didn't seem likely. "Can you scroll back to where the courthouse address is? I'll need to write that down to put it into my GPS for tomorrow."

After Jack wrote the info down, she said, "You text me tomorrow as soon as you find out, either way. Even if I'm in class, unless I'm in the middle of that test, I'll step out into the hall and call you back."

Jack smiled. "I will."

"What if it turns out to be him? What if they really did change their name from Hausen to Wagner?"

"Oh, I'm fully expecting it to be true. There's no doubt in my mind that the serial killer is old man Wagner, and that the good senator isn't so good after all."

# 46

It was the following morning. Vandergraf was sitting in a golf cart with the Senator. Last night, he had tried for hours to reach him. Finally, the Senator sent a text just before Vandergraf had gone to bed: *Tee-time 8am. Talk in between holes. Have to sharpen my game. Playing 18 holes with Mr. B after lunch.*

Turned out, the Senator had been spending some quality time last night with a multibillionaire donor—nicknamed Mr. B.— whom he had been courting for months. He'd turned off his cell phone.

Now, Vandergraf and the Senator were out on the course doing a warm-up round, so the Senator wouldn't look so bad when he got with Mr. B. after lunch for another eighteen holes.

Looking at the scenery now, Vandergraf had to admit—it was a beautiful morning for golf with one exception. It was barely 9:00am and the air was already damp. Southern humidity is a terrible thing. He wished Senator Wagner wasn't such a stickler for style, insisting they wore long pants like touring pros. Vandergraf thought Wagner might think better of the idea if he could see the widening band of sweat on his rear end.

He still hadn't talked to the Senator about the phone call from

Officer Campbell yesterday afternoon. He'd tried to as soon as they headed out to the first tee, but the Senator had stopped him. "Is this life or death?"

Vandergraf didn't know what to say. "Potentially," he'd said.

"If it's only *potentially*, then I want to finish my morning coffee before you *potentially* ruin my morning."

Wagner sipped his coffee nice and slow.

They were approaching the fourth hole, a dogleg to the right, bending at the two-hundred-yard mark. Vandergraf had figured Wagner should have added at least three more strokes to his score that morning. He'd caught him kicking his ball to a better lie that many times. Vandergraf enjoyed the comments Wagner made after the dirty deeds. "Didn't think I'd pull that shot off," he'd say, wiping his brow. Or, "That's what they call shotmaking, my boy."

Vandergraf watched the Senator sip his tall mug again, hoping it was the last one. Had to be close. It was Vandergraf's turn to tee off. He'd made par on the last hole, beating the Senator by a stroke. He yanked the head cover off his driver and slid it out of his bag.

"I hate doglegs," Wagner muttered, still enjoying the shade in the golf cart.

Vandergraf knew Wagner's best drive wasn't quite two-hundred yards and usually sliced to the right. On this hole, anything less than the Senator's best swing would put him in the woods. Hard to fake a lost ball. Vandergraf had a suggestion that would help the Senator avoid this, but Wagner didn't respond well to golf advice. Vandergraf kept his mouth shut, put his ball on the tee, went through his pre-shot routine and let her fly.

"Nice Harold," Wagner said, watching the ball soar off the tee.

It wasn't nice, Vandergraf thought. It was perfect. "It'll do," he said, feigning humility. The ball sailed right down the middle of the fairway over three hundred yards, bounced and rolled toward a perfect approach shot to the green. He'd never have hit like that when he first started working for the Senator. Opting instead to intentionally play a few notches below Wagner's game on every hole.

He glanced at the Senator still sitting in the cart, to see if he'd give him the green light to start talking about the real reason he'd come out here.

Not yet.

Wagner got up, walked to the back of the golf cart and pulled out his driver. True to form, he walked up to the tee, did that little pitter-patter with his feet and butt-wiggle dance of his, and swung the driver. They stood and watched as the ball sliced to the right. He swore as the ball careened into the trees about a-hundred and seventy-five yards away.

"I don't know, Senator. I think you can play out of that one," Vandergraf said.

Wagner, recovering his poise, replied, "I'm sure of it. I think it hit a tree. Maybe it took a nice bounce in my favor."

As they rode along in the cart, enjoying the breeze, Wagner was finally ready. "So, Harold, tell me about this potentially ruinous development that was so urgent you had to drive all the way out here this morning?"

"Well, I know you don't like a long build-up, so I guess I'll just jump in. Are you aware of any journal your father might have written before he died, that he might have left out at the cabin?"

Wagner's face instantly grew serious. He pulled the golf cart over and hit the break. "What did you say?"

"That's what Officer Campbell called about. That history professor who's renting out your cabin, he showed up at the police station again yesterday afternoon. This time with his girlfriend. Campbell's not in the inner loop, so he's not able to sit in on the meetings they had with the detective. But he was able to pick up some important details from things he overheard in the hallway. The detective mentioned to his partner that this couple was coming in any minute, and said something about her having finished translating this journal. A few minutes later, in comes this couple and Campbell says she's holding a small, well-worn leather book in her hand, along with an old scrapbook. Then all of them go into this meeting. The doors are closed, so he can't hear anything else. But after it was over, unlike the last time when it was clear the police were talking about not pursuing this any further, this time they're all chummy. The professor, his girlfriend and the police. Campbell got the impression they were encouraging him to look into something else they had discussed in the meeting and to get back with them soon. As you know, I don't know what any of this is about. But it seems things are heating up, and I'm thinking we should be doing a little more than just observing."

The Senator's face became very grave, but Vandergraf still couldn't read how he was processing all this. "Was I wrong to interrupt your golf game with this?"

"Not only were you not wrong to interrupt me," Wagner said, "had you known what this was really all about you would've said yes to my first question, not *potentially*." Wagner whipped the golf cart around and started heading down the cart path toward the clubhouse, as fast as the cart would go.

So, the Senator considered this a life and death matter. He wished the Senator trusted him enough to stop playing these games and would simply tell him what this was all about. He felt like he'd earned that much by now.

Wagner's eyes stayed locked on the path ahead. "I agree, this new development means we're past the point of mere observing. It's time to act, decisively. Do you know where Mr. Strickland is?"

Vandergraf almost smiled. "I've already called him, sir. In fact, I started paying his retainer yesterday. He was finishing up a delivery and planned to arrive back in town today. I told him not to leave again, that I suspected we would need him soon and to keep his cell phone charged and with him at all times."

"Good. It's time to put a stop to this little adventure our history professor has begun. We must keep this from going any further." They approached a sharp curve. He slowed the cart down, brought it to a stop and looked at Vandergraf. "Strickland must retrieve that journal and the scrapbook and get them both to me immediately, no matter what it takes. Do you understand what I'm saying?"

Vandergraf nodded. "I do, sir."

"No matter what it takes."

# 47

After abruptly ending their round of golf, Vandergraf and the Senator got cleaned up in the locker room and headed toward their cars. Few words were spoken. Their cars were in separate sections of the parking lot. Vandergraf could tell the Senator was just about to say some parting words, so he decided to jump in and take a chance. If there was ever a time Wagner would open up and share his family secrets, this was it.

"Senator, before I call Strickland and set this new mission in motion, is there anything more about this situation you can tell me? I'm not asking to satisfy my curiosity. I feel if I really understood what we're dealing with, I'd be able to make better decisions without having to constantly involve you like this." They stopped walking. "I can handle whatever it is, sir. And I hope you know by now, you can trust me."

Vandergraf already knew enough inside information about the Senator's activities to send him to prison for a very long time. Vandergraf had also committed enough felonies and misdemeanors on the Senator's behalf to ensure he'd be thrown in prison for just as long a time, if not longer.

The Senator stood there looking at him. Finally, he spoke. "I can't tell you everything, but you're right. As much as I am able to trust anyone, I trust you. The contents of those two items, the scrapbook and the journal, contain enough information to destroy my career, to destroy everything I've worked for since the day I graduated college. I would be ruined, and the hefty salary I'm able to pay you for your services would instantly dry up."

Vandergraf had figured this much by himself. It was obvious just from observing Wagner's reaction. "But why? What's in them? Why do they matter so much?"

The Senator looked away then down at the ground, then back at Vandergraf. "You never met my father. In some ways, we are polar opposites. In some ways, I suppose, we are very much the same. He was a ruthless man fueled by a lifetime of rage. It's a very long and complicated story, but the bottom line is…we came here from Germany not long after the Berlin Wall fell, so that my father could exact his revenge on the World War II pilots who destroyed his family. He was well on his way to achieving this goal when his health failed."

"You told me once he had a massive stroke," Vandergraf said.

"That's what happened. I was here, attending the university. He wanted me to pick up where he left off. To complete his life's work, as he called it. There's just no way I could. For starters, I didn't even believe in it. War is war. It's a terrible thing. Inhumane and unthinkable things were done on both sides. By soldiers acting under orders. I wasn't a Nazi, or even a communist. I'm a capitalist. I like money and power, and the things they can buy. But I told him I would do as he asked, just as soon as I finished college. He showed me this journal he had been keeping and a scrapbook filled with newspaper clippings. He said he would hide them in the cabin for me, in case something happened to him. I think he knew he was dying."

"Did he tell you where?"

"He did. I'm sure he did. But I wasn't listening. It's not like I was going to do anything with it. And sure enough, before I graduated he had another major stroke. He became a total invalid after that, couldn't even talk. He stayed that way until he died."

"Did you ever read the journal? Do you know what it says?"

The Senator shook his head no. "But I didn't have to. I knew what he was doing. He talked about it all the time. I know without a doubt, whatever it says will totally ruin my career, all my plans. I can't let that happen. I won't let that happen. Do you understand?"

"Perfectly," Vandergraf said. "I won't fail you, sir."

Rob Strickland sat alone in a booth in Denny's restaurant on the west end of Culpepper, sipping the last dregs of a cold cup of coffee. His cell phone chimed on the table.

He read the number and name. His occasional boss, Harold Vandergraf. He knew the real head honcho wasn't Vandergraf. It was Senator Wagner. Strickland didn't mind serving at their beck-and-call. Not that he believed in the Senator, or cared one bit about his politics. The money was just so good. Sometimes he made a month's salary for just a few days' work. He was making more sitting there at Denny's than he did driving that truck.

He threw down a five-dollar tip and made his way to the cashier. Once outside, he stepped out of earshot and called Vandergraf back.

It rang a few times. "Hey there, Rob. Thanks for returning my call so quickly."

"Yeah, well…."

"Like I expected. Things just got real. Got a job for you, a big one. And I need you to get on it right away."

"I'm all ears," Strickland said.

"Have you ever done anything for us out at the Senator's cabin?"

"Can't say I have."

"Well, I'm about to give you two addresses. Write these down. The first one is the cabin." He also gave Strickland some verbal directions since the cabin was off the beaten path. "The second is a condo called The Whispering Hills. I checked. It's got the usual condo security, shouldn't be too much of a problem for you to get in. Fact is, I'm hoping you won't even need to go to the second place, that you'll find everything you need at the cabin."

"First question. What am I looking for? Second question, am I likely to encounter any people at either place?"

"I don't want you to, if you can help it. This needs to be done nice and quiet. The Senator doesn't want any publicity."

"Okay, got it." Strickland took that to mean he wasn't being given permission to hurt anyone. But Vandergraf and the Senator both understood, sometimes that was impossible to avoid. "I still don't know what I'm looking for."

"You're looking for two things. An old scrapbook filled with newspaper clippings and a small leather journal. Getting both of these items is of the utmost importance. Apparently, they have something to do with the Senator's father. There's a guy—a college professor—who's been staying at the cabin. I guess he's found these two things and has been talking to the police about whatever's in them."

"What is in them? Why do they matter?"

"Not important. What is important, is that you get them back ASAP. I'm hoping this professor has brought them back there. To the cabin, I mean."

"Do you know where I'll find them *in* the cabin?"

"No. But they're in there. Somewhere. Unless the professor brought them home to his condo. If you don't find them in the cabin, go there."

"Can I tear the place up looking for them? Or am I supposed to do it without leaving a trace?"

"Do it cleanly. The best thing would be, you get these two items and no one even knows you were there."

"But you know, the best thing hardly ever happens. I need to know you're okay if the worst thing happens."

There was a long pause. "Do whatever you have to do. The Senator wants these items back no matter what. And you can't get caught, and no one can see your face."

"By *no matter what*," Strickland repeated. "Do you mean—"

"I think you know exactly what I mean."

# 48

Jack almost ran down the marble steps of the County courthouse in Columbia, South Carolina. He couldn't wait to call Rachel. In his hand he held a photocopy that proved what he and Rachel had already believed. Senator Burke Wagner had started his life with a different name.

*Ernst Josef Hausen.*

Wagner had been named after an uncle he had never met. An uncle who had died in the Dresden bombing. And the man they had been referring to as *old man Wagner* was actually Luther Wilhelm Hausen, born in Dresden, Germany in 1937. The court records said the name change had become official on February 14th, 1992. Which was ironic. February 14th was the day the American B-17s had attacked Dresden back in 1945.

The same day Luther Hausen's family had been killed.

Jack hurried across the street toward a shady spot provided by a row of maple trees and pulled out his phone. He quickly found Rachel's picture and phone icon under his favorites tab and pushed the button. She picked up in two rings.

"Jack?"

"It's me. Guess what I'm holding in my hand?"

"You found it?"

"I found it. Proof positive."

"For both, the father and son?"

"Yep. Luther Hausen, and his son…Senator Ernst Hausen. The name change became official in 1992."

"Are you going to call Sergeant Boyd?"

"As soon as I get off with you."

"Wow…it's real then. This thing really happened. The Senator's father really is, or was, a serial killer."

"And the Senator knew all about it. At the very least."

"This comes out, his career is finished," she said.

"At the very least," he repeated.

"What time are you heading back?"

"I'll probably get on the road in about twenty minutes. Get some coffee first and top off the gas tank. Took me just over two hours to get here, but I think I'll celebrate a little and take the scenic ride home."

"How long will that take?"

"About another forty minutes."

"Are you gonna drop off the court records at the police station?"

"I'll probably bring them over in the morning. But I'm going to take pictures of them right now and send them to Joe just before I call him."

"I wonder what they'll do."

"I'm not sure. Like they said in our meeting, most of what the father did is FBI territory, or else the police departments in the cities where the men were killed."

"I know," she said. "I'm wondering what they're going to do about Senator Wagner. He was here in Culpepper when it all happened, going to school."

"You're right. I don't know. I guess we'll just have to wait and see."

After they hung up, still standing there in the shade, Jack took the photos then texted them to Sergeant Boyd, with this message: *Call me if you get these in the next few minutes. They are what you think they are. If I don't hear from you, I'll call you once I get on the highway.*


Rob Strickland's favorite vehicle to drive was his red 1995 F250 Ford pickup. But that's not what he drove when he did jobs for the Senator. He drove a silver 2005 Toyota Corolla. Mainly because it looked like ten other cars. If he drove his red pickup on jobs, people would remember it, right off. It'd stick out like a zebra in a horse race.

Being invisible was its only benefit, though. It was a four-cylinder piece of crap on these hills. No pickup. No power windows. No frills at all. Like GPS, for instance. Strickland didn't think anyone had ever even heard of GPS back when this Corolla was made. They didn't put them in cars anyway. He had GPS on his smart phone but didn't bring it out on jobs, either. He always picked up a cheap burner phone. And to stay on the safe side, he always pulled the battery out of it unless he was calling someone.

So here he was, navigating the winding roads around the hills and lakes of Culpepper glancing down at a paper map with handwritten instructions to the Senator's cabin.

If he was reading this right, around two more S-curves the turnoff should show up on the right. He was liking all the trees on both sides of the road. Not so much that he cared about trees; he cared about not seeing people when he was up to no good, which pretty much described all his work for the Senator.

Sure enough, there was the break in the trees, the turnoff on the right. He drove down the dirt road, so bumpy it made his jaw rattle.

Stupid Corolla. His truck would glide over this stuff like he was water skiing. After a few minutes, he came to another break in the trees, another dirt road, veering off to the left. This must be it, the road to the cabin. Said it right there in the instructions: *You'll see the cabin in a clearing off to the left.*

This dirt road was narrower but a lot smoother. Sure enough, he quickly came to a clearing. The lake filled his windshield. Out his right window, there was the cabin. Thankfully, he didn't see any cars. Vandergraf didn't want him to get into any confrontations unless they were unavoidable. Just get in there and out with those two items. Shouldn't be too hard, considering the size of this cabin.

It was pretty small. Looked more like a shack to him. He couldn't imagine anyone thinking this might be a good place to come and get some work done. But hey, it didn't matter to him. He was there for just one thing. He pulled the car close to the little building and got out. He listened for a moment, just to be sure he was alone.

No sounds. Good.

Vandergraf had given him a key, so he pulled it out. When he got to the door, he jiggled the handle and it opened right up. So far, this was easy money. It was fairly dark inside, except for a ribbon of light coming in from a lone window on the left wall. He felt for a light switch, but there was none. As his eyes adjusted to the dimmer light, he noticed a single bulb hanging from the center ceiling rafter, a pull chain dangling from it.

He pulled and it instantly glowed a dingy yellow. Couldn't be more than forty watts. But he could see everything, which wasn't saying much. It was just one big room. Bed in one corner, table and chairs in the other. In between them, a potbellied stove. Something like a kitchen counter made of butcher block was tucked into the third corner. Beside it, a freestanding slop sink.

He didn't see any signs of life, any evidence that it was even being lived in. Made him wonder if the professor had already moved back home to his condo. Vandergraf had said he was renting it for the month. Just to be thorough, Strickland walked all around looking for the journal and scrapbook. He lifted, opened and looked under everything he could. Didn't find a thing.

Clearly, what he'd come here for wasn't here.

He put everything back the way he'd found it, pulled the chain to turn out the light, and backed out through the front door.

Now it was on to the condo. He'd better find the goods there. Otherwise, he didn't see any other way to get them without confronting the professor in person.

That would escalate things quite a bit.


Jack drove south on I-26 about twenty minutes west of Columbia when his phone rang. It was Sergeant Boyd returning his call. Just before answering, he reminded himself not to call him that. "Hey Joe, thanks for getting back with me."

"Sorry I missed you. I was doing some interviews. I checked my cell phone when I got back to my desk. Looks like your drive to the courthouse proved fruitful. I can't say I was totally surprised by what you found. But still, seeing it there in black and white makes it pretty official."

"I know. I had the same reaction. The question now is, what comes next?"

"I've got a friend I used to work with when I was a detective in Pittsburgh. He's been with the FBI the last few years. Think I'll start by calling him. Tell him the story, see where he thinks it should go next."

Jack liked the sound of that. "I know you both thought most of the father's part of the story involved FBI territory, since the murders happened in different states. But what about the local part? Senator Wagner, or rather Ernst Hausen, was attending Culpepper at the time. His father's home base was that cabin I'm staying in. The son knew everything the father was up to and never did a thing to stop it, or even report it. Seems like those things would be crimes, don't you think?"

"I think you're probably right. But there's an old saying, when unloading the Ark, start with the elephants not the mice. What the father did is huge in comparison to the son's involvement. I'm sure the FBI will see it that way, too, and so will the DA. So let's start with that. Once I hear back from my friend, I'll set up an appointment with the DA, tell him the whole story. I'm sure he'll see any criminal allegations involving the Senator right away. The important thing now is, what to do with the evidence you've uncovered. You still have them, right?"

"In a way. I put them back where I found them in the cabin."

"You mean in the safe, under the floorboards?"

"I wanted everything to look just the way it was supposed to. Didn't want to take a chance in case anyone stopped in when I wasn't there. Both the Senator and my next-door neighbor have keys." There was a long pause. Jack added, "Do you disagree?"

"Not completely. Legally, I can't tell you what to do with it. Not until we have a search warrant. But with these documents you uncovered today, we're a whole lot closer to establishing probable cause. I'm just concerned about the meantime. The only evidence we have that proves everything is that scrapbook and journal. Know what I mean?"

Jack thought he did. If he understood it right, Joe was asking him, unofficially, to get those two items out of the cabin and hide them someplace safe until they reached a point where they could secure them legally. "I got you, Joe. I'll take care of it when I get back to the cabin tonight. In the morning, I'll bring the courthouse documents to the station."

# 49

Rob Strickland sat in his car a block down from The Whispering Hills condominium complex, the main residence of this professor, Jack Turner. The sun had started to set but there was still plenty of light. The street was relatively quiet. He didn't see anyone out walking around. It was a gated community, providing a just-for-looks level of security, which included one very old man reading a book in the guard house.

After driving around the place twice, Strickland had noticed a thick section of woods bordered the west side. A stone wall also outlined the perimeter. That was his way in. No fuss, no hassle. He was only there to pick up the two items, which he could easily carry in his hands.

He got out of the car, walked across the street and down the sidewalk until he reached the spot where the stone wall turned into the woods. Glancing back and forth down the street to make sure he was still alone, he backed into the shrubs until they completely covered him. He turned and hurried along the edge of the stone wall until he found a tree with low-hanging branches standing adjacent to the wall. On the other side, a row of hemlock trees would hide him nicely from the neighbors. He climbed until his head cleared the top of the wall then waited till it was obvious no one was looking.

In no time, he was over the stone wall and landed in a patch of mulch. He walked through the hemlock trees toward Turner's building like he was just any resident out for a walk.

He passed an elderly woman across the street walking a poodle and waved. She waved back and kept walking.

Turner's unit was on the left. He walked through a breezeway between two buildings, turned right and came to his building. He stopped long enough to confirm Turner's car wasn't in either of his assigned parking spaces. Vandergraf had said Turner rode a sporty blue BMW. Two minutes later, Strickland was standing in front of Turner's door. Good, just a regular deadbolt. He pressed his ear to the door, listening for any signs of life. Nothing. He took out his tools and had the deadbolt sliding away in less than a minute.

He opened the door, stood and listened. The only sounds were bubbles floating up through the filters of a large aquarium. He waited in the hall a full minute, just to be sure. Certain he had the apartment to himself, Strickland set about searching for the journal and scrapbook.

Most people called Jack's next-door neighbor Mrs. Carlson. At the moment, she sat in her late husband's favorite chair, a sagging recliner, watching a movie on the Hallmark channel. Her aging poodle, Ralphie, was sound asleep on his favorite spot on the sofa. Mrs. Carlson was thinking about hitting the pause button and fixing herself something to eat.

In any case, she needed to get up. An alarm had gone off twenty minutes ago reminding her to take her dinner-time dose of heart medicine. She'd better do it or she'd forget. Some days she struggled taking the medication at all, especially her before-bed dose. Maybe if she didn't, she'd die quietly in her sleep and finally get to join her husband Bill. Then she wouldn't have to sit there every night alone, missing him.

As she walked into the kitchen, she remembered the pain from the heart attack she had last year, and how terrified she felt lying there before the paramedics came. Which is why she kept taking the medicine, even at night. Otherwise, what if she just lay there in her bed, suffering alone for hours?

That would be awful.

She walked over to the fridge resolved to keep taking her medicine. She reached for the freezer door. That's when she noticed it. A yellow post-it note she had put there herself. *"Don't forget— feed Jack's fish before dinner!"*

Why had she agreed to do this?

Why? Because Jack had asked her so nicely, that's why. And he had the sweetest eyes, almost like her son Robbie's. "But what if one of the fish dies while you're gone?" she'd asked him. They were such fragile little things. "That's fine," Jack had said. "I won't blame you. I know that happens with fish."

"What if they all died?" she'd said. "Then you won't have to come over and feed them anymore," he'd said smiling. He was such a nice young man.

"God," she prayed as she walked over to fetch the jar of fish food, "You can take me anytime you want, just not his fish."

She picked the jar off the counter and walked back into the living room. "Darn." She looked at the TV. She'd hit the mute button instead of the pause button. Now she'd have to backtrack and figure out where she'd left off in the movie.

Jack's fish would have to wait a few more minutes.

Strickland had quickly walked through Turner's whole apartment—twice—and hadn't found what he came there for. That either meant Turner had the items with him, like in his car, or he'd hidden them somewhere in here. Strickland doubted that, but he couldn't face Vandergraf empty-handed. He had to be sure. The easiest thing would be to tear up the place, make it look like a break-in. That way he could leave without having to clean up or try to remember where everything went.

Turner had left all the drapes closed, so it was fairly dark. Strickland had turned on all the lights, rather than open the drapes and chance being seen. He started searching in Turner's bedroom. First, he rummaged through the closet, then he emptied a few drawers on the bed. Nothing. Turner had a desk over in the far corner. He went through that. Still, nothing. He went through the second bedroom, clearly a guest room. Everything in there was empty.

He walked through the darkened hallway into the living area. His eyes shifted to the big screen TV. It sat atop a nice hutch with drawers running down both sides. He looked through all of them. Nothing but DVD's. He pulled out a small pile and tossed them scattershot across the living room rug. Just for effect.

He slowly panned the room until his eyes rested on a closet in the hallway he hadn't noticed before. There's a possibility. He slid open the closet door. Just a row of coats, a vacuum cleaner, an umbrella, and a box of sweaters on the shelf. The least he could do was throw the sweaters all across the room.

This wasn't done for effect. Strickland was getting frustrated. He had to find those items. They were paying him a lot of money, and the only way they'd keep doing that is if he got results. He'd never failed them before.

He wasn't about to start now.

Mrs. Carlson walked over and, still standing, grabbed the remote to get the TV situated. She knew if she sat down, she wouldn't get up again.

Well, better go feed the fish, she thought. Get it over with. She tightened up her robe as she walked to the front door. She took a look at herself in a hallway mirror. "Hope nobody sees that," she said aloud.

So what if they did, what would they think? Just an old lady in a robe, right? Who did she care to impress at her age? She reached for the doorknob, then remembered—the key. Where had she put the key? For crying out loud, she had put it somewhere special so she wouldn't forget, and now she couldn't remember. See? More proof she had lived too long. When you start forgetting things like that, you've been on the earth too long.

Then she remembered. It's on the windowsill above the sink.

All the way back into the kitchen.

Oh well. The fish have waited this long. They could wait a couple more minutes.

# 50

Strickland set the glass down on the kitchen counter. He was so thirsty. He had been wearing gloves so there was no chance of leaving fingerprints. But he wondered ... what about *lip prints*? There's no such thing, right? But there was DNA. They could snag him with that. So, he'd bring the glass with him. The ice tea tasted so good, he poured himself another.

As he drank, he opened the refrigerator door to put the pitcher of iced tea back. For a second, he thought he heard something in the hallway. He stopped drinking. Now, silence. He started to drink again—there it was again. He froze. Someone was putting keys into the front door. The door was opening.

Quietly, he set the glass down, then squatted on the kitchen floor. He couldn't see the door from where he was, but there was no doubt about it—someone had just walked in. He heard the front door close over. He reached behind him and pulled his gun out of his waist band.

He suddenly became aware of how many lights were on in the place. He wished he could flip the switch in the kitchen, but that would immediately give him away. He felt so exposed standing in that bright kitchen. Why hadn't he worn a ski mask? He'd gone to the trouble of dressing in black, of wearing gloves, but he had forgotten all about a mask. Now, whoever it was would probably see his face, so he would have to shoot them.

He really didn't want to kill anybody today.

"What a mess!" someone said, the voice of an old woman. At least it wasn't Turner.

"I take all those nice thoughts I had about you back, Jack," she said. "I never took you for being such a slob."

He heard her footsteps shuffling across the carpet. "Okay, little fishies," the woman said sweetly. "Anybody dead in there? You better not be."

What terrible luck. He knew things had been going too smoothly. She was there to feed the fish. He tried to calm himself down. Maybe he should sit tight. Maybe she'd just feed the fish and head back out again.

"You boys were hungry, weren't you?" she said.

A few moments of silence. Was she done? Was she leaving?

"Why are so many lights on?" she said. "It's such a waste."

That did it.

She was going to walk around the apartment now, turning out all the lights. Which meant she would be in the kitchen any second. It was time to make his move. He stood and walked quietly across the kitchen floor. His finger rested gently on the trigger.

As he came to the doorway, he couldn't hear where she was, but saw she wasn't in the living room. He turned the corner and peered into the dining area. She was standing no more than fifteen feet away, next to a hutch, reading something. As he looked more closely, he saw a stack of mail on the hutch beside her. The old lady was just being nosy, reading Turner's mail.

Her nosiness might have just saved her life.

She was facing away from Strickland, toward the bedrooms. He knew he couldn't walk through the living room and rush out the front door without being spotted. But he had an idea. If it worked, he wouldn't have to shoot her.

Putting his gun back in his waist band, he readied himself for the plunge. In a flash, he leaped from his hiding place and ran toward the woman. He grabbed her by the shoulders. She shrieked. "Be quiet old girl," he muttered, as he manhandled her toward the master bedroom. He kept her face looking away from him.

"Oh, God. Please, no," she said.

"Open the door," Strickland demanded.

She obeyed. "Don't hurt me," she pleaded.

"I'm trying not to." He threw her on Jack's bed. She landed face down, on top of the pile of clothes Strickland had tossed there earlier. Before she had a chance to turn around, he quickly backed out and shut the door. "Don't come out for fifteen minutes," he yelled through the door, "and you'll be fine."

Strickland had to get out of there. He started down the hallway, then remembered he'd left the glass with his lip prints on the counter. He ran into the kitchen, grabbed the glass then headed for the door.

Once outside, he walked briskly down the sidewalk toward the section of the stone wall where he'd come in, trying to look much calmer than he felt.


Back on Jack's bed, Mrs. Carlson slowly turned over. Her heart was racing, she could feel the pounding throughout her body, especially in her chest and head. Suddenly, a surge of pain shot up from her chest and through her arm. She knew what was happening.

"Oh, Jesus. Please help me."

She reached for her heart, as if grabbing her chest would

somehow relieve the intense pain. Surprisingly, it did. In the next moment, all her pain subsided, giving way to a deep and relaxing joy. She hadn't felt this good in years. A smile came across her face.

The thought came: *This is it.*

But it didn't scare her. She uttered a quiet prayer. "Jesus, this isn't so bad. It's really quite nice. Will I be seeing Bill soon?"

Then she closed her eyes.

# 51

Rob Strickland drove through a Wendy's in the downtown area of Culpepper, then pulled into a shady parking spot in the town center to eat. He rolled down the windows to take advantage of the nice breeze. He was also buying a little time before calling Vandergraf with the bad news that he still hadn't found what they were paying him to find.

By the time he'd finished off his burger and fries, he had still not figured out what to say when he called. Was it time to break into Turner's car? Should he follow him a few days, see if he was carrying the items around with him?

He took out his phone, stared at it a few moments then made the call.

"Mr. Strickland. I've been waiting for your call."

He sounded cheerful enough. That was about to change. "I don't have good news for you. I've searched the professor's cabin and his condo and haven't found any trace of the scrapbook or journal. He must be keeping them in his car or something."

"Hmmm. I was hoping for a quick resolve to this," Vandergraf said. "No matter. We have to fix this. There's no other choice." He paused a moment. "I thought for sure you'd find them in the cabin.

That's where the Senator thought they'd be. You sure you looked everywhere for them?"

"In the cabin? Yeah. Of course, there wasn't much to look at. Just one big room. Looked more like a shack to me."

"What are you talking about? It's a pretty nice cabin."

"I beg to differ," Strickland said. "I'm a pretty basic guy, but I think even I'd like something nicer than that. It's rustic times two."

"Wait a minute," Vandergraf said. "You said shack. There is a shack on the property, in between the main road and the cabin. When you turned off the paved road, did you keep driving down the dirt road until you came to the clearing where the cabin is?"

"I'm not sure. I came to a dirt road on the left, turned down that, drove through some woods and came to a little clearing. That's where I saw this shack. It was right on the water, like you said."

"Strickland…that's not the cabin. You turned too soon. I didn't say turn left at the first dirt road. I said keep driving till you come to a clearing on the left, and you'll see the cabin right there by the water. You haven't even searched the cabin yet."

"Oh. Guess I got a little mixed up with your directions. But that's good news, right? I can head out there now. Won't take me more than twenty minutes. Unless the guy's there. That happens, I might have to wait him out. But that probably means I can still finish this thing. Maybe even today."

Vandergraf sighed. "Well, please go out there and take care of it. Then call me back when you've found the items."

"If he's there, you don't want me going in after it, right?"

"No. We don't have to play hardball yet. I'd rather this not get messy. At least not at this stage."

"Got it. I'll get back with you soon." Strickland started up the car and headed for the road leading out of town toward the cabin.

Fifteen minutes later, he turned right onto the same dirt road he'd driven on earlier that day. This time, he drove right past the dirt road on the left. Sure enough, about a block away the road opened into a clearing. The lake was on the left, the cabin on the right. It was nice. Definitely not a shack. Best of all, no BMW parked nearby. No cars at all, as a matter of fact.

To be on the safe side, he turned around and headed back toward the dirt road leading to the shack. Thought it would be better to hide the car down that road in case Turner came back while he was there.

After hiding the car, he jogged past the shack along the water's edge until he came to the cabin. The place was still quiet. The door was locked but the key he'd been given opened it. He went inside. It was empty, but it was obvious someone was staying there. He needed to do a thorough search but decided against tearing the place up like he had done at Turner's condo. Having both places torn up in the same day would rule out the idea of a break-in at the condo. Cops would figure out that someone must be searching for something.

That wouldn't be good.

Strickland started his search in the upstairs loft.

When Jack arrived back at the cabin, it was totally dark. And he was totally exhausted. No chance of doing anything with the remnants of this night but grab a snack and head off to bed. He set his things down on the dinette table and decided he did have enough energy to call Rachel and update her about his phone call to Joe.

"I was hoping you'd call," she said. "At least, so I'd know you got in okay."

"I did. But I'm wiped out. But hey, it's for a good cause."

"So how'd your call go with Joe?"

"Perfect," Jack said. "He had the exact reaction I was hoping for. Between this evidence of the name change and the items from the safe, the case is pretty solid. He's gonna call an FBI friend, run the whole thing by him. Then set up a time with the DA to see how he wants to handle the local part."

"You mean about whether or not to charge the Senator?"

"Yeah. He agrees there's criminal activity there. But he's not sure how the DA will see it." Jack just noticed something. He had been pacing around the living room as they talked. He walked back toward the dinette table. "That's odd."

"What is?"

"My laptop bag. It's on the dinette table. When I left, I put it on the chair. And my box of Dresden research material." He had left it sitting on the dinette table. It was still there, but, "the lid isn't snapped down. It's just resting on top, and it's a little crooked."

"You sure you didn't just forget?"

"Pretty sure. Definitely sure about the research box lid." He noticed something else. "My bedroom door is open. I closed it this morning before I left. Somebody's been in here."

"Are you sure?"

"Yeah, I'm pretty sure. Let me check something else." He unzipped the top of his laptop bag. "Good. Still there."

"What is?"

"My laptop. It wasn't stolen. Seems to me, if someone broke in, they'd definitely steal something like that. But instead, it's like they just…moved it. I don't understand. Can I call you right back?"

"Sure. But don't forget."

"I won't."

Jack spent the next ten minutes walking through the cabin seeing if anything was missing. Nothing was. He did find several more examples of things that had been moved, some just slightly. He called Rachel back.

"Well, this is very strange. I'm one hundred percent convinced somebody's been in here while I was gone. But I can't find a single thing missing."

"Why would anyone do that?"

"I don't know. I wonder if it was Bass, the next-door neighbor who looks after the place. Maybe he just came in when I was gone. You know, being nosy."

"Are you gonna say something to him tomorrow?"

"I don't think so. If it was him, he didn't really bother anything. But I gotta say, between him being next door and this cabin's dark history, I'm pretty sure I won't be buying this place when my month is up."

Rachel laughed. "I guess not. Although it is a shame. It's a really nice place. And I love that fire pit outside."

"I know. Well, anyway…I better go."

"Glad you made it home okay."

"Me too. I'll call you tomorrow sometime. Love you."

After hanging up, Jack had another thought about his mystery visitor. He went into the living room, slid the recliner back, pulled back the throw rug and popped off the loose floorboard. He reached down and felt the safe right where it belonged. But he started thinking about what Joe had said earlier about how critical this evidence was.

He lifted the safe out, set it on the floor and opened it. After bringing the scrapbook and journal to the dinette table, he put the living room back together again. He couldn't be sure there was any connection between all these events but, to be on the safe side, he decided to lock these things in the trunk of his car.

Right now, not in the morning.

# 52

Rob Strickland had just finished eating breakfast at Cracker Barrel. It was early. Mainly because he'd hardly slept last night. He hadn't found the scrapbook and journal in the big cabin either. He'd looked everywhere. He didn't have the nerve to call Vandergraf about it last night. But he'd have to call him this morning. If he didn't, Vandergraf would be calling him.

All things considering, it could have gone much worse. He'd avoided a disaster when that old lady walked in on him at the condo. But it ended up okay. He didn't have to shoot her, and he was sure she hadn't seen his face. Of course, it's not like he could share that small victory with Vandergraf.

He was about to slide out of the booth when his phone rang. Crap, it was Vandergraf.

"Strickland, where are you?" Vandergraf's voice was sharp and angry.

"What do you mean, *where am I?*" Strickland said. "How about, *good morning, Rob. How's it going?*"

"What happened last night?" Again, Vandergraf's angry voice.

"What's eating you?" Strickland asked. "How about you go get your morning coffee, then call me back."

"How about you tell me what happened at that history professor's condo last night, and tell me why you didn't mention anything about it when we talked?"

How did he know about anything going wrong at the condo? "Would you please tell me what's going on? Yesterday evening you were nice as a spring rain. Now, you're all in my face. What's going on?"

"Strickland, what happened at the condo yesterday? Something involving an elderly woman?"

"You know about her?"

"Sadly, I do. And so do the police."

"The police? How are the police involved?" Strickland stood, dropped a twenty on top of his bill, nodded to the waitress. "You keep the rest," he whispered and headed out the front door.

"Then you don't even know?"

"Know what? What are you talking about?"

"I was a little curious," Vandergraf said. "So I drove by Turner's condo complex this morning. There's all these police cars and emergency vehicles there. And their lights are flashing. So I stopped and asked the security guard at the gate what was going on. He said the police found an elderly woman—he identified her as a Mrs. Carlson. She was lying dead on Jack Turner's bed. Turner's not there. The guard said he hadn't been there for over a week. He said the police are thinking it looked like she surprised a burglar, but they aren't sure yet. He didn't know how she was killed. If she was shot, or what. But you know, Strickland, don't you? So I'm asking…what did you do?"

"I didn't do anything to her!" Strickland yelled.

"The guard said one of the cops mentioned since they'd found her on his bed, they weren't sure if she had been sexually assaulted,"

"WHAT?" Strickland yelled. Someone in the parking lot turned to look. He quickly turned his back and lowered his voice. "You think I raped an old lady? That's crazy. I wouldn't do that. I did everything I could not to hurt her."

"Well, guess that didn't turn out so well. She's dead."

"Well, she wasn't when I left. I was almost finished searching the place when she walked in. I guess she was there to feed his fish. I was in the kitchen, so she didn't see me. But I knew she would any minute. When I saw her back was facing away from me, I shoved her into the bedroom and closed the door. Before she could get a look at my face. That's all that happened. Then I left. Well, first I told her not to come out for fifteen minutes. But I swear to you, I didn't touch her."

There was a long pause on the other end, then Vandergraf said, "Okay, let's both calm down here."

"I can't believe the old lady's dead. She must have had a heart attack. That's all I can think of."

"Maybe so. But you know what this means, don't you? Heart attack or no heart attack."

Strickland knew. "I ain't a murderer," he said. "I just did what you guys hired me to do." He said that last comment as a subtle reminder that, if he went down for this, he would not go down alone.

Vandergraf seemed to get what Strickland was saying, because the accusing tone left his voice. "Well, let's just stop for a minute and think this thing through. Did anyone else see you besides this elderly woman?"

Strickland thought for a moment. "There was this other old lady walking her dog on the way in. We saw each other for a second at the most, but she was across the street. I couldn't even tell you what she looked like, so there's no way she could ID me."

"Was she the only one?"

"Yes. I'm sure of it."

"Well, the autopsy will confirm that you didn't hurt her, that she died of a heart attack or maybe a stroke. Since she died of natural causes, there won't be as much outrage as if she'd been shot. How old do you think she was?"

"Seventy or eighty, at least."

"You wore gloves?"

"Course, I wore gloves."

"Well, I think we can weather this thing."

"It was an accident," Strickland said. "I did what I did so I wouldn't have to shoot her. I even pushed her down on the bed so she wouldn't fall on the floor."

"Okay," Vandergraf said. "Let's drop it for now. What's done is done. So, did you at least get back to Turner's cabin? The real one?"

"I did. Scoured the place, top to bottom, but no luck. Couldn't find any trace of the journal or that scrapbook."

Vandergraf sighed. "We have to get them. It has to be done. It might be necessary to intensify your search."

"You mean…"

"If they're not in Turner's condo, and they're not in the cabin, he must have them in his briefcase, or in his car. Which means you have to take things to the next level."

"I can start by breaking into his car," Strickland said. "That I can do without making a scene. I'll just follow him a while and do it when he parks somewhere easy. But if they're not in there, you know what comes next."

A short pause. "I don't care," Vandergraf said. "You have to get those items, no matter what it takes."

"I just want to make sure we understand each other," Strickland said.

"I think we do," Vandergraf said. "Just don't get sloppy." He hung up.

"The old lady wasn't my fault," Strickland said to no one as he put his phone back in his pocket.

# 53

As usual, Jack allowed himself to wake up when his body was ready. He got out of bed, washed his face with cold water and drifted out to the kitchen to turn the coffee pot on. He could tell by the amount of light coming in the windows that he'd slept longer than usual. Glancing at the microwave clock, he saw it was 8:35am.

While the coffee brewed, he decided to give Rachel a call. That's when he realized he'd forgotten to charge his phone. It was completely dead. He plugged it in. He'd call her after his coffee.

When it came on, he stared at the screen to check if anyone had tried to reach him. He had two texts and two phone calls, both that morning. Clicking the texts first, he discovered they were both from Sergeant Boyd, a few minutes apart. Both said the same thing: *Jack, call me as soon as you get this.* He looked at the phone calls. Again, both from the sergeant, both a few minutes apart. He called him back right away.

"Jack, how soon can you get here? I'm at your condo."

"My condo? Why are you there?"

"I've been trying to reach you. There's been an incident here. An elderly woman is dead. Would you be surprised if she was found in your apartment this morning?"

"Mrs. Carlson?"

"I believe that's her name. Someone found her this morning. Actually lying on your bed."

"What? You're kidding? Of course you're not kidding."

"Do you know what she was doing at your place?"

"Probably feeding my fish. The poor lady. She lives next door. I asked her to stop by once a day to feed the fish. How did she die?"

"We'll have to wait for the autopsy to be sure, but it looks like natural causes to me. No evidence of foul play on her body. Hank and I are both thinking she didn't just die because it was her time. I've gotta ask you something…would you say you keep your apartment pretty neat or pretty messy?"

"On the neat side, I guess. Why?"

"I thought so. The other thing that doesn't add up is finding her on your bed. I'm told the door was closed."

"Yeah, that doesn't make sense. The aquarium's in the hallway. I can't believe she's dead. Although I'm not sure I've ever met anyone more eager to leave this life. She talked about it all the time, wanted to be with her husband. But why did you ask if I was neat or messy?"

"Because your apartment is a total mess," Boyd said. "Hank and I both think she interrupted a break-in, and that whoever was here scared the life out of her, literally. Probably shut her in the bedroom and closed the door. Then the heart attack came, or whatever else killed her."

"A break-in?" Jack couldn't believe it.

"Nothing else makes any sense, Jack. How soon can you get here? I'd like you to do a quick inventory, see if you can see if anything's missing. I've looked around. None of the usual things have been taken, which is strange if this is a robbery. Some pretty valuable things are right out in the open. But even if nothing was stolen, if someone broke in here and that resulted in this woman's death, it graduates to murder. I guess it's possible she surprised the thief before he could grab anything, or else he got spooked and took off."

Jack felt his stomach tying in a knot. "Or else it wasn't a break-in at all. Just staged to look that way."

"Staged? Why would you say that?"

Jack explained what happened last night, the obvious examples that someone had been inside the cabin moving things around while he'd been on his day trip to Columbia. "And now you're telling me someone was inside my condo, and the place is all torn up. But nothing is missing. Joe, these things have to be connected. That can't be a coincidence."

Joe didn't answer right away. "I don't believe in coincidences," he finally said.

"Can I tell you what I'm thinking?" Jack said.

"Somebody is looking for something."

"Exactly."

"Although, I have no idea how that is possible. Nobody has been talking about this thing involving the Senator except you, me, Rachel and Hank. And I'd trust Hank with my life."

Just then, Jack had a flash of his confrontation at the arcade with those two thugs, Paco and Jeff. He remembered what they'd said. "Speaking of Hank, did he ever tell you about me getting jumped at that arcade by two guys?"

"He did," Boyd said. "You came in to look at mugshots, if I recall. He also said you whupped them pretty good."

"But did he tell you what they said to me?"

Boyd paused. "No, I don't remember anything that was said."

"That's because neither one of us thought there was any way it could be connected. But that was the same day I had come down to the station to tell you guys all about the evidence I had found at the cabin. Then a few hours later, I'm blowing off steam at this arcade when these two guys come after me. They acted like it wasn't some random thing. Like they had come in there specifically after me."

"What makes you say that?"

"Because one of them said they heard I'd been digging into somebody else's business. *'Putting your nose where it don't belong'* was the actual quote. He said I was asking questions and stirring up trouble. *'We're here as a friendly warning. It's time for you to butt out.'*"

There was a long pause. "I'm sure at the time," Boyd said, "it seemed impossible to Hank for those things to be related. But in light of what just happened here at your condo and at the cabin, I gotta believe they go together. I don't know how. I can't imagine our station being bugged. I mean, who would want to do it? Almost nothing ever happens in this town. But Jack, I think we need to start acting like, somehow, the Senator has found out about this. And that he has resources in play to try and shut this down. Considering the consequences of the things you've uncovered, I can certainly understand why."

"So, what do you suggest, Joe?"

"Where is the scrapbook and journal now?"

"In the trunk of my car."

"That's no good. I know yesterday I suggested you move them from the cabin. But the fact is, a greedy teenager can break into a car trunk."

"Where do you suggest I hide them?"

"Officially? I still can't tell you. Because until I can get a warrant, I don't have control of the evidence. I'll see what I can do to make that happen, but until then—"

"I just thought of something," Jack said. "It's an oddball idea, maybe even a stupid one. But if the Senator sent someone to search the cabin for the scrapbook and journal, that has to mean he doesn't know where his father hid them."

"How do you know he doesn't know?" Boyd said. "Maybe he looked under the floorboards when you were in Columbia yesterday, and didn't find them because you had them in your trunk."

"I didn't have them in my trunk yesterday, remember? They were under the floorboards. I put them back in the safe the day before. I didn't take them out until last night when I got home. When I realized someone had been in the cabin, that's when I put them in my trunk, just before I went to bed."

"Then I guess you're right," Boyd said. "The Senator doesn't know where his father hid them."

"And since he's already searched the cabin and come up empty," Jack said, "maybe I should just put them back where they belong. Maybe that's the safest place for now. What do you think?"

"I think I can't tell you what to do, not officially. Officially? I think you're onto something. There's also this, which slipped my mind yesterday...when I do get a search warrant, it will be for the cabin, not for your car."

"You still need me to head over to my condo then? To do that inventory? Since we both don't think it was a real robbery."

"I think you should still come over here to confirm this break-in is real. Like I said, even if nothing was stolen, an innocent woman died, so that makes this a serious felony. Maybe you could still stop by the station before you go there, to drop off those documents you found at the courthouse in Columbia. But there's no need to hurry. The only hurrying I'd do, if I were you, is to follow through on that idea you just had."

Jack knew what Boyd meant. Get the journal and scrapbook out of his trunk and back into the safe.

# 54

As Jack moved those two items from his trunk to the safe, he wrestled with something else he knew he had to do, but dreaded. Call Rachel. She'd be pretty upset hearing what had happened yesterday and instantly recognize the danger. But he had no choice. After putting the living room back together, he picked up his phone and called her.

"Good morning, Jack. This is a pleasant surprise."

How he wished it was. "Morning, Rach." He couldn't think of a way to say it.

"Is something wrong?"

"Yeah, there is. I'm okay, but something's come up. Something pretty serious. You know how I thought last night someone had been in this cabin, and I found a bunch of things had been moved around?"

"Yes."

"Turns out, I was right. I got off the phone with Joe a few minutes ago. He had been trying to call me all morning."

"Oh? What about?"

"He was calling from my condo, of all places."

"Why from there?"

"Someone broke into it yesterday—probably the same guy. Only this time he wasn't so careful. Joe said the place was all torn up. But the worst part is, they found my next-door neighbor dead…on my bed."

"What? Oh, no…."

"She wasn't murdered, not exactly. They think she had a heart attack, or maybe a massive stroke. She was there to feed my fish."

"I remember you telling me when you asked her."

"Hank and Joe both think she walked in on a burglar. I guess he must've frightened her, literally, to death. But he said there weren't any marks on her. She hadn't been beaten or physically hurt by whoever did it."

"But still," she added, "that poor woman. It's so sad she had to die that way, even if she wasn't killed on purpose. They're going to treat it as a murder, right?"

"They are. Joe wants me to head over there this morning and do an inventory, see if anything's missing. He doesn't think there is. Neither one of us thinks this is a real robbery."

"You think whoever it was, is looking for that scrapbook and journal?"

Rachel was always so sharp. "Yep. I think the robbery was staged. We both think that. Which means, somehow, the Senator found out about what we've been up to, and he's sent someone to try and get the things I found in the safe."

"Jack, this is starting to get scary. If the Senator does know, he knows how damaging these things are to his reputation. I don't think he's going to stop looking until he finds them."

"I agree. Which is why I think you should go visit your folks in Charlotte for a few days."

She didn't say anything for a few moments. "Maybe we both should. I can't believe we're even talking about something like this again."

She was referring to what happened last year. "I can't go with you, Rachel. Not yet. Joe's going to contact an FBI friend and talk to the DA about the case. He also needs to get with a judge about a search warrant. He's gonna try and get all that done today. He needs to be able to take possession of these things legally. So, I've got to stay here until then."

"Where are they now?"

"Back in the safe." He explained why. Then he said, "I think once these two things are safely with the authorities, the danger for us disappears. We're not the threat, these documents are."

"You think that can happen today?"

"That's the plan. But we have to assume whoever's looking for these things is going to keep looking. That's why I'd feel better if you were out of town."

"Then you know how I feel about you staying here," she said.

"I do. But I don't have a choice, at least until I get these things safely into Joe's hands. As soon as I do that I'll head out of town and meet you at your folk's place."

"I wish you were coming with me." Then a pause. "I can't believe we're actually having to do this."

"I know. But I'll be okay. This isn't like last year. For one thing, I know how to take care of myself now. And I have a gun and a permit to carry it, which I'm going to start doing until this thing is over. Anyway, it doesn't seem like these people are as ruthless as the ones we were dealing with last year. Nigel Avery would've shot that woman without hesitation, or killed her some other way. This guy just shoved her into my bedroom closed the door. He wasn't even trying to kill her."

"Still…you leave town the moment Joe says he's got the warrant."

"I will."

"There's another reason to leave as soon as you can," she said. "I was just watching the weather. There's a major thunderstorm system moving in from the west. It's supposed to arrive here just after dark."

"I'm hoping to be gone long before that. Well, I better get going. I've got to take a quick shower, drop off those courthouse docs at the police station and head over to my condo. Maybe I'll get something to eat on the way."

"Okay. I'll call my mom, let her know I'm coming. But stay safe, Jack. Don't dig into this thing anymore. Please. Just get those things to Joe, and meet me at my folks."

"I will. I promise."

# 55

Ten minutes ago, Strickland drove his silver sedan through the winding country road that joined Culpepper's downtown area to the cabin on Lake Sampson. He'd parked by the edge of the woods nearest the old shack, deciding to walk through the woods to the cabin where Turner was staying.

The whole while, he kept replaying in his mind the scene at Turner's condo yesterday with the old woman. He mentally walked through the entire episode, play-by-play, just to make sure he hadn't forgotten any significant detail. Although he still felt restless, he had assured himself there was no way that what happened could be traced back to him.

At the moment, he was hiding in the woods but had a fairly clear view of Turner's BMW and the cabin's front door. He wished he could study the man's behavior patterns more, but there just wasn't time. He didn't know how long Turner would remain in the cabin. Strickland could have the trunk opened, the two items removed and be back here in the woods in about four minutes. Maybe less.

Of course, he had his gun tucked into his waistband just in case. Didn't need the silencer, not out here. With so many hunters nearby, an occasional gunshot didn't rattle anyone's nerves.

After a few more minutes with no visible activity taking place in the cabin, Strickland decided it was time to make his move. He had just taken a few steps when the front door opened. He froze. Turner came out, turned and locked the cabin door. Now he was heading to his car. He had nothing in his hands, which meant the scrapbook and journal were likely still in the trunk.

As soon as Turner got in his car, Strickland hightailed it out of there, running back through the woods the way he came. He planned to follow him, all day if need be, till he got his chance to get in that trunk.

Strickland had followed Turner back toward town. He got nervous when Turner stopped at the police station, but he was in and out of there in two minutes. Next, he drove through a McDonald's, then turned right and headed out on another country road hugging the outskirts of town. After a few minutes, Strickland knew where Turner was going. Back to his condo. It came up on the left. Strickland held back, allowing Jack to go through the security gate on his own.

He decided to repeat his own method of entry, the route he discovered yesterday. He parked along the curb, got out and headed through the woods, trotting alongside the big stone wall. Soon he had climbed the tree and peered over the wall, waiting till the coast was clear. He hopped over and, once again, stood in front of the row of hemlock trees. Stepping between two of them, he walked nonchalantly down the sidewalk toward Turner's building.

He was surprised when he reached Turner's parking places to find them occupied by government vehicles, not Turner's car. Must be crime scene guys or other people investigating the old woman's death. But where was Turner's car?

He kept walking past his assigned spaces, searching the cars parked all around. Finally, he found it in a guest spot two buildings away. The extra distance turned out to be a blessing in disguise. Turner's BMW was far away from the action. Strickland wouldn't have to worry about someone, especially someone with the police, coming back to their car and spotting Strickland breaking in.

When he reached Turner's car, he slowed his pace, walked past it until he reached a pool fence about fifty feet away. Turning as casually as possible, he now had a full view of the lot where Jack's car was. No one in sight. He walked back to the car, circled it twice, peering into the windows on the second pass.

No luck.

No journal, no scrapbook. Had to be in the trunk.

He walked across the parking lot to buy some time to recalibrate, make sure he was still completely alone. He was, so this time he headed right for the driver's side door. Pulling out a special gadget he'd purchased last year, he slid it into the key slot, fiddled with it for three to four seconds, heard the door unlock then opened it a few inches. No alarms sounded. He looked around one more time. Still alone. Opening the door halfway, he squatted down and unlatched the trunk.

He walked back, opened the trunk lid and peered inside. It was very neat. Too neat. He could see almost the entire carpeted floor. There were a handful of things stored around the edges. He moved them all but could already tell, there was no leather journal or old scrapbook stored in here. He even lifted the carpet to check out the area around the spare tire. No room for anything but a tire.

Slamming the trunk lid down, he swore. Then quickly looked all around. *Don't lose your cool.* No one seemed to see or hear him. Where could Turner have put them? This was supposed to be so easy. He stepped away from the car, knowing his last option for completing this task without going after Turner had just come and gone.

As he walked down the sidewalk, he noticed a bright red car had just turned into the parking area. He kept walking toward the hemlock trees about a hundred yards away. The car drove past him, a beautiful brunette behind the wheel. She didn't look at him, but he couldn't help look at her. He kept walking.

As he reached the trees, he looked back to see something surprising. The red car had pulled in beside Turner's BMW. Then Turner came out from a breezeway between two buildings. The girl got out of the car, saw Turner and waved to him. He saw her, waved and headed toward her. As soon as they reached each other, they hugged and kissed.

My, my. Must be Turner's girlfriend. He watched as they walked hand-in-hand back toward Turner's building.

He disappeared between the hemlock trees and climbed back over the wall, heading for his car. Seeing them together had just given him the perfect solution to his dilemma.

# 56

"This is a nice surprise," Jack said. "Way better than saying goodbye on the phone." He and Rachel had just turned a corner on the sidewalk and were very near his building.

"Well, I just figured it's not that far out of the way. I'm heading back to my apartment to pack an overnight bag and hated the idea of driving out of town without seeing you."

"I'm glad you did. You sure you want to come inside? Not much to see. Just imagine someone walking around my apartment throwing everything around for twenty minutes."

"Have you found anything missing?"

"No, and I'm not expecting to. My guess is, the Senator is paying his hired man a pretty good wage. Probably doesn't need any of the junk I have. But he wanted it to look like a break-in. Poor Mrs. Carlson just got in the way."

"It is sad, but you told me many times how often she's talked about going to heaven."

"To be with her Bill. I know. That's keeping me from getting too sad about it. Knowing how happy she is right now. Of course, her dying like this has just complicated my life a little bit."

"How so?"

"The animal control officer left a few minutes before you got here. Mrs. Carlson had an old dog named Ralphie. Dogs that age don't always get adopted. So I told her, I'd take him. But with all this mess going on, I can't take him just yet."

"Awww, that's so nice of you. Have you ever owned a dog?"

"Not since I was a kid. But I just didn't feel right letting him spend the rest of his days all alone. Especially since his owner died helping me. Besides that, the manager told me Ralphie's the reason they found Mrs. Carlson. He wouldn't stop barking and a neighbor complained because Ralphie never barks. When they opened the door to check on him, he ran right to my door and kept scratching at it with his paws."

"Poor thing. Well, that's good to know he doesn't usually bark."

"Yeah. He seems like a really calm little guy. I called the Humane Society and explained the situation. They're gonna charge me a kennel rate to keep him for a few days, till all of this blows over."

As they approached his front door, Rachel noticed it was wide open. "Well, if you leave it like this, no wonder people break-in."

"I left it open because there's still a couple of forensics guys in there doing their thing. I can't really clean up until they give me the okay. That's supposed to be soon. I figured I'd hang loose here, then after I get things put back together maybe Joe will call saying he got the warrant."

They walked through the front door and down the hall. Rachel surveyed the scene. "Man, what a mess. You sure you don't want me to stay here and help you clean up?"

"No. It won't take me that long. It looks worse than it is. But if you don't get on the road pretty soon, you're going to run into some rush-hour traffic by the time you reach your parents' house."

"I'd also like to beat that storm. I hate driving on the highway when it's raining that hard."

"Well, here's a small piece of good news. I checked my weather app. It looks like the northern tip of the storm cell is going to hit here, but it doesn't reach Charlotte. If you leave pretty soon, you might miss it altogether."

Strickland sat slouched in the front seat of his car, his eyes locked on to the entrance gate of the condo complex. This went on for about fifteen minutes. Finally, some action. The gate lifted. A red car passed under it and turned right. It was her. She was coming this way.

Strickland slouched further in the seat until she passed by. Then he quickly sat up, turned the car on and made a U-turn. Thankfully, she wasn't a speeder, so he caught up to her in no time at all.

The brightness of her car made it easy to track as they drove around the winding roads carving a pathway through the hills along the outskirts of town. In about ten minutes, she'd turned left into an attractive apartment complex. So he did, too.

He stayed back allowing at least one building between them and continued like this until she pulled into a parking spot on the right. He quickly pulled into one of the empty spaces on the left. He resumed his slouched position and watched as she got out of the car, walked up to a front door, unlocked it and disappeared inside.

How long would he have to stay here? He better not fall asleep.

A few minutes into his wait, his phone rang. Crap, it was Vandergraf. No use ignoring it. He would just keep calling. Strickland picked up the phone.

"You haven't called me yet, Rob. I'm assuming that means you haven't secured the two items."

"Not yet. But I'm very close."

"What's the old saying," Vandergraf said, "close only counts in horseshoes? Close doesn't do it for me, Rob. We need that scrapbook and journal. What's holding things up?"

"I still don't know where he's stashed it. I searched the cabin, the real cabin not just the shack. I searched his condo. And a little while ago I searched his car, including the trunk. Nothing."

"Then you know what you have to do next."

"I do. And I'm on it. I've got a plan in motion that is guaranteed to work. I will have that stupid journal and scrapbook in your hands before this day is done."

# 57

Hank Jensen took a seat in Joe Boyd's office. Joe had just buzzed him a few minutes ago, asked him to come in. "What's up, Joe? Guess it's got something to do with what Jack and Rachel are working on?"

"It does." Boyd handed Hank some documents. "Take a look at these."

"What are they?"

"Jack dropped them off this morning. He got them at the courthouse in Columbia yesterday afternoon. I guess you could call these…the smoking gun."

Hank looked them over. "Geez, this is for real then. The Senator's real name is Ernst Hausen, born in East Germany? And his father really was a serial killer. Man, this is going to make some waves."

"I think the waves have already started."

"What do you mean?"

Joe told Hank about the staged break-in at Jack's condo, resulting in Mrs. Carlson's death. Then about Jack's certainty that someone had been searching through his cabin yesterday while he was in Columbia. Hank instantly saw the connection.

"But how could the Senator know anything about all of this yet?"

Boyd looked up, over Hank's shoulder. The front door of his office was wide open. "Maybe that's how," he said pointing at the door with his head.

"You think we got a—" Hank reached over and closed the office door. "—you think we got a mole in here? Someone who works for the Senator?"

"I don't know," Boyd said. "Hard to imagine. Nothing ever happens around here. Would be easy money for somebody."

"Well, nothing happens," Hank said, "until now."

"Whether we do or we don't," Boyd said. "Somehow Wagner found out. I know it wasn't you or me. And it sure wasn't Jack or Rachel. But from now on, let's handle things under the assumption that someone around here is on Wagner's payroll."

"I agree. So, what do you want me to do with this?" He held up the courtroom documents.

"I think with those docs in your hand, and what Jack has shown us, we have probable cause to get a warrant for the Senator's cabin. Jack and I talked about how this guy is searching. We're pretty sure the Senator doesn't know where his father hid the journal and scrapbook. The sooner I get them under lock and key, the better. Why don't you start working on getting the warrant from the judge? I'll try and set up an appointment with the DA, get him up to speed. I've also got an FBI friend—an old partner of mine in Pittsburgh. I'm gonna run this by him, get his advice."

"On what parts might be their turf and what things are ours?"

Boyd nodded. "Let's make this case our priority. Especially since we know the Senator's got at least one guy working on this, maybe more. We need to get that evidence in our hands before they get hold of them. That happens, and they'll be gone for good."

For the last five minutes, Boyd had been sitting on hold with the District Attorney's office. A secretary had already informed him he would not be speaking with the DA, not this morning anyway. He was tied up working on a major case. Boyd knew of the case and had mentioned to her the case he wanted to speak to the DA about would become even bigger than that one. She said she'd put him through to the Assistant DA, a guy named Hoffman. Boyd had worked with Hoffman before and knew he was considered to be the DA's right-hand man.

Finally, someone picked up. "Hello, this is John Hoffman. Who am I speaking with?"

Boyd introduced himself.

"Joe, I remember you. All right to call you Joe?"

"Sure Mr. Hoffman."

"Call me John. So, what's up? All I heard was, something urgent."

"Yeah, it's not just urgent. It's going to be big, in terms of media attention. I don't normally get your office involved until we're close to bringing charges. We're almost there. Thought I'd give you guys a heads up now, because of who's involved."

"Okay, you got my attention."

"It's Senator Wagner. I've got solid evidence that—now this is going to be hard to believe at first—that Wagner's father, now deceased, was a serial killer in the 1990s. And that the Senator knew all about what his father was doing—he was attending the university then—and did nothing about it. He didn't try to stop it, or even say anything about it. The father killed at least eight people in several different states over a period of three years. He may have killed more than that, but this is what I know so far."

Hoffman didn't say anything for a moment. "You're not kidding about this."

"I wish I were."

"How solid is your evidence?"

"Rock solid. I've seen it with my own eyes. I need to get a search warrant, which we're working on right now, so I can secure this evidence. But it's real, John." Boyd spent the next five minutes filling Hoffman in on the case.

"Wow," Hoffman said. "You're right, when this breaks it's going to be huge. I mean, even if we've got no criminal case against the Senator, the press will eat this up. It'll go national, for sure. Wagner's political career will be over."

"Are you saying, you think we have no case against the Senator himself?"

"No. That will depend on the nature of the evidence you have, and how much we can prove. I'm sure the DA will want to hear what you have. But obviously, having a dad who killed a bunch of World War II heroes, and the way he killed them? And before that, he worked for the East German version of the KGB? Talk about skeletons in the closet."

Boyd said he agreed, that Wagner's political career was toast.

"But it seems to me," Hoffman said, "that the biggest fish to fry here has to do with the father, not the son. And seems like it will involve the FBI more than it does us."

Boyd agreed. "My next phone call after this is to the FBI."

"Well Joe, thanks for the call. I'll definitely pass all this on. I'm sure the DA will want to meet with you very soon after we talk. Even if the evidence isn't all collected now, when you come, bring what you got. And do me a favor, keep us in the loop with anything that comes from the FBI side."

"I will. Thanks for taking my call."

# 58

Boyd spent the next fifteen minutes trying to get hold of his friend from the FBI. But no luck. He was able to leave a decent enough voicemail in two places, so he was confident he'd get a call back soon, hopefully today.

The main thing, of course, was getting that search warrant. He was about to call Hank for an update when another concern came to mind. He started thinking about Jack and Rachel's involvement in this case. And the likelihood that the Senator already knew something was up. He was certain Wagner was behind the break-in at Jack's condo, and whoever had gone inside Jack's cabin when he was in Columbia.

Boyd considered himself a good judge of character. Wagner was a ruthless, ambitious, self-serving politician. Men like that don't take kindly to someone threatening their position or future plans. He decided to call the Senator's office directly, see if he could talk to Wagner himself. Send something of a warning shot across the bow of his boat.

Harold Vandergraf had just received a disturbing phone message from his receptionist. Apparently a detective with the Culpepper PD was on line two, insisting he needed to speak with the Senator right away on a matter of extreme importance. She had been properly trained and knew to divert all such calls to him.

He took a deep breath and pressed the button. "Hello, this is Harold Vandergraf, Senator Wagner's aide, whom am I speaking with?"

"This is Sergeant Joe Boyd with the Culpepper PD. I told the receptionist I needed to speak with the Senator himself. I'm not sure why she connected me with you."

Vandergraf was pretty sure he knew what this call was about. "I'm the Senator's personal aide. I handle all his affairs. She connected us because she knows that also, and she knows the Senator is completely unavailable right now. I'm guessing since you mentioned this was of extreme importance, she didn't want to put you off, so she directed you to me. Anything you say to me will be held in strict confidence, and I will personally deliver the message to the Senator, just as soon as that is possible."

"Well, I guess if you're his trusted aide then you probably already know what I'm calling about. It has to do with a young professor, Jack Turner, who teaches over at the University, who also happens to be renting a cabin from the Senator. Is this starting to ring any bells?"

"No, I'm afraid not, Sergeant."

"Well then, how's this? His condo was broken into yesterday. Nothing was stolen, but an elderly woman surprised the intruder, and she died of a heart attack on the spot."

"Sergeant, that sounds like a terrible thing to happen, especially to that poor woman, but I don't see—"

"As it turns out," Boyd continued, "that same day, another intruder or possibly the same one broke into the cabin Jack is renting while he was gone. My hunch is, the condo was a staged break-in.

The intruder was searching for something. Something he did not find in either place. Is any of this starting to connect Mr. Vandergraf?"

Vandergraf didn't answer. His mind was scrambling for the right thing to say.

"I thought it might," Boyd said. "The reason I'm calling is to let the Senator know that he needs to leave this young professor alone. Tell him, for me, that if any harm comes to Jack Turner, I will know he's behind it. I will hold him personally accountable. I will come after him myself and not stop until he pays for anything he has done. Are we clear on this?"

"Crystal clear, Sergeant. But again, I have no idea what you're talking about, and I'm sure the Senator doesn't either. It almost sounds as if you're making a threat. Is that your intention?"

Boyd paused. "An interesting comeback, Mr. Vandergraf. First, you deny having any knowledge of what I'm talking about, then you're worried about whether I'm making a threat. Obviously, if you are not involved and have no idea what I'm talking about, then you have no cause to worry about anything I've said. But I will say it again. It's really very simple. Leave Jack Turner alone."

He hung up.

Vandergraf set his receiver down. Clearly, this represented an escalation. The only question was whether to involve the Senator directly or handle it himself. The standing rule of providing the Senator plausible deniability in matters like these only went so far. Vandergraf had always done his job well. And he'd always protected the Senator's reputation.

So far.

If this matter resolved properly, everything remained intact. On the other hand, if things were beginning to unravel, Vandergraf followed an even greater, more primary rule. It was the same thing referees tell boxers just before a fight.

*Protect yourself at all times.*

He pulled out a pad of paper and began writing out a number of scenarios, different ways this situation could go down. It quickly became apparent only one path kept Vandergraf's primary rule intact.

# 59

Strickland sat in his silver sedan for almost twenty minutes waiting for Turner's girlfriend to come back out of her apartment. He didn't know her name. Not that it mattered very much. He expected their time together to begin and end today.

Finally, the door opened. The brunette came out pulling a small rollaway suitcase. He watched her load it up in the backseat of her bright red car, get in and back the car out. The suitcase was a good sign. Meant she was likely heading out of town. All the roads outside of Culpepper were winding country roads. Lots of trees, few houses, lots of privacy.

He slouched in the seat as she drove by then quickly turned the car on and began to follow. As soon as they turned right at the gate leaving the complex, he reached down between his legs and lifted his gun and ski mask from their hiding place. He set them down on the seat beside him.

They continued to take roads leading north away from town. In less than ten minutes, things began to look just the way they needed to. Now all Strickland needed was a nice straight stretch of road. As soon as it presented itself, he put on the ski mask, lowered the passenger window, grabbed his gun and began to pass her on the left.

When he was directly across from her, he slowed down to match her speed. She looked over at him just as he raised the gun and pointed it at her head. Her eyes open wide and a look of fear came over her face. Her car jerked, forcing Strickland to react quickly to avoid being sideswiped. She corrected, and he did the same. All the while keeping the gun aimed at her head. "Pull over," he yelled. "Now!" He glanced forward. The road was still clear. He screamed out the same words again.

This time, she obeyed.

He pulled his car off the road in front of hers and quickly popped the latch on his trunk. Before she could react, like dial 911 on her phone, he darted out of his car and hurried to hers, holding the gun at her head. "Young lady," he yelled, "get out of the car. Now."

"Why? What's going on?"

"I won't ask you again. Out of the car now. Leave your phone."

She did and got out, putting her hands up.

"Put your hands down. Walk over to the back of my car. Do it now."

"Why? Why are you doing this?"

"I'll explain later. What is your name?"

"My name? Rachel."

"Okay, Rachel, if you do what I say, I won't hurt you." He lifted the trunk lid. "Get in." She hesitated. He grabbed her neck and began to force her down.

"Okay, I'll do it." She got in the trunk. "Where are you taking me?"

He closed the lid, removed his ski mask and yelled, "Not far. Less than ten minutes. You'll be fine. Stop talking. I'll tell you more when we get where we're going." Putting his gun in his waistband, he headed for the front seat.

As he drove off, he could hear her crying through the backseat.

Now it sounded like she was talking, too. Did she have a second phone? Her hands were definitely empty when she got into the trunk. Should he pull over? "Who are you talking to?"

"God," she yelled back. "I'm just praying."

"Well stop, or do it quietly."

After a few minutes, he could barely hear her. Even her cries.

Vandergraf knocked twice on the Senator's office door, then walked in. He'd already buzzed him to say they needed to talk. The Senator knew Vandergraf never interrupted him without good reason. Just before reaching the Senator's desk, Vandergraf reached into his coat pocket and turned on a digital recorder. Just in case.

The Senator looked up from his iPad and swiveled in his chair to face his aide. "Okay, Harold. What's up?"

"There have been some significant developments on this matter about retrieving your father's journal and scrapbook."

"By significant developments, I hope you mean you have secured these items like we discussed."

"Not yet. The situation is proving to be a lot more complicated than we expected. Now the police are involved."

Wagner's face instantly became alarmed. "The police? If the police are involved, the press is next. What in the world is going on, Harold? This wasn't a difficult assignment."

Vandergraf took a seat and brought the Senator up to date. Nothing he said relaxed the look on his face. If anything, his scowl grew more intense.

His first reply was, "It doesn't sound like Mr. Strickland is up for this assignment. These new complications stem from his poor judgment. I'm afraid you're going to have to take first chair on this."

"I was thinking the same thing, sir."

"My sense from what this Sergeant Boyd told you is, they don't have any hard evidence yet. If they did, he wouldn't be calling with a warning. He'd be knocking on our door. He's buying time. Maybe waiting for a warrant. Maybe, waiting for his evidence to build. The point is, we can't wait any longer. You have to make this go away…today. Or no later than tonight. This has to be taken care of. I think you understand, by now, the terrible consequences both of us face if my father's papers go public. You need to get them—now—and destroy them. If you have to, burn them. It's not like they're family heirlooms. In fact, I'm fine if you want to put them in the cabin and burn the whole thing down. I'll probably get more from the insurance money than I will from selling it."

"I'll take care of it, Senator. Personally."

"I'm afraid that's only half the story," Wagner said. "That'll take care of our legal liability. But we have to assume at this point this professor and his girlfriend have already seen everything in the scrapbook and journal. Even if, or when, you destroy this evidence I can't take the chance that they will go public with their allegations."

"Or," Vandergraf added, "that they haven't made copies."

"Exactly. So you know where I'm going with this?"

"I do, sir. You want me to take them out. What about Mr. Strickland?"

"Same thing. I'd say he's outlived his usefulness to us, wouldn't you agree?"

"I would."

"Then take care of that also."

# 60

Strickland turned off the main road onto the dirt road leading to the shack and cabin. He hadn't heard a peep from his guest in the trunk for the last five minutes. Soon he came to the left turn that went to the shack. He drove for about a block in between tall rows of trees, then the lake came into view. The sky overhead was a dull gray. When he came to the clearing, he pulled his car as close to the edge of the woods as possible.

Before getting out, he put the ski mask back on. He held the gun in one hand as he opened the trunk. "We're here. You can get out."

She did. As she stood, she looked around. "Where is this?"

"Someplace safe," he said. "Safe and quiet. Turn around and pick up that roll of duct tape in the trunk. It's there on the right." She did. "Rip off a piece about six inches long." She did that. He took the tape from her and put it across her eyes, pushed it in nice and tight. He could tell it frightened her. "I'm only doing this for your own good. You see my face, and you have to die. Simple as that." Oddly, that seemed to calm her down.

After pulling off his ski mask, he said, "I'm going to lead you into that shack. I'm sure you saw it when you got out of the trunk. Then I'm gonna tape your hands and your feet so you can't go anywhere.

If you scream or make any noise, I'll tape your mouth, too. Understand?"

She nodded her head. "But why are you doing this?"

"You and your boyfriend, the professor that teaches at the college, you both took something that doesn't belong to you. My job is to get it back. I've been trying to do that without involving you. That became impossible. Simple as that. You're my leverage. Your boyfriend gives me what I want, you go free. He doesn't? Well, let's don't think about that. Don't ask me any more questions. That's all I'm gonna say."

His phone rang. He looked at the screen. It was Vandergraf. Finally, he would have something positive to tell him. "Come on," he said to Rachel as he led her toward the shack. After a few steps, he answered the phone. "Hey, good timing. Well, almost. Can I call you back in about two minutes? I've made some real progress."

Vandergraf said fine and hung up.

He opened the door. It was really clouding up outside. Just in the last few minutes, some dark clouds had started showing up off to the west. Made the cabin even darker. He found the chain hanging from the single bulb in the center and pulled it. Looking around, he noticed an old armchair and a narrow cot against the wall. He told Rachel about them and asked her which one she wanted to sit in.

"The chair, please."

"Fine with me." He moved her into place. "It's right behind you. So sit." He quickly taped up her feet. For good measure, he taped her arms to the arm rests. "You stay put while I call this guy back."

Making sure he was far enough away, he picked up his cell and called Vandergraf back.

"So what's this new progress you've made?" Vandergraf said.

Strickland explained the situation. When he finished, he waited for something positive coming from Vandergraf. But all he got was silence. "Nothing? You've got nothing to say? I got this thing halfway wrapped up. There's no way this guy Turner doesn't make the exchange. I saw them together back in his apartment. He loves this chick. I bet he comes right over as soon as I make the call."

"I'm sorry, Strickland. I'm just a little distracted. You have made real progress. And you're sure she can't ID you?"

"Totally."

"You can call Turner, let him know you have her. In fact, that would be a good idea, make sure he doesn't turn the journal and scrapbook over to the cops. But don't set up the exchange just yet. We have a little time."

"But why do we need a little time?"

"Well, for one thing. It would make a lot more sense and be more to your advantage to make the exchange once it starts getting dark. There's a reason why the majority of crimes are committed in the dark. Harder for the bad guys to be seen. Easier to get away. All kinds of reasons."

"Yeah, I suppose."

"I'm not talking the middle of the night," Vandergraf said. "But you don't want to do something like this in broad daylight. Besides, you won't have to wait long. There's a big storm coming in from the west. It's been on the news. It'll probably be plenty dark by sundown."

"Guess that's not too far away."

"Do me a favor, though. Give me a call when you've solidified the time with Turner. Let me know what the plan is."

"Alright, will do. This thing's gonna happen this time. Not expecting any more glitches from here."

"Good. Call me soon." Vandergraf hung up.

Vandergraf sat forward in his chair, crossed a few things off on his legal pad, added a few to the bottom of the list. This really was a positive development, though not in the way Strickland had meant. Vandergraf didn't doubt that Turner would make the exchange for Rachel. He'd do that in a heartbeat. What he liked about the plan was, it put all three of them—Turner, his girlfriend and Strickland—in one place at the same time.

And not just any place. But a secluded section of woods well outside of town. Vandergraf had checked the weather report. He wasn't exaggerating about the storm. A powerful cell was heading their way right around sundown. The weatherman said to expect quite a show. Lots of thunder, lots of lightning, and some powerful gusty winds.

The kinds of things that make gunshots pretty hard to hear.

# 61

It had been almost an hour since Rachel had left Jack at his condo. The forensics team had finished their work and had given Jack the all-clear signal to clean up his place. As expected, it took about thirty minutes. Also as expected, Jack had confirmed nothing had been stolen.

Sergeant Boyd hadn't called him yet saying he had gotten the warrant. Jack was about to head back to the cabin but decided to call Rachel first, just to see how she was doing on the road. After locking the condo up, he took out his phone to call her as he walked to the car. Her phone rang and rang; she never picked up. It's possible she had the volume turned down and the car stereo turned way up.

He tried texting her instead: *Just called to see how you're doing. Guess you're enjoying a little music and didn't hear. Nothing urgent. Just wanted to chat. Call whenever. Still no word from Boyd. Heading back to the cabin. Love you much.*

He'd barely put his phone back in his pocket when it rang. He quickly pulled it out, expecting to see her face on the screen. It wasn't her. And it wasn't Sergeant Boyd, either. Jack didn't recognize the number. Maybe it was Hank Jensen. He and Jack had talked before, but Jack had never saved his number.

"Hello, this is Jack Turner."

"Hello, Mr. Turner. You don't know me. But I know you, sort of. I know, for example, you and your girlfriend have been butting your nose into things that are none of your business."

"What? Who is this?"

"Doesn't matter. Like I'd tell you anyway. The thing is, I've been told you have taken a couple of things from a certain cabin that don't belong to you. The owner wants them back. In a serious way. You know the things I'm talking about. Some kind of old journal and scrapbook."

Jack couldn't believe it. He instantly thought about what that punk, Paco, had said at the arcade. Almost the exact same warning. Should he play dumb?

"I've also been told," the man continued, "that you can take care of yourself pretty good. So I've taken some precautions. Or you could say I created *an incentive* that I think will convince you to cooperate fully and quickly with what I'm about to say."

Jack wondered what he meant. "This has to do with Senator Wagner, doesn't it?"

"Like I said, you know what I'm talking about. I want both of those things handed over, tonight, at 6:30. There's a little wooden table on the porch at the cabin. You can set them there, then take off. Go somewhere else for about half an hour."

"Now why would I want to do that?"

"Why? Because I think you're in love." He chuckled. "And the woman you love, Rachel...I have her. My guess is, you would like to see her again, alive."

Jack felt like he'd been punched in the stomach. Could this be true? "Rachel's not even in town. She left an hour ago."

"That's not quite accurate. She *tried* to leave town would be a better way to put it. I followed her, till we came to a nice lonely stretch of road. I convinced her to pull over and get into my trunk.

If you want proof, drive north on 441 about ten minutes past town. You'll see her bright red car parked on the side of the road. Matter of fact, maybe you should go out there even if you do believe me. Both her keys and cell phone are inside. And it's not locked. Eventually, someone's going to figure that out and drive off with it."

Jack's stomach turned, and his face felt hot. The man wasn't lying. *Oh God, don't let anything happen to Rachel.*

"I can tell by your silence that you believe me. That's good. You should believe me. Right now, she's fine. I've got her in a safe place. She'll stay fine and safe, unless you don't do what I say."

"Now you listen to what I say." Jack tried to control his words. "If you've hurt her, or if you do anything to her, you will die today. Do you understand me?"

"You don't need to threaten me."

"You said it yourself, I can take care of myself pretty good. Well, I take even better care of those I love. My life is nothing without her. Do you understand? I couldn't care less about this journal and scrapbook. I care about her. You hurt her, you are dead."

"Well good. Not the part about you killing me, the part where you could care less about the journal and scrapbook. So, we understand each other. I haven't hurt Rachel, and I don't want to. You bring those two things to the cabin at 6:30, set them on that table on the porch and leave. Thirty minutes after that, I will call you and tell you where you can find Rachel. It's as simple as that. Oh, and this goes without saying. You involve the cops in this, it's over. I mean, Rachel. I'll kill her."

He hung up.


Jack saw Rachel's car up ahead on the right, just as the caller described. His mind had been racing and his heart pounding constantly since that call. If anything happened to Rachel….

He pulled in behind her car. Images of what must have happened here began swirling in his head. The fear she must have felt. Being forced into the trunk. And being driven away to…where? How long was she in there? He said she was in a safe place. Was that place somewhere in town? He said no cops, or he'd kill her. Should Jack call Joe? Should he drive down to the Senator's office and make a scene? Force him to tell Jack where they had taken her?

He got out of the car and walked to the driver's side. The window was halfway down. He opened the door. There was her cell phone on the front seat, the keys still in the ignition. He turned the car on enough to raise the window. Then he took her phone, her keys and locked it up.

He leaned back on the fender as a wave of panic overtook him. His eyes filled with tears. He couldn't lose Rachel. She was the love of his life. The guy said he didn't hurt her and didn't plan to. God, he prayed, let that be true. As he walked back to his car, he began to calm down. A clear thought broke through the haze.

*Call Joe. You can trust Joe.*

Once in his own car, he found Joe's number on his phone and pushed the button.

Joe picked up fairly quickly. "Hey Jack, great timing. I was just about to call you. Hank secured the search warrant. Are you at the cabin? Probably better for me to come out there and get them."

Jack didn't answer. He was trying to think of what to say.

"Jack? Did you hear me?"

"Yeah."

"What's wrong? You sound upset."

"I'm way past upset."

"Why, what happened?"

"Rachel has been kidnapped."

"What?"

"Kidnapped. Rachel's been kidnapped. I got the phone call about twenty minutes ago."

"Do you know who?"

"Not the man's name. Who he works for."

"It's the Senator, right? I can't believe it. This guy's worse than I thought."

"It is. My guess is the call came from the same guy who broke into my condo, and the cabin."

"He say what he wants? Never mind. I know what he wants. This thing is getting out of control. I still haven't heard back from my FBI friend. As soon as we get off the phone, I'll call him again."

"No, don't do that. He said no cops. I really shouldn't even be talking to you."

"Jack, they always say that. Because they know if we get involved we won't stop until we catch them. He's just trying to manipulate you, Jack."

"It's working. But I knew I had to call you. Can't we just do this, you and me?"

"I don't know. I don't like the sound of that."

"Please, Joe. We get a whole squad of guys involved, somebody makes a mistake and he gets wind of it? It could be all over for Rachel. You could get Hank involved. I'd trust him, too."

"I can't believe the Senator would do something so stupid. He's more desperate than I thought."

"How about it, Joe? You, me and Hank? And that's it."

"Alright, tell me what you know. What's the plan?"

# 62

The promised storm came early.

With it, came dark clouds and heavy winds. It hadn't yet begun to rain. But clearly, it would soon. Jack had spent a horrible afternoon in his condo. There was nothing to do but think. And wait. And pray. Pray that the plan he had worked out with Joe would succeed.

The main thrust was to make sure Rachel was safe. Nothing they did would compromise that goal. But Boyd had thought of a way to still secure the journal and scrapbook after Rachel had been freed. It depended on a number of things happening just right. Then he'd said the chances of all those things going right were slim and none.

It was 6:20pm.

Jack pulled into the clearing, saw the cabin up ahead. Now that his car was no longer surrounded by trees, the sky wasn't as dark. But the storm clouds were more visible on the western horizon. He wondered how much time they had before the hard rains began to fall.

Mostly, he wondered how Rachel was doing. He couldn't keep his mind off her. She must be so scared. This man would pay for what he put her through, put them both through. Joe said the aggravated kidnapping charge alone could get him life in prison. Life without parole when you threw in Mrs. Carlson's death, if they proved he was the same man who'd broken into Jack's condo.

Jack had been imaging a different kind of punishment for this guy…all afternoon.

He was just about to unlock the cabin door when something caught his eye out on the lake. A flicker of orange light, on one spot in the water. Was it someone fishing? Maybe holding up a lantern? Could it be the kidnapper, watching for Jack to complete his task?

In case that was it, Jack went inside, turned on a few lights and snuck out the back door. Walking through the trees, he came around the other side of the cabin closer to the waterline. He could still easily see the orange light. It was the only bright spot on the lake. But now he could also see, it wasn't a boat or a lantern. It was a reflection from something on the shore.

Then it dawned on him…the old shack. That's where the light was coming from.

Suddenly, it went out.

But he was sure he was right. He thought about it some more. What if that's where the kidnapper was? What if that's where he'd brought Rachel? Nobody lived there. After Rachel had asked about it, Jack had called the realtor and found out it was part of the property. But the realtor had also said they never rented it out.

So why was there light coming from the shack just now? And why did it just go out?

He was speculating, of course. But it made sense. Maybe the kidnapper was hiding there, and he'd turned out the light so he could make his way through the woods to spy on Jack, make sure Jack put the journal and scrapbook where he'd been told to, on the porch table.

He glanced at his watch. Only five minutes left. He'd better do that now. Walking back through the woods the way he came, he snuck back into the cabin through the back door and headed straight for the living room. In no time at all, he was pulling the safe through the floorboards. He brought it to the dinette table, opened it and pulled out the journal and scrapbook. Walking them to the front door, he stopped briefly and reached behind his back to get a feel for his Glock, nestled in his waistband. The man hadn't asked him to do this, but Jack turned on the porch light, to make sure the man could see Jack placing the items on the table.

Jack opened the front door, brought the two items over to the table and set them down. Now he was supposed to leave. To go somewhere for thirty minutes. He wished he could call Joe and tell him of his suspicions about the shack. But he knew, Joe was already hidden somewhere nearby in the woods, was already watching him and everything he did.

The plan was for Joe to stay hidden until the kidnapper came for the journal and scrapbook. Then to follow him until he made the call to Jack, telling him where to find Rachel. Jack was to text Joe as soon as Rachel was safe, freeing Joe to arrest the kidnapper. Hank was in town, with another team waiting for word from Joe to go after Harold Vandergraf and the Senator.

That was the plan. But plans never turn out right. That's what Joe said.

Jack couldn't worry about that now. He had to stay focused on his part. Drop the things off and drive away. Wait for the kidnapper's phone call. As he drove down the tree-lined dirt road, the sky grew darker again. The winds were picking up. Small branches began to break off and fly sideways between the trees. One startled him, bouncing off the hood of his car.

Jack slowed down as he drove past the dirt road on his right that led toward the shack. It was all he could do not to drive down that road. His gut told him that the orange light he had seen reflected off the lake came from the shack. The shack that was supposed to be empty. Empty and dark.

But he kept driving until he reached the main road. Then he got an idea. The kidnapper was going to call his cell phone, which meant Jack could be anywhere he wanted when the call came. He quickly found a place to pull over and got out of his car. Anticipating the events of this night, Jack had dressed all in black. He was very glad he did now. He took out his phone and, using the GPS, got a sense of where the shack was. He began walking in that direction through the trees. As he did, he pulled out his Glock and held it in front of him. He stayed closer to the waterline for better visibility.

In about fifteen minutes, he had reached the opening in the trees for the clearing around the shack. The shack was just up ahead.

It was totally dark inside.


Joe Boyd had arrived twenty minutes ago, dressed in dark hunting garb. Using the GPS on his smart phone, he had navigated through the woods and was now positioned near the cabin, set back about twenty feet in the woods. He'd arrived just as Jack had turned the porch light on then came outside to put the journal and scrapbook in place.

He'd watched Jack drive off just as he'd been told. Boyd had his gun ready and pointed toward the porch.

All he could do now was wait.

# 63

Carefully and as quietly as he could, Jack walked toward the shack. His gun straight ahead, his index finger resting as close to the trigger as he dared. He didn't hear a sound.

That is, until he came close to the doorway.

Now he heard something. Muffled sounds. An occasional bump. Was that someone moaning? He had to go inside. If he had figured this right, the kidnapper wasn't here. He should be at the bigger cabin by now, ready to snatch the journal and scrapbook.

Jack decided to come in low in case he'd guessed wrong and the kidnapper fired his gun chest-high as the door opened. He closed his eyes, said a quick prayer and turned the knob until it clicked. He pushed the door open, grateful that it didn't squeak. He breathed a sigh of relief when it reached the halfway point.

No gunfire.

He stepped inside. Now he could hear better. There was definitely someone in the room. Someone positioned against the far wall. But they didn't say anything. He reached up where a light switch should be, but found none. Must be on a pull chain.

He took a few more steps. Still no reaction to his presence. He wished he had a flashlight but, wait…he did. The flashlight app on his phone. After pointing his gun toward the far wall, he tapped the app and the light came on.

"Rachel!" He said as quietly as he could.

It was her, and only her with him in the room. She was sitting in a chair, her eyes and mouth covered by strips of duct tape. Her feet were also taped, her arms to the chair. He put his gun in his waistband, set the phone on a cot next to her, hugged her with one hand and gently pulled the duct tape off her face with the other.

"Jack," she cried as soon as her eyes focused. "I can't believe you're here."

He freed her arms and she quickly reached down, tore off the tape around her ankles. They hugged tightly.

"We have to get you out of here now," he whispered. "The guy could come back any second." He glanced at his watch. "He's probably at the cabin right now getting the journal and scrapbook. Are you hurt? Can you walk?"

"I'm a little stiff, but he didn't hurt me."

"Then we need to go." Jack helped her stand. He tapped the flashlight app off, plunging the room into darkness once more. He picked up his phone. "Hold my hand tight and follow me. We're going back through the woods toward my car. It's out on the main road."

They stepped outside onto the dirt. Just then, an incredibly bright flash of lightning struck very close, followed instantaneously by a loud crack of thunder. It startled both of them and they dropped to the ground.

"That was thunder, right?" Jack said.

"Yes, but it sounded a little bit like a rifle shot."

"That's what I thought. C'mon. We need to get into the woods."

Right on time, Boyd watched a dark figure emerge from the trees on the far side of the clearing, heading straight for the front porch. He was carrying a gun and his head swiveled back and forth nervously with each step. When he reached the porch, he seemed satisfied that he was alone and stuck the pistol in his waistband. He saw the items on the table and went right for them. Boyd waited for him to pick them up and step back off the porch. As soon as he did, Boyd came out from his position with his gun pointed at the kidnapper's chest.

The plan was, for Boyd to follow him until he called Jack. But Joe had thought about it. He didn't want to take a chance of this guy leaving the scene and somehow getting away.

"Freeze," Boyd said, not yelling but loud enough to be heard over the wind. "This is the police. You're under arrest. Don't even think of going for your gun."

The man obeyed, turned his head toward the sound of Boyd's voice.

The next moment, there was a bright flash of lightning and a loud bang of thunder. It was so close, Boyd instinctively hit the ground. So did the kidnapper, but something about the way he went down looked strange. The journal and scrapbook flew out of his hands.

*Did he just get shot?*

Boyd began to lift himself off the ground and was just about to call out to the man when another shot rang out. A bullet whizzed right by his head and struck the tree behind him. Joe rolled away in the opposite direction and headed for the trees. Another shot, clearly from a rifle. The dirt beside him flew up in the air.

Who was shooting at him? When he reached the safety of the trees, he looked back at the man he'd thought was the kidnapper. He hadn't moved. Boyd couldn't be sure because of the dim light, but it looked like he'd suffered a massive head wound.

Boyd thought about backtracking through the woods to get more firepower from his car but, just as he moved, another rifle shot hit the tree right behind his head. The guy obviously had a scope.

Boyd was pinned down.

When they reached the edge of the woods, Jack and Rachel heard more loud bangs. Obvious gunshots. Several rang out over the next few seconds, all in the direction of the cabin. "C'mon, Jack. We have to get out of here."

"I can't, Rachel. Something's wrong. I think Joe's in trouble."

"What? Why? Is he by himself?"

"Yes. I don't have time to explain. But please, trust me. Here." He handed her his phone, swiped the screen revealing a GPS map. "Follow this through the woods. It will take you right to my car. It's not far."

"Jack, I can't leave you like this."

"Rachel, you have to. Joe came out here to protect us. I don't know what's happening, but I can't leave him stranded. As soon as you get to the car, start driving toward town. Call 911 and tell the dispatcher about what's going on. Tell her Joe Boyd's in trouble and to send Hank Jensen's team out here. Go quick."

She looked toward the woods then back at him. She flung her arms around his neck. They hugged and kissed. "You stay behind the trees," she said.

"I will."

"Do not get shot, Jack Turner."

"I won't. I promise. Now go."

# 64

Jack decided the quickest and quietest route back to the cabin was on the beach near the waterline. When he reached the spot in front of the fire pit, he saw the porch light he'd left on in the distance. And what looked like a body lying still in the dirt about ten feet away. It didn't look like Joe. Seemed too long. He didn't have to wonder very long.

"Sergeant Boyd," a voice yelled from the tree line to his right, maybe twenty-five yards away. "There's no use running from me. As you've probably guessed, I've got an infrared scope. I know you're behind that big oak tree. I saw you run there. You move six inches either side of it, I've got a nice head shot."

"That you, Mr. Vandergraf?" Boyd yelled back. "Have you really thought this through? You willing to kill a police officer for your boss?"

"That wasn't part of the plan," Vandergraf said. "You weren't part of the plan. You toss your gun down, I'm willing to let you run back through those trees toward your car. The only thing I want is on that front porch. That old journal and scrapbook. That's all I'm here for."

Jack's heart began to pound. He was standing out in the open. If this guy, Vandergraf, had an infrared scope, all he had to do was look toward the lake and he could take Jack out with one shot. Thankfully, at the moment, he was preoccupied looking the other way toward Boyd.

Boyd began to talk again. "You think I'm stupid, Vandergraf. You didn't come out here with an infrared scope on your rifle just to fetch a couple of old books. You just killed a man right in front of me. My guess is, he's the guy you and the Senator hired for this little mission. I throw down my gun, there's no way you're going to let me make it back to my car."

"No, I guess not," Vandergraf said, then laughed. "The good news is, I hear head shots are almost painless. Over in the blink of an eye. But if I have to chase you through the woods, I might have to shoot you four, five, six times to put you down. That would be a shame, and very painful. Truth is, you weren't even supposed to be here. My orders were to take out my guy here, that history professor who started this whole mess, and his girlfriend. I don't know what happened to them. Guess I have some more work to finish tonight after you and I are done here."

Jack had heard enough. Enough to know exactly where Vandergraf was, and enough to know what he had to do next.

As quietly as he could, Jack closed the gap between them. As he got closer he saw Vandergraf pointing his rifle in Boyd's direction, one eye locked on the scope.

"Hey Vandergraf," Jack yelled.

Vandergraf turned, lowered the rifle slightly, a look of shock on his face.

"Wondering where I am? I'm right here." From less than fifteen feet, Jack fired his gun, twice, at Vandergraf's head.

Vandergraf dropped dead on the spot.

A long moment later. "Jack," Boyd yelled. "Is that you?"

"It's me, Joe." Jack walked up to Vandergraf's lifeless body, kicked the rifle away. "You can come out now. I think both the bad guys are dead."

Boyd emerged from the woods then from the shadows into the clearing, gun still in hand. "I'm so glad you came back. I was sure this was it for me."

"Rachel and I heard the shots. I had my gun with me, just in case I needed it for her."

"Is she alright?"

"She's shaken up, but she looked good. She said the guy didn't hurt her." Jack pointed to the body that had already been lying there. "I'm guessing this was her kidnapper."

"Looks like it," Boyd said. "And the guy you shot is Harold Vandergraf. Senator Wagner's aide. And I'd say, Wagner's hit man. No doubt that's who's behind this. I'm gonna call Hank. He's got a team ready to arrest the Senator."

"I think he's on his way here. I turned Rachel loose to take my car and my phone. I asked her to call 911 and tell them to send Hank and a team here. Of course, then, I didn't know how this would be going down."

"You did the right thing." Boyd stuck out his hand. "I owe you my life, Jack."

After shaking it, Jack thought about what happened last year and said, "I guess we're even now. Say, are you gonna call Hank on your phone?"

"I was but, here, take it. I can call him from my car." He looked down at the scene. "Nothing's happening at the moment. You call, Rachel. Let her know you're fine. She's suffered enough anxiety today."

"Thanks. I'll stand here till you get back." He watched as Boyd faded back into the trees then called Rachel.

She picked up right away. "Joe, is Jack okay?"

"It's me, Rach. I'm using Joe's phone. I'm okay. We're both okay. Both the bad guys are dead. So you're totally safe now." He heard her begin to cry on the other end. "I'm going to stay here for a little while. Guess I have no choice, since you're in my car."

"I'm hanging up," she said. "I'm turning the car around. I'll be right there. Where are you?"

"The cabin. The real cabin, not the shack. But you don't have to—"

"I'll be right there," she said, still crying. "I'm so glad you're okay. I'm going to hang up now."

"Don't drive fast," Jack said. "There's no hurry now."

"I won't," she said. "I love you."

"I love you, too. So much."

Jack put the phone in his pocket, his Glock back in his waistband. He looked out over the lake. The sight was actually quite beautiful, totally unlike the scene around his feet. A last glimmer of sunlight poured out through the storm clouds. In the distance, multiple sirens rang out through the trees.

# 65

One Month Later

The media frenzy surrounding this case finally began to subside.

It had made the national news three days in a row, the regional and local news for another week. Joe Boyd and Hank had been interviewed on both *Fox News* and *CNN*. In the Fox interview, Boyd had mentioned how Jack had saved his life, bravely taking out the shooter who had him pinned behind some trees. That went over big. Bigger still the part when Joe described how Jack had rescued Rachel from the kidnapper.

Once that news got out, producers from *Fox and Friends* hounded Jack for an exclusive interview with him and Rachel. It was the perfect angle for the morning show. Man risks his life to save the woman he loves. Didn't hurt that both of them were young and attractive. Jack and Rachel had finally agreed when they were told the interview would be brief and that they could tape it from the local news station.

That interview had led to at least two-dozen more phone calls from other media outlets begging to cash in, but Jack and Rachel had turned them all down. Jack's agent and publisher had begged them to say yes. "Think of the publicity for your next book."

All Jack could think of was getting their lives back to normal. Neither he nor Rachel had any interest in extending their fifteen minutes of fame.

Of course, Senator Burke Wagner's political career came to an abrupt halt two days after the shootout at the cabin. On the morning of that first day, he had feigned shock and surprise at the horrible misdeeds of his young aide, Harold Vandergraf, and the "thug" he had hired, Rob Strickland. How could he be blamed for the illegal activities done by those he'd employed?

Later that afternoon, a search of Vandergraf's apartment yielded a digital recorder found in the lapel pocket of a suit jacket spread across Vandergraf's bed. The very first recording was the conversation between Vandergraf and the Senator, where the Senator can be clearly heard giving Vandergraf instructions to kill Jack, Rachel and Strickland. When the DA heard the recording, he promptly set up a meeting with Wagner and his defense attorney.

Needless to say, it had the desired effect. Wagner had immediately agreed to resign his state senate seat that day and was begging for a plea deal. The other story, the big cold case file Jack and Rachel had uncovered involving the Senator's father?

It hadn't even made the news yet.

Jack was headed down the hallway right now toward Boyd's office for a briefing about that, and to hear some other news Boyd wanted to share with him in person. Jack had some news of his own he wanted to share.

When he walked through Boyd's doorway, Boyd was already there at his desk. Hank Jensen sat in the other office chair. Both rose to their feet to shake his hand. Jack had noticed Hank's overall attitude toward him change dramatically since that night at the cabin.

"You're looking pretty spiffy," Boyd said to Jack, as he and Hank sat down again. "I'm sure that's not on account of me."

"No, right after this I'm picking Rachel up for a special dinner at River Bend restaurant."

"Yeah, well, those clothes are just about right then," Boyd said. "River Bend's Kate's favorite place. We went there one night with the whole family on our vacation about ten days ago."

"I'm glad this thing didn't mess that up."

"Me, too," Boyd said. "Though, it almost did."

"Did you find a decent cabin to rent on the lake?"

"We finally did. Way on the other side, far away from the cabin you were staying at. Had a great time. Did some fishing with the kids and swimming. Some nice fires at night. Guess it goes without saying you aren't going to buy that one from Wagner."

They all laughed. "Hardly," Jack said. "Already got my month's rent back from the realtor."

"You still looking for one?" Hank asked.

"Honestly? No. Rachel and I talked about it. I still like the idea, but I'm narrowing down my search to some decent lakefront property. After my last two cabin experiences, I don't think I'm open to buying anyone else's place. We're going to get one of those cute little cabin kits and put one up from scratch. A place where all the stories will be ones we make ourselves."

Hank laughed. "Now this relationship is sounding serious."

Jack smiled.

"I can perfectly understand that," Boyd said. "How's Rachel doing these days? How's she coping with the trauma now that all the hoopla has started to settle down?"

"She's doing a little better. She spent the last week with her folks in Charlotte. They're great people, so that helped. Her dad suggested something to her that we've talked about before. She's much more willing to consider it now."

"What's that?"

"Buying a handgun and taking classes for a carry permit. She's ready to do that, so I told her I'd go through it again with her."

"I think that's a good idea," Boyd said.

"Give her some peace of mind," Hank added.

"How are things with you and the college? How did they react to all this publicity you've been getting? I know you said you were getting a little concerned about it."

"I was but, fortunately, the publicity has been mostly positive. Some of it very positive. So they're doing okay with me."

"Well, that's good. Because you're about to get some more positive publicity. This should all be local stuff. That's one of the reasons I asked you to come in. The mayor wanted me to tell you about it in person."

"The mayor?"

Boyd nodded. The city council took a vote and it was unanimous. They're pretty proud of what you did that night at the cabin. We're all pretty proud of you, Jack. Me more than anyone. So, they're going to give you the Culpepper Brave Citizen's Award. Comes with a nice little check too. Though I don't know how much. All the city and county bigwigs will be there. Chief of Police. Mayor's going to give it to you himself. Hank and I will be there."

"Really? Wow. Well, what can I say? It's not really my cup of tea, doing things like that. But you're right. Definitely can't hurt things between me and the University. It should definitely soften the blow when I tell them I didn't get very far with my doctoral dissertation research. Although I did get some great new ideas about which direction to go. Which reminds me...you ever hear back from your FBI friend?"

"Oh, yeah," Boyd said. "Almost forgot. That's the other reason I wanted to see you. I told you I ran the whole thing by him right after it happened, sent him copies of everything. He called me yesterday saying he heard back from some people in their Cold Case Division. There's definitely some interest in this. He thinks they're going to pick the case up and run with it."

"That's great," Jack said. "I was hoping so. That'll really help me with this new direction I'm planning for my dissertation on Dresden. And for the book I'm working on. Might be how I write the final chapter." Jack thought of something else he had been wondering about. "By the way, did you ever figure out who the mole was here? Somebody had to be tipping off Vandergraf and the Senator about our conversations."

Boyd shook his head. "Never did. But I have a hunch I know who it is."

"Of course," Hank added, "Not that it matters much anymore. That side job of his ended when we put Wagner in handcuffs." Hank stood and walked around Jack. "Well, gentlemen, I've got some place I have to be." He stopped at the doorway and looked at Jack. "Before I leave, something I need to say. I'm sorry, Jack, for doubting you like I did when you first came in here with all this. Anything else comes up down the road, I promise, I won't give you a hard time." He smiled, held out his hand.

Jack shook it and he left.

No one said anything for a moment. "Well, is that all?" Jack said.

"That's all I had," Boyd said.

Jack stood and pulled something out of his pocket. "Okay, how about I share some news with you before I go." He held out a little black velvet box and opened the lid.

"Whoa, Jack," Boyd said. "Tonight's the night?"

"Going to ask her at River Bend, between dinner and dessert."

"What's that, a half-carat?"

"A whole one," Jack said. "Think she'll say yes?"

Boyd laughed. "No mystery there, Jack. Congratulations, my friend."



Later that evening, Jack couldn't take his eyes off Rachel as they walked through the doors of the River Bend restaurant. She looked absolutely gorgeous. After pulling out her chair and just before taking his own seat, he reached into his pocket and felt the little velvety box. How was he ever going to keep it together through dinner?

"What?" she said, catching him staring at her yet again.

"You look amazing," he said. "And by the way, order whatever you want for dinner…but let me pick out the dessert."

# Author's Note

*Remembering Dresden* is actually the 2$^{nd}$ book in the *Jack Turner Suspense Series*. If you've read it first, no harm done. I wrote it so that it would work just fine as a stand-alone book. But I think you'd really enjoy reading the first book, *When Night Comes*. What happened in that book is referred to throughout this story by Jack, Rachel and Sergeant Boyd.

Here's the link for *When Night Comes*. You can download it now and start reading it within minutes:

http://amzn.to/1xNat4G

I've already begun developing Book 3 in this series.

If I'm a new author to you and you haven't yet read any of my other novels (besides this one, there are over 15 others in print), let me start off by saying thanks for reading *Remembering Dresden*. I hope you thoroughly enjoyed it.

The *Jack Turner Suspense Series* opens up something of a new door for my writing. I'm more known for writing inspirational novels that include strong emotional and/or spiritual themes (think Nicholas Sparks-type books with better endings). But I've always enjoyed reading suspense novels and decided to see if I could write both. The great response from readers to *When Night Comes* made that possible.

For those of you who've read and enjoyed my other more inspirational novels, you are familiar with my character-driven storylines, strong romantic threads and, still, lots of page-turning suspense. You'll find all of that in my *Jack Turner Suspense* novels.

To make it easier to tell the difference between the genres, my suspense novels will have a totally different kind of cover than my other books. I decided to do things this way rather than to write under a different name.

# Want to Help the Author?

If you enjoyed reading this book, the best thing you can do to help Dan is very simple—*tell others about it*. Word-of-mouth is the most powerful marketing tool there is. Better than expensive TV commercials or full-page ads in magazines.

Dan would greatly appreciate you rating his book and leaving a brief review at any of the popular online stores, wherever books are sold. Even a sentence or two will help.

# Sign up to Receive Dan's Newsletter

If you'd like to get an email alert whenever Dan has a new book coming out, or when a special deal is being offered on any of Dan's books, click on his website link below and sign up for his newsletter.

From his homepage, you can also contact Dan or follow him on Facebook, Twitter or Goodreads.

http://danwalshbooks.com

# Want to Read More of Dan's Novels?

**Suspense Novels**
    The Discovery (stand alone - looks like Inspirational novel)
    What Follows After (stand alone - looks like Inspirational novel)
    When Night Comes (Jack Turner Series – Book 1)
    Remembering Dresden (Jack Turner Series – Book 2)

**Inspirational Novels**
    The Unfinished Gift (Homefront Series Book 1 – Christmas story)
    The Homecoming (Homefront Series Book 2)
    The Deepest Waters (stand alone)
    Remembering Christmas (stand alone – Christmas story)
    The Discovery (stand alone)
    The Reunion (stand alone – set during the Christmas season)
    Keeping Christmas (stand alone – Christmas story)

**Restoration Series with Gary Smalley (Inspirational)**
    The Dance
    The Promise
    The Desire
    The Legacy

To get a sneak peek at Dan's other novels or see what others are saying about them, click on this link, then click the book cover you're curious about:

http://www.danwalshbooks.com/books/

If you'd like to write Dan, feel free to email him at dwalsh@danwalshbooks.com. He loves to get reader emails and reads all of them himself.

# Acknowledgments

There are a few people I absolutely must thank for helping to get *Remembering Dresden* into print. Starting with my wife, Cindi. Not just for her encouragement and support. Over the years, her editing skills grew to where the editors at my publishing house requested I not send in a manuscript until she's gone through it. Once again on this novel, I promoted Cindi to senior editor. She provided excellent help on edits with the storyline and characters.

I want to also thank my great team of Beta readers, who caught many things Cindi and I missed, even after several passes. Thank you Terry Giordano and Jann W. Martin

I also must absolutely thank my friend and fellow author John M. Wills for all his help on the police details in the novels. John spent the better part of his life protecting and serving fellow Americans as a police officer in Chicago then with the FBI. Besides his books, John also writes book reviews for the New York Journal of Books, and he writes monthly articles on Officer.com. Check out his books at any online bookstore.

Dan Walsh

# About The Author

Dan Walsh was born in Philadelphia in 1957. His family moved down to Daytona Beach, Florida in 1965, when his dad began to work with GE on the Apollo space program. That's where Dan grew up.

He married Cindi, the love of his life in 1976. They have two grown children and three grandchildren. Dan served as a pastor for 25 years, then began writing fiction full-time in 2010. His bestselling novels have won many awards, including 3 ACFW Carol Awards (Book-of-the-Year) and 2 Selah Awards. Three of Dan's novels were finalists for RT Reviews Inspirational Book of the Year.

CPSIA information can be obtained
at www.ICGtesting.com
Printed in the USA
LVHW01s1120150918
590254LV00002B/93/P

9 780692 677216